PLAY WITH ME

Book Three in the

With Me In Seattle

Series

By

Kristen Proby

PLAY WITH ME
Book Three in the With Me In Seattle Series
Kristen Proby

Dedication:

This book is dedicated to my brother, Mike Holien. There has never been a prouder big sister! You make me laugh, and you're totally okay with me being the favorite. I love you, baby brudder.

Prologue

Ms. McBride,

Thank you for your inquiry regarding Will Montgomery and the rest of the team appearing at your hospital. Our organization receives thousands of similar requests each year, and unfortunately, Mr. Montgomery is unable to fulfill every request. He is not available at this time.

Regards,

Susan Jones
Public Relations, Seattle Football Organization

Nice.

This makes the fifth rejection from the elusive Will Montgomery in the past two years. My kids will be disappointed again.

I clear the email from my phone screen and throw it in my handbag, climb out of my car and head into Red Mill Burgers, my favorite place to indulge in a big, juicy burger and fries.

I stand in the back of the line and contemplate the latest in a long line of rejection letters from the Seattle professional footbal team. I am a nurse at Seattle Children's Hospital, and my teenagers would love nothing more than to meet their sports heroes. I thought celebrities got off on photo ops like this. All I'm asking for is a couple of hours; they don't have to spend the night for Pete's sake.

I glance to my right, and sitting right in the middle of the tiny restaurant is none other than my college buddy, Jules, and her brother, Will Motherfucking Montgomery.

Sonofabitch!

I love Jules. She and Natalie and I were good friends in college, so I will absolutely go say hi. I just wish I didn't have to speak to her arrogant ass of a brother in the process.

I place my order and saunter over to my friend.

"Jules?" I ask, my hand on her shoulder.

"Meg!" She immediately jumps up and pulls me into a warm hug. "Oh my gosh, I haven't seen you in years! How are you?"

I glance nervously at Will. "I'm doing very well, thanks. It's great to see you." She looks great, as always, but her eyes look a little sad. I wonder what's going on…

"Will, this is Megan McBride, a friend of mine from college. Meg, this is my brother, Will."

Will stands, his tall frame towering over me, and offers me his hand. Crap, I have to touch him? Digging deep, I find the manners instilled in me and shake his hand politely. "I know who you are."

He just nods and takes his seat again.

"What have you been up to?" she asks me.

"I'm a charge nurse at Seattle Children's Hospital in the cancer unit." I grin at her, keenly aware of Will's eyes on me, running up and down my body, over my loose-fitting white blouse, belted over black leggings and my red cowboy boots. He makes me nervous.

"That's awesome! Good for you, girl. Are you still singing?" she asks with a smile.

"Uh, no." I shake my head and gaze down at the table. "Not since college."

"You sing?" Will asks, his eyebrows raised.

"She has a fantastic voice," Jules replies proudly. She always was so sweet and supportive.

"Thanks, but you know how it is," I respond with a shrug. "Life takes over and things get busy." *And best friends leave you behind to start a band of their own.*

Will and Jules exchange a look, and suddenly she hits me with, "Are you married?"

I let out a loud laugh. Not hardly. "Hell, no."

"Can I get your number?" Will asks bluntly. Arrogant ass. I'll bet women fall all over him everywhere he goes.

I narrow my eyes, unable to hide my contempt for this man. "Hell, no."

Will's jaw drops and he smirks, then shakes his head. "Excuse me?"

"I don't think I stuttered," I respond, then lay my hand on Jules' shoulder and force a smile for my friend. "It was great to see you. Take care, girl."

"You too, Meg."

As I turn and walk away I hear Will murmur, "What the hell was that all about?"

Jerk.

I collect my brown-bagged burger and fries and head back out of the restaurant to go home and enjoy my only night off this week. I pray I don't get called into work.

Chapter One

"To Nate and Jules," Luke Williams raises his champagne flute in the air and keeps one arm around his beautiful wife, Natalie. Everyone follows suit, toasting the happy couple. "May your love continue to grow. We wish you nothing but all the happiness in the world."

"To Nate and Jules!" The guests echo and sip their drinks in celebration. Nate McKenna, tall and dark and not just a little intense, folds his stunning blonde fiancé into his arms and kisses her senseless in front of all of us, amid whistles and applause and Will Montgomery, Jules' brother, yelling out, "Get a room!"

I sip my sweet pink champagne and glance around the extravagant Olympic room of the Edgewater Hotel. For the hundredth time, I ask myself what I'm doing here. I was shocked to receive the invitation to Jules Montgomery's engagement party. Jules and Natalie and I all hung out quite a bit in college, and it was great to reconnect with them a few months ago, but I certainly wasn't expecting an invitation to come mingle with their family and close friends.

I'm in a room with Luke Williams for fuck sake. The movie star.

The room is decorated in Tiffany blue and white with simple white flower bouquets on the tables, white table linens and Tiffany blue napkins and touches here and there. It's incredibly classy.

It's completely Jules.

It's a late summer evening, and not quite dark out yet, so we have an amazing view of the Puget Sound, the sky just beginning to change to pink and orange, reflecting on the water. The glass doors are open so guests can come in and out at their leisure, enjoy the veranda and the late summer view, or come inside and dance.

"Meg, I'm so happy you could come." Natalie taps my shoulder and pulls me into a big hug. "I've missed you, girl."

"Me too," I respond, holding her close and then pulling back to admire the lovely woman before me. "You look fantastic. Marriage and motherhood agree with you, my friend."

And it's true. Natalie's green eyes shine with happiness and contentment, her dark chestnut hair is pulled back away from her face in waves, and she is wearing a fantastic black sleeveless gown.

"Thank you. I love that dress. Your style hasn't changed a bit," she responds with a grin. I look down at my pale silver strapless dress with handkerchief hemline and strappy silver sandals.

"Not much of anything has changed," I respond with a shrug.

"Except your hair, as usual," Natalie laughs, pointing at my auburn hair streaked with chunky blonde highlights, and I chuckle with her.

"My hair always changes, and this is pretty tame for me. The kids enjoy it, and well, you know… once a rocker chick, always a rocker chick."

"You know," Natalie grins smugly. "I still have those photos we did of you with your guitar, and nothing else."

"Oh God," I giggle at the memory of playing around in Natalie's small college studio all those years ago. "You might want to burn those."

"No, I'm just thinking we should shoot them over again. You didn't have that back then," she points to my inner arm and I follow her gaze to the tattoo on my inner upper arm.

"Maybe someday."

"So…" she begins but is interrupted by her husband. "Oh, Meg, this is my husband, Luke. Luke, I'd like you to meet an old friend of mine and Jules, Megan McBride."

"Hello, Megan, nice to meet you." He offers me his right hand and I feel my cheeks flush slightly before I respond, placing my hand in his to shake. But instead, he raises it to his lips and kisses my knuckles.

"Um, it's nice to meet you too, Luke."

He flashes me his movie-star grin, the one that used to grace every magazine cover in the country, and then excuses himself when Caleb, another of Jules' brothers, calls to him.

"Um, Nat?"

"Yeah," she replies with a satisfied sigh.

"You're married to Luke Williams."

She chuckles and nods her head. "I am."

"How the fuck did that happen?"

"Long story. I'll fill you in over wine one night."

"It's a date."

"There you are!" Jules exclaims and wraps one of each of her arms around us into a group hug. "Meg, I'm so glad you made it!"

"I wouldn't miss it. Although, I was surprised to get the invite."

"You're my friend. I wanted you here." Jules grins and searches the room until her eyes find her man's.

"He's very handsome, Jules. And completely gone over you." I murmur and follow her gaze.

"Yeah, he is. It's mutual."

"I'm happy for you." I sip more sweet champagne.

"Thanks." Her smile is wide and happy, and it's true, I am so happy that she found her guy. They are great together.

"When do we eat?" Will asks from a table not far from us. I've been doing my best to ignore Will Montgomery, aka Football Quarterback, aka arrogant ass all night. I've managed to stay out of his way and avoid another introduction, but I've felt his eyes on me all night, which I don't get. I'm surely not his type, and it's no secret that I'm not interested.

"The buffet is ready to go, Miss Montgomery." A pretty, curvy blonde walks up to Jules with a wide smile. "Dinner is ready when you are."

"Perfect, thank you, Alecia. Be sure you and your assistant eat too."

"Oh, we will." Alecia laughs and walks away, consulting her iPad.

"God, I love that woman." Jules exhales and smoothes her hands down her floaty red chiffon strapless dress.

"She's amazing," Nat agrees.

"Who is she?" I ask.

"Party planner," Jules replies. "I found her when I hosted Nat's baby shower a few months ago. She's also doing the wedding. She's a genius."

"She's my fucking hero," Will grumbles and follows after Alecia. "I'm starving."

"You're always starving!" Jules yells after him and laughs.

* * *

How I ended up at Will's table is a mystery to me. In fact, I'm sitting with all of Jules' impossibly handsome brothers, a sweet woman named Brynna, and Jules' sister-in-law, Stacy, who is lovely and very pregnant. Like, pop any day pregnant.

Everyone is laughing, joking with each other, and they all look incredible.

Why the hell didn't I bring a date? Most likely because the last time I went out on a date a tsunami hit Japan.

Pathetic.

"So, Megan, what do you do?" Jules' brother Matt asks me.

"I'm a charge nurse at Seattle Children's Hospital."

"What department?" he asks and cuts into his steak.

"I work with teens on the cancer care floor." I take a bite of roasted potato and a sip of wine. I'm going to need more of this.

"How long have you done that?" Matt asks and I notice Will scowl. What the hell is his problem?

"I've been a nurse for about six years, in this position for two."

Matt fills my wine glass and offers me a kind smile and I find myself returning it.

"You're young to have such an important job," Will comments kindly, but I roll my eyes and ignore him, earning another glare from him.

"So, if Stacy goes into labor, you can save the day," Caleb suggests and we all giggle.

"No, I'm not an O.B. nurse. But I can call an ambulance," I respond.

Stacy rubs her belly and grins. "It's okay, guys, we still have about a month to go."

Isaac leans down and kisses his wife's cheek and whispers something in her ear, making her grin.

These men are all seriously charming. Jules and her family's gene pool is impressive.

Matt pours me another glass of wine and I immediately sip it, pushing my plate aside. I'm too nervous to eat anyway.

In the middle of a conversation with Stacy I realize I'm beginning to feel a bit light headed, so I excuse myself and head to the bathroom to press a cold cloth on my forehead and refresh my lip gloss.

"Meg, wait up."

Shit.

I try to make it into the ladies room ahead of him, but Will just follows me in and locks the door.

"What the hell are you doing?" I ask him with an eyebrow raised.

"You don't like me very much, do you?" He leans his tall, six foot four frame against the door and crosses his arms over his chest. He took his suit jacket off long ago, leaving him in a pink – *pink* – dress shirt that looks surprisingly hot on him, with no tie and black slacks. The sleeves are rolled up, showing off muscular forearms. His dark blonde hair is overlong and messy, and his blue eyes are running up and down my body before landing on mine.

"I don't know you well enough to like or dislike you."

"I call bullshit," he says calmly.

"It doesn't matter." I shrug and turn to the sink to wash my hands and apply my lip gloss, while Will's eyes never leave me.

"What?" I ask and turn around.

"Why don't you just tell me what I did to piss you off so I can go ahead and hit on you?"

I burst out laughing, making him scowl, which makes me laugh even harder.

"You really are an arrogant asshole, aren't you?"

"No, I'm not." He's dead serious, not finding this situation funny at all.

"Yeah, you are. I don't want you to hit on me."

He shrugs as if what I want is of no consequence. "I'm not an asshole, Meg. What did I do to offend you so much?"

I stop laughing and clear my throat, and take a moment to just really look at him. He looks sincere. But I will never get the looks of disappointment in my patients' eyes out of my head.

"It doesn't matter," I repeat.

Will pushes himself off the door and crosses to me, pinning me against the bathroom counter, his hands resting on the granite on either side of me at my hip. He doesn't touch me, but leans in so his nose is just about twelve inches from mine.

"It does matter," he murmurs.

"Why?" My heartbeat has just gone into overdrive and oh, God, he smells so good. I'm blaming my fuzzy head on the over-abundance of wine I've consumed with very little food.

"I need you to tell me what I did to piss you off so I can apologize." He leans back, just a few inches, and his eyes travel down my body leisurely. I can feel the heat from his gaze and I feel my skin warm. His eyes travel back up to my face and he pins me with his hot blue gaze. "You look amazing in this little dress with your heels and your auburn hair all curly and messy around your sweet face."

"Um…" What was the question?

"Tell me." He insists.

"Tell you what?" I whisper.

He grins and whispers back, "What I did to piss you off, Meg."

"I've repeatedly sent messages to your PR people for the past two years asking for you and your team to come up and see my kids. Every request has been shot down, saying that you're not interested."

He frowns and slightly shakes his head. "I've never received anything from PR about going to Children's."

"Right," I respond sarcastically and try to pull back so I can't smell his musky scent. It's doing things to me.

I want to lick his neck.

"I'm not lying. They field a lot of requests for me. It was never passed on to me."

Oh.

Well, crap.

"Why didn't you just have Jules talk to me about it? Or get my number from her?"

"Right," I snort. "First, she's my friend and I'm not going to use her for stuff like that, and second, why would I call you? I don't know you."

Will smiles softly and raises a hand to my face, tips my chin up with his forefinger, making me look him in the eye. He's so tall, he towers over me, but he's leaning down to me. His bright blue eyes watch me lick my lips and when I bite my lower lip he inhales sharply and pins my dark eyes in his gaze.

His hand lightly cups my jaw and he raises his other hand to lightly brush my hair back off my shoulder, and I am just lost in his eyes. I can't move. I should push him away. I don't do this. I don't let strange men touch me in public restrooms while their entire family sits outside chatting and laughing and eating.

But I can't look away.

He lowers his face to mine, brushes my lips ever so gently, smiles down at me in that cocky way that he's known for, and sinks into me, burying his hands in my hair, holding my face so he can move his mouth against mine.

Holy shit, he's good at this kissing stuff. His lips are soft, yet firm, and that somehow makes perfect sense to me. They move with precision and purpose, across my lips and back again. I moan and wrap my arms around his waist, lean into him, and Will groans against me and suddenly this kiss has turned into not just want, but need. His tongue invades my mouth, twirling and dancing with my own. I reach up, wrap my arms around his neck and twist my fingers into his gloriously soft hair and practically climb up him, trying to get closer.

Finally, he cups my ass in his large hands and lifts me up. My legs wrap around his waist and before I know it, my back is braced against the door, Will is leaning on me, keeping me firmly in place, and is still kissing the shit out of me.

Holy fuck this man can kiss.

"God, you're sweet," he murmurs and nibbles and kisses his way across my jawline to my ear and down my neck. "We could have a lot of fun together, baby."

Baby? And just as if I've been doused with a bucket of cold water, I come to my senses. I'm about to get it on in a public restroom – ew! – with Will Montgomery.

No!

"Stop," I demand, my voice firm.

Chapter Two

"You don't want me to stop."

He pushes his pelvis against my center and I bite my lip to stop the moan that wants to come from my throat.

"I said stop, Will."

He pulls back and looks me in the eye, panting, his eyes narrowed. He shakes his head as if he's clearing it and gently lowers me to the floor. My knees almost buckle beneath me, and he steadies me, his hands on my shoulders.

"What's wrong?" he asks.

"I'm not doing this with you. Ever."

He steps back, runs those fantastic hands through his hair, takes a deep breath and clenches his eyes shut. "Okay." He swallows hard. "I'm sorry. I thought you were interested."

"Let's get something straight right now. I'm not some stupid sports groupie who's dying to get into your pants and I'm not your *baby.*" God, I hate being called that.

"I apologize again, for the misunderstanding regarding my PR people, and for this." His voice is steady now, his breathing under control and he shoves his hands into his pockets. *Wow, he's handsome.*

I lick my lips, still tasting him on me.

"If you'll step aside, I'll leave you alone." I suddenly hate this polite coldness I'm getting from him. I wish he'd take me in his arms again and kiss me, and I hate *myself* just a little for it.

Maybe he's not as bad as I thought, but he's not for me.

I quickly move out of his way, and he unlocks the restroom door. Before he opens it, he looks back at me and offers me a half grin, winks, and leaves me alone.

My eyes find my own in the mirror. They're a bit glassy from too much wine and lust. My hair is just a bit messy, but I styled it that way to begin with, so no biggie. Aside from my lip gloss having been kissed off, I look the same as I did when I walked in here.

So why does it feel like everything is about to change?

* * *

"Okay, what are we drinking to this time?" I ask and look around the table at my friends and their men. All of the parents left the party a few hours ago, and all that's left are Jules and Nate, Natalie and Luke, Stacy and Isaac, Brynna, Matt, Caleb and Will. All of the other guests have gone home, leaving the eleven of us to drink shots and laugh and catch up.

I haven't had this much fun in a long time.

If I drink this next shot, I just might forget the escapade in the bathroom with Will.

Maybe.

Probably not.

Speaking of Will, he keeps watching me, sipping a beer, quiet. But I ignore him and lift another shot of tequila in the air. So far, we've toasted babies, rock and roll, tattoos, shopping, and shopping again.

"Here's to orgasms, and the three I'm going to have tonight!" Natalie exclaims, earning fits of giggles from the rest of us girls while the boys – all except for Luke – grumble about TMI.

"To orgasms!" we all concur and slam the shot.

I stopped using the training wheels of lime and salt three shots ago.

I glance back over at Will, who's now in a deep conversation with his brother Caleb, and despite my clearly drunk state, my thighs clench just at the sight of him. Geez. He's all broad shoulders and muscles and blue eyes and his shaggy dark blonde hair is all messy from his fingers, and mine, and I want to give it a good tug.

I should have done him in the bathroom.

Stop it! That's just drunk and horny Meg talking.

"So, Meg," Jules slurs as she leans over toward me and plops her arm around my shoulders. "Why are you still single, my beautiful friend?"

"Because my job is my relationship, my equally as beautiful friend."

"That sucks."

"It's fine." I wave her off and take a sip of my fifth margarita. Damn, I really should have eaten more at dinner.

"Does your job give you orgasms?" Natalie asks as she crawls into Luke's lap.

"No," I giggle.

"Then it's not fine," she responds smugly.

No, it's not fine, but it is what it is. I need to change this subject.

"You should sing something," Jules claps her hands and bounces in her seat.

"You are all starting to kill this really great buzz I've got going on."

"Sing!" Jules demands.

"I can barely talk. No singing. I haven't sung in a long time anyway."

"Okay, then let's dance." Jules stands, and then wobbles. Nate pulls her in his lap, laughing down at her.

"I think it's time I take you up to the room, baby." She cups his face in her hand and smiles up at him.

"Okay. Can I have some orgasms?"

"I think I can make that happen," he replies with a smirk.

"No fair!" Natalie exclaims. "I want orgasms!"

Dear God, did we always talk about orgasms when we were drunk in college?

"Then let's go up to our room too, I'll give you those orgasms." Luke kisses Nat's cheek and stands with her cradled in his arms.

Jesus, Luke Williams is in the same room with me, talking about orgasms.

This is crazy.

"I'm out too." I slam one last shot, grab for my purse and stand. The room spins a bit, but I brace myself on the back of a chair and take a deep breath.

"You're not driving are you?" Nate asks.

"I'll call a cab."

"I'll take you home." Will stands and is suddenly at my side, gripping my elbow.

"You drank too," I remind him.

"I had one beer. I'm fine."

Oh.

"Really?"

"I'm in the middle of a season, Meg, I can't drink much."

"What kind of season?" I ask as the room spins slowly around me. I'm vaguely aware of snickering happening around me but I'm too drunk to kick anyone's ass.

"Football," he says gently and brushes my hair behind my ear.

"You want to play football?" I'm so confused. "I'm too drunk to play football."

Will laughs and shakes his head. "No, sweetheart, I will play football on Sunday. With my team. Remember?"

"Oh, yeah. You're a football star." I wave him off and turn toward my friends. "He's a big time football player. Did you know?"

Natalie giggles at me. "Meg, you're funny. I'm glad you're hanging out with us again."

"Dude, you got her?" Caleb asks.

"Yeah, I got her," Will confirms.

"Who you got?" I ask.

"You, drunk girl. Come on." He turns to lead me toward the exit, and I start to follow him, but for some reason my feet don't work very well.

"Um, Will?"

"Yeah?"

"I lost my feet."

"What?" he laughs and pinches the bridge of his nose.

"I can't find my feet."

Why is everyone laughing at me? This is serious!

"Okay, I've got you." He lifts me effortlessly into his arms and cradles me against his chest.

"You don't have to carry me."

"If I want to get you in the car and take you home, I think I do."

"I thought you wanted to play football." I yawn and lean my head against his shoulder. Hmm… he still smells good.

"Not tonight."

"I think I'm drunk."

"What was your first clue?" he chuckles.

"Don't make me hurt you, Mungumry."

"Yeah, you scare me."

* * *

"What kind of car is this?" I ask.

"It's a Shelby."

"Is Shelby your girlfriend?" I ask, mortified. Holy shit! I made out with a guy who has a girlfriend!

"No, this car is a Shelby Mustang, Megan."

"Oh. Then who is your girlfriend?"

"I don't have a girlfriend."

"Why not?"

"No time." He shrugs. "No one has interested me, until very recently." He mutters that last part, and before I can ask him what he means by that, he pulls up to my townhouse.

"Thanks for the ride."

"You're welcome. Stay there."

I don't think I could get out of this car if I wanted to. It sits really low to the ground, but it's nice. The seat is comfortable.

Suddenly the passenger door is open and Will is leaning inside, pulling me out of the car. He gets me to stand, and then lifts me again.

"I could probably walk now."

"I doubt it. Just don't throw up on me, please."

Well, I didn't feel like throwing up until he said something. Now my stomach is rolling and I have that icky feeling in the back of my throat.

Fuck!

"Where are your keys?" he asks.

"Handbag."

"Do you want me to get them?"

"Yes." *Just breathe. Just breathe and you won't throw up.*

"Okay, I'm going to stand you by the door. Just lean on the wall for a second."

Is he speaking English? I don't understand him, all I can concentrate on is not throwing up. He shuffles through my bag and produces my keys.

"This one." I point to the house key and he unlocks the door and scoops me up again, carrying me inside.

"You don't have an alarm system?" he asks with a frown.

"No."

"Why not?" he demands.

"Too expensive. Fuck, put me down."

He lowers me to the floor and as soon as my feet hit the ground I sprint to the bathroom, and hurl about two bottles of tequila into the toilet.

It never tastes as good coming up as it did going down.

Oh, sweet Jesus, make it stop. My stomach convulses and shudders, and I feel a sweat break out on my skin.

Suddenly my hair is scooped back off my face and a cold cloth is pressed to the back of my neck.

Fuck, I forgot he was here. How mortifying.

"You can go," I mumble and rest my forehead on my arm, still cradling the toilet.

"I'll stay." His voice is firm and maybe a little grim.

"I'm okay, Will."

"I'm not leaving you like this, so shut it." He gently lifts my head and presses another cold cloth to my forehead, making me moan in delight.

"That feels good."

"I know. Are you done throwing up?"

"I think so."

"Okay, let's get you in bed."

"Hey!" My head jerks up and I pin him with a glare. "You're not getting me into bed."

"Yeah, I am. Don't worry, sweetheart, no hanky panky." He grins and I groan as another wave of nausea hits. I'm suddenly bone-tired.

"Okay." I stand and he wraps an arm awkwardly around my waist. He's just too tall for his own good. "I'm fine, Will. The worst is over. You can go."

He glares down at me and wipes my face with the cool cloth. "I'll make sure you're asleep before I leave."

"Why? I haven't exactly been nice to you."

"Because I'm not an asshole, and the sooner you realize that, the better."

I frown at him, not understanding him at all. He opens the drawers in my dresser, shuffling through clothes and socks, then turns to me with a scowl.

"Where are your pajamas?"

"I don't wear pajamas."

"So what do you wear to bed?" he asks and plants his hands on his hips.

"Nothing."

He closes his eyes and exhales deeply, then searches through my drawers again until he finds an old t-shirt and throws it at me. "Here, put this on."

"Why?"

"Because I'm climbing in that bed with you, and you can't be naked or I *will* be an asshole." He looks almost angry.

"Turn around," I murmur. When he's facing the other direction, I quickly unzip and step out of my dress and pull the t-shirt over my head. I'm not wearing panties, but the t-shirt is long enough that you can't see so I don't care. "I don't think I can take my sandals off without falling over."

Will turns to me and his eyes soften. "You look so young right now."

"I'm sure I look like shit, but okay. Sandals?"

"Sit." He kneels before me and takes my shoes off, and then tucks me into the bed. He unbuttons his shirt, lets it fall off his shoulders and drapes it on my desk chair. Holy muscled body, Batman.

"Your place is nice," he mutters.

"Hmm." I close my eyes to block out the delicious image of a mostly-naked Will. I hear the zipper of his pants and the rustling of him stepping out of them, and then the bed dips as he crawls in beside me. He turns me away from him, and pulls my back against his front.

"Sleep."

"Why are you still here?" I ask sleepily. I should demand that he go, but damn if this doesn't feel good.

"I don't know," he whispers.

* * *

~Will~

She instantly falls asleep, tucked against me, her breath slow and even. Why am I still here? Good question. I got her home and in bed safely, she'll just sleep it off and be fine in the morning, albeit a bit hung over. But lying here with her feels right, and for the first time in a long, long time I feel protective over a woman that I'm not related to.

She's different. She doesn't care about my job or my family connections.

And she told me no. That was new.

I smile and kiss the top of her head, enjoying the smell of peppermint in her hair and the way her soft hair feels against my nose. She sighs deeply and wiggles against me, pushing that tight, round ass against my groin. Her t-shirt rides up and I can feel her ass.

Her warm, naked ass.

Fuck me.

This little hazel-eyed woman has a body made for sex, a sharp wit and a killer smile. The dimple in her right cheek is fucking adorable. It's too bad for me that she's forever frowning at me.

I wonder what it will take to make her smile more, and trust me. Because I've got to see her again.

Meg whimpers softly and turns in my arms, burrows her face against my chest and wraps her arm around my waist, hanging on tight. I brush her hair off her cheek and kiss her forehead before falling asleep myself.

Hell yes, I'll see her again.

Chapter Three

Two weeks later

"Meg, there's a call for you on extension forty-six hundred."

"Okay, Jill, thanks." I set the chart I've been documenting medication doses into in its slot at the nurses' station and pick up the phone.

"This is Meg."

"Megan McBride?" a polite female voice asks.

"Yes, can I help you?"

"I hope so. This is Susan Jones. I'm with the Seattle football public relations office."

Oh, hell. My stomach flips over and my upper lip begins to sweat.

"Hello."

"I'm calling on behalf of Will Montgomery. He would like to accept your invitation to come up to your department at Children's and meet your staff and patients."

I rub my forehead with my fingertips and bite my lip. "Okay. I can make arrangements for that."

"Great. He'd like to come up on Wednesday."

"Of this week?" My voice is much squeakier than normal, but I can't help it. He wants to come to my job in two days?

"That's right."

I sigh in resignation. The kids will be so excited; there's no way I can say no.

"Okay, what time?"

"Around one O'clock?"

"Okay, we'll be expecting him."

I hang up and stare at the phone. *Fuck me.* Will Montgomery is coming here in two days. It's been two weeks since the moment in the restroom. Since my colossally embarrassing drunk display.

Since waking up the next morning, naked, in my empty bed.

I really need to ask him how the hell I ended up naked. If my blurry memory serves, I climbed in bed in a t-shirt.

And then, to cap off an incredibly confusing evening, Will had my car delivered to my townhouse the next morning so I didn't have to take a cab to go collect it from the hotel.

Sweet? Maybe.

Yet, not a word from him since then. Of course, he's a busy professional football player, and it's football season, and maybe he's just not interested in me after the way I laid the bitch-act on.

I couldn't blame him if that were the case. Not to mention, I did make it clear that I would never, ever be intimate with him.

I'm an idiot.

And now he wants to come to my job and meet my patients. It's probably just a ploy to get some publicity. He'll undoubtedly bring some press with him, have his photo taken with sick kids, and it'll make him look great on Channel 7 News.

Arrogant ass.

* * *

"He's here. Security just called up." Jill grins and does a little dance. She and I have worked together since day one. She's a pretty petite blonde with dark brown eyes and a voluptuous figure. She's also happily married and has three kids, but not averse to flirting with hot football players.

Who can blame her?

"Okay, I'm going to walk out to the elevators and meet him. Remember, act surprised."

She winks at me and I walk over to the elevator lobby. I gave my kids' parents a heads up about today's guest so they could come and take photos and meet the athlete themselves, but I decided to make it a surprise for the kids.

Finally, the elevators open and I can just stare. He's brought four of his teammates, all dressed in blue jeans and their team jerseys, pushing carts full of gifts, baskets wrapped in bows and cellophane, full of their team gear; hats, jerseys, pajamas, flags… you name it. They have stuffed animals and games, too.

I look up into Will's bright, happy blue eyes and I can't stop the grin that splits my face in two.

He's spoiling my kids!

"Hey, you're the prettiest nurse I've ever seen." He offers me that cocky grin and follows the other guys out of the elevator. They are all so tall and broad, making me feel tiny next to them.

I look down at my simple blue scrubs and laugh. "Right because scrubs and ponytails are all the rage these days."

He leans down to kiss my cheek and whispers in my ear, "Hottest nurse I've ever seen."

Well, then.

I clear my throat and Will introduces me to his teammates; Jerrel Sanders, Thomas Jones, Kip Sutherland and Trevon Wilson.

They are all incredibly polite and look a little nervous, hands in their pockets, shuffling on their big feet, looking about the hospital corridor.

"Thank you so much, all of you, for coming. I haven't told the kids you were coming; I wanted it to be a surprise. But the parents know, so they could bring their cameras and stuff." The guys all nod and I look around the lobby. "No press?"

Will's face sobers. "No, no press. This isn't a photo-op, Meg. We're here because we want to be."

"How did you talk your PR lady into that?" I ask, surprise ringing through my voice.

"She works for us, not the other way around," he responds simply and grabs a rolling cart full of goodies for my kids. "Lead the way."

I lead the guys into the corridor, a wide smile on my face, and wink at Jill who is standing at the nurse's station, her arms folded around her middle.

"Let's start with Nicholas. He's played football until this past winter when he got hurt on the field and it was discovered that he as osteosarcoma." The guys all frown with concern. "Bone cancer," I murmur and knock on Nick's door.

"Yeah," I hear him call.

I crack the door open and shield his view from the guys behind me. "Do you have a sec?"

His eyes light up and he grins at me. He's got such a crush, it's cute. "I always have time for the hottest nurse here."

I open the door wide and step aside so the guys can move into his room, and Will leans down to me on his way by and whispers in my ear, "See? Hottest nurse."

Nick pales, his jaw drops, and then he starts to laugh. "Oh, my God!"

"Hey, man." Will approaches him first and offers his hand to shake. "It's a pleasure to meet another player."

"I'm not playing anymore," Nick murmurs.

"Once a player, always a player, dude." Will grins and sits next to his bed. "What position did you play?"

"Quarterback," Nick responds shyly, not able to look Will in the eye. Nick's hair is gone, and his once strong body looks weak in the large hospital bed.

"Were you good?" Will asks.

"Fuck yeah, it was only my junior year and I had offers from USC and Florida State," he says proudly.

"Damn, I'm sorry, man."

I step out of the room and let the guys chat it up with Nicholas, give him gifts and just make his day.

Hell, make his whole life.

About an hour later, the players file out, smiling and joking with each other and with Nick. Will offers me a sweet, sad smile. "We need to talk later," he mutters.

I frown and cock my head to the side. Talk? About what? I don't have time to question him.

"Okay, guys, if you're comfortable splitting up for a while, there are a lot of kids anxious to meet you. I have extra nursing staff on hand today to lead you around and introduce you to kids and their parents."

"Sounds great," Sanders responds and offers Jill a cocky grin. "Lead on, sweetheart."

They each grab baskets full of gifts and follow my staff to various parts of the department, and I laugh as I hear whoops and cries of excitement coming out of the rooms.

"This is awesome, Will. These kids will remember this for the rest of their lives. Thank you."

"My pleasure. I'm gonna stick with you, if you don't mind. Where to next?"

* * *

Okay, the man is good with kids. He's kind and a good listener. He has patiently posed for dozens of photos, flirted with my girls, made the guys feel like he's their buddy, and just been generally awesome today. All five players eventually made it to every room and talked with every patient. Now, we're all gathered in a common area that we have set up for families, where they can come and rest. It's recently been remodeled, and it proudly boasts about two-thousand square feet of plush leather couches and recliners, an enormous big-screen television mounted to one wall, tables and chairs near outlets for laptops and plenty of space to spread out.

Now the oldest patients who are able to leave their rooms are scattered around the space, at the suggestion of Kip, so the kids can ask questions and have a little more time with the team before they leave for the evening.

They've already been here for a staggering five hours.

"Meg, I need some help with an IV in room twenty," Dr. Sanchez whispers to me so she doesn't interrupt the Q&A session.

"No problem." I follow her back to the room and help her, and then when I return to the lounge, I stay out of sight so I can listen.

"So, do you have a girlfriend, Will?" A pretty sixteen-year-old patient named Liza asks with a shy smile.

"No, I don't, sweetheart."

"Why not?" someone asks.

"Well, there is one woman I'm interested in, but I don't think she likes me back."

"Well then she's stupid," Liza retorts, and everyone laughs.

"No, she's smart," Trevon jokes, punching Will in the shoulder.

"Who is it?" Nick asks him.

"Actually, you know her," Will begins and I bite my lip and feel my eyes widen. *Holy shit!* "I'd love to get to know Meg better."

"Well then ask her out," someone out of my line of vision advises him.

"I don't think she's interested in me."

"We can help," Liza offers. "We know her really well."

"Um, okay." Will suddenly sounds nervous and I grin.

"She loves music," my patient, Bree tells him.

"And chocolate," offers Mike.

"And she likes hugs," my thirteen-year-old Jason chimes in.

"But if you fuck with her, I'll tear your heart out of your chest, cancer be damned," Nick states clearly, harshly.

"Nick!" his mom exclaims. My feet are rooted to the floor. I should go take care of this, but I can't move. I want to hear Will's response. Silence fills the room and I picture the two guys, one almost a man and one a grown up, staring at each other.

Finally, Will says, "You know, Nick, I already had a lot of respect for you just from our chat earlier today, but now I just think you're badass. You're a good man. You don't need to worry about Meg."

I walk into the room in time to see Nick nod soberly and look at the floor. The other four players' smirks have left their handsome faces, and are instead looking at Nick with respect.

"Okay, everyone," my voice is bright, not giving a clue that I just heard the conversation about Will and me. "I know you probably have a lot more questions for our guests, but I think it's time we let them off the hook. They've spent a lot of their time with us today."

There are a few groans, but the room erupts into applause.

"Thank you!" The kids call out, and all five players look a bit embarrassed, but boast huge, proud smiles.

34

"You're very welcome," Will responds when the applause dies down.

"Good luck on Sunday," Bree's dad calls out. "I have money riding on it!"

"We'll see what we can do," Sanders responds.

I follow the players back to the elevators, Will and I lagging behind the others. He takes my hand in his, but I pull away and look around.

"Not at my job, Will."

"Oh, so I can hold your hand outside of work?" he asks with a cocky grin.

"I didn't say that." Damn him.

"Walk me to my car." He murmurs down to me, so only I can hear.

"You didn't ride with the others?" I ask.

"No, Trevon stopped at the training center on his way here to get the Hawks gear, and we all met here."

"Okay."

When we reach the parking garage, Will's teammates each hug me tight.

"You do not have an easy job, little lady," Kip mutters, his face grim.

"Days like today make my job fantastic, Kip. Seriously, thank you, all of you for coming today. You just don't know what you did for those kids."

"Why haven't you asked us to come before?" Jerrel asks and Will coughs, choking on his own spit.

"Actually, I have. Several times. But I always got a no."

"Fucking Susan," Trevon mutters darkly. "From now on, contact us directly. I'm assuming you have Montgomery's number?"

"Uh, no." I shake my head and press my lips together.

"Well, hell, I'll give you *my* number," Kip grins. "And not just to visit you at work."

"Back up, Sutherland," Will warns. "I got this."

"Good." Kip winks at me and the guys all go climb in their own vehicles to leave, wave at us and are gone.

"So," Will murmurs and steps toward me. Despite the magnetic pull I feel, I take a step back.

"I should go back up."

"I want to see you, Meg." Well, he's blunt, isn't he?

"I don't think that's a good idea," I murmur.

His eyes narrow and he crosses his arms over his chest. "Why not?"

"This is a busy time for you, Will, and my job is busy too. Hell, I haven't heard from you for the past two weeks, so I just assumed…"

"Number one, don't assume. Ever." His voice is hard and immediately grabs my attention. "Number two, yes, we're busy, but we can find the time. And number three, I'm interested."

"How did I end up naked the morning after the party?" I blurt out, ashamed that I can't remember. His eyes twinkle mischievously.

"You woke up naked?" he asks, a half-grin spreading on his handsome face.

"Yeah, but I remember you making me put the t-shirt on."

"You were still in the t-shirt when I left that morning. I told you, no hanky panky."

"I'm surprised that you didn't try anything."

"Oh, trust me, sugar, having your tight, naked ass cradled against my dick was damn alluring." He steps closer to me and tips my chin up with his fingers. "But I wouldn't take advantage of you when you don't have your wits about you. When I take you, you'll know exactly what we're doing, what you're feeling, and I won't stop until your legs are shaking and the neighbors know my name."

Holy fucking hell.

He brushes his lips over mine once, then twice, before cupping my face firmly in his big hands and sinking into me, kissing me soundly. God, it's just as good as I remember, if not better, and I didn't think that was possible.

If I were wearing panties, they'd be soaked; I'm panting, and I just want to climb him. He pulls back and gently brushes loose hairs off my face.

"You're so sweet, baby."

Shit.

I step out of his embrace and rub my hands down my face, trying to clear my head.

"Will, I'm only going to tell you this once. Please, don't ever call me baby. Ever." My voice is controlled, firm. He scowls at me.

"Why?"

"I don't like it."

"Why?" he asks again.

"My deadbeat father used to call me that, during the few times I saw him, and it gives me the yucks. Just don't, okay?"

"Okay. Never again." He shrugs and smiles at me. "Sorry."

I shake my head and start to retreat back to the elevator. "I have to get back."

"I'll call you," he promises, but I just shake my head again and smirk.

"Sure you will," I respond sarcastically, wave, and disappear into the elevator.

Chapter Four

"Meg, these just came for you."

I'm sitting at my computer, responding to email and drinking a Starbucks, settling in before I have to take report from the night shift nurse and dig into work. Jill hands me a huge bouquet of flowers, pink roses with calla lilies. I bury my nose in them and breathe them in.

I know who they're from, but pull the card off the plastic holder and grin at the note.

You forgot to give me your number. Mine is 206-555-3598. Use it, please.

So, he's a little bossy.

"You gonna call him?" Jill asks from behind me, clearly reading over my shoulder and I laugh.

"I'll text him for now."

"Hell, I'd do a lot more than text him. Have you seen him?"

I roll my eyes at her and tuck the card in my scrub pocket. "I was here yesterday, remember?"

"The kids are still talking about it. They were really nice." Jill grabs a chart and begins making notes.

"Yeah, they were." I murmur and pull my phone out of my pocket. I add Will's number to my contact list, but instead of adding his name, I label it *Football Star*. I smirk and open a fresh text screen.

Thank you for the beautiful flowers.

I hit send and finish my email and coffee, and begin taking report from my co-worker.

About an hour later, I feel my phone buzz in my pocket.

You're welcome. Dinner tonight?

He doesn't waste any time, does he? Tonight is my only evening off through the weekend. Starting tomorrow I'm working swing shifts until Monday, and let's be honest, I want to see him.

Sure. I'm off work at six.

"Good for you, girl." I whirl at Jill's voice and glare at her.

"Do you always read over my shoulder?" I demand.

"No, but now that I know there's going to be juicy stuff to read, I will be." She winks and sashays past me into a patient's room.

I'll pick you up at seven.

* * *

"You look fantastic," Will smiles when I open my front door to him. I'm in a white BoHo-style chiffon dress with a soft lace overlay, the hem hitting me mid-thigh, and my brown cowboy boots. Several long necklaces hang around my neck, a chunky cuff bracelet sits on my left wrist, and my hair is down.

"What did you do to your hair?" He asks.

I chuckle run my fingers through it. "I added a few pink strands. The kids at work think it's fun, and so do I."

"Me, too." He smiles softly and steps back, ushering me out the door.

"Holy shit, you have a Shelby Mustang!" I gasp as I close the door behind me. Will stares down at me and then starts to laugh.

"It's the same car I drove you home in after the party, Meg."

I blink up at him and then gaze longingly at his car. I rode in a Shelby and don't remember? Impossible!

"Please tell me I didn't throw up in it."

"Thankfully, no." He grins down at me and tucks a pink strand of my hair behind my ear.

"Where are we going?" I ask as he follows me down to his spectacular car and opens the door for me.

"I thought we'd just go to a place downtown for dinner and maybe take a walk by the water front."

Instead of sitting in the leather seat, I walk to the rear of the car and gaze at the snake emblem, the chrome, hell, even the tires are pretty.

The car is black, all black, with tinted windows, making the chrome look even shinier. I feel my eyes glass over and I sigh.

"Meg?"

"Huh?" I glance up into Will's amused blue eyes and shake my head ruefully. "I'm sorry, what?"

"Are you okay?" he asks with a chuckle and moves to me, settles his big hand at the small of my back, and between his touch and this car, I can't breathe.

"This is a Shelby." I state, as if that explains everything.

"I know," he responds. "Are you a motor-head?"

"No, I just really, really love your car." Jesus, I love his car. This car is sexy as hell. Suddenly, I picture myself going down on him in the front seat as he drives and I gasp, squeeze my thighs together and run my fingers through my loose hair.

"What just went through that amazing head of yours?" he asks, his eyes narrowed, as he grips my shoulders and turns me to face him. I swallow.

"Nothing." I lie.

"You're a horrible liar."

"Let's just say, this car is really sexy, and does things to me," I respond, not looking him in the eye.

"Really," he drawls and smiles widely. He takes a tiny step closer, and tips my face up to look at him. His other hand snakes around my waist and he starts to lower his face to mine, but I step quickly out of his embrace.

"Don't get any ideas." I warn him and walk over to the open passenger door. He steps in front of me, blocking my way.

"Why not?" he asks.

"This is only a first date," I remind him.

"So?"

"So, no ideas, Montgomery." I try to look stern, but can't help but smile at him. He's just too... Will.

"Don't tell me you have that stupid girl three-date-rule?"

I shrug, but don't answer.

Hell yes, I have a three date rule!

"Can we count the engagement party as the first date?" he asks as he steps back and allows me to slide down into the plush seat.

I'm sitting in a Shelby! Holy fuck.

40

"No," I respond when he gracefully lowers his long frame into the driver's seat.

"But I took you home," he reminds me with a sly grin.

"But you didn't take me *there*, so it wasn't a date."

"What about yesterday at the hospital?" he asks and merges into traffic.

"Anything that includes my job is not a date." I laugh and run my hands along the dashboard. "This car is my every fantasy," I whisper.

Will's head whips around and he stares at me, his jaw dropped and then he starts to laugh, a huge, loud belly laugh and I join him, giggling like crazy.

"Great, so now you're just using me for my car."

"You'll live." I shrug. "So, how is Jules? I haven't had a chance to call her since the party."

"She's good. Busy with their new business, and planning the wedding. I don't know why they think they have to get married so soon." He frowns and I want to run my fingers through his messy hair, but link my fingers together and keep them firmly in place in my lap.

"Did they set a date?"

"Yeah, for early October."

"Why so soon?" I ask, surprised. That's only a couple months away.

"Who knows? This is my sister we're talking about. She said her whole life she wasn't interested in getting married, then she falls for a guy and now she can't get married fast enough." He frowns and pulls the car into a parking garage.

"Maybe she's just ready to get married."

"I guess."

"Don't you like Nate?" I ask and turn in my seat to watch his face.

"I do. He's a good guy, and he obviously loves my sister." He backs into a parking space and I smile widely at him.

"What?" he asks.

"So, you're just being an overprotective big brother then?" I tease him.

He frowns and then grins. "Yeah, can't help it."

"Jules is good, Will." I pat his thigh and he captures my hand in his and kisses my knuckles, one by one, and just like that my stomach clenches and my breath catches and I wonder how the fuck I'm going to hold out for two more dates.

"Your fingertips have little callouses on them," he murmurs.

"It's from the guitar."

His blue eyes meet mine. "I'd love to hear you play some-time."

"Sometime," I respond and grin.

"I love that dimple in your cheek." He leans in and kisses my dimple softly once, then again and backs away, still clutching my fingers, to pin me with those fiercely blue eyes. "Do you feel this too?" he whispers.

"Oh, yeah," I immediately respond. It's futile to deny it. I want him so much it hurts.

"Good. Come on, I'm hungry." Will climbs out of the low car and briskly walks around to the passenger side, opens my door, and offers his hand to help me out.

"I seriously love this car."

"I'll let you drive it home," he replies and links our fingers together.

"Seriously?" I gape up at him as he leads me down to the street.

"Sure, why not?"

"It's a Shelby." I state again, slowly, so he can understand the words coming out of my mouth.

"Honey, it's just a car."

"It's a Shelby." I shake my head. "I'm not driving it. If I wreck it, I can't afford to replace it."

"Do you get into many car accidents?" He narrows those eyes down at me and I giggle.

"No. But with my luck, this would be the time."

"You'll be fine. Besides," he winks down at me, "I have insur-ance."

He's so confident. His voice, the way he walks, the way he carries himself. So confident.

And sexy as all get out.

That ass alone should be illegal.

But I really love his shoulders and arms. He's perfectly sculpted, shoulders are broad, arms so strong. Hell, he lifted me like I was nothing.

And, thinking about that makes me go wet again.

Calm down, Meg. This is only Date One.

He's led me into a sports bar in downtown Seattle. I recognize it. It's upscale, full of professional sports memorabilia, televisions on various sports shows and games, and large, dark furniture.

Given the time of day, the place is pretty full of business men and other locals unwinding after a long workday.

Will leads me to a booth and sits opposite of me.

"Have you been here before?" he asks.

"A few times, yeah."

"They make a good burger here."

"You eat burgers?" I ask, surprised. I would think that with his rigorous training schedule he'd be on a strict diet.

"Not too often, but yeah, I do. I burn a lot of calories every day, so I pack a lot of food in." He offers me a menu.

Instead of reading it, I gaze over at him and he meets my eyes. I run my eyes over his face, those broad shoulders and arms, and down to his long-fingered hands. He's delicious in a gray t-shirt and jeans. When my gaze returns to his, his face is sober, his eyes molten blue, and I can't tell if he's pissed or just really, really turned on.

"Keep looking at me like that and the fucking three date rule will be out the window, Megan."

Make that really, really turned on.

"Hey guys, what can I getcha?" A waitress sets waters down before us and takes out her notebook.

"What would you like?" he asks me without looking at the waitress, his eyes still on fire.

"Whatever you're having is fine," I respond and swallow hard.

"Two cheeseburgers with fries, please."

"Hey, you're Will Montgomery!" The waitress exclaims.

And before my eyes, Will transforms. He smiles his cocky smile, his eyes calm, and he immediately slides into celebrity mode. I've seen it on TV, but this is my first glimpse in person.

"How are you, sugar?" he asks her.

"I'm great. Good to see you again." She winks at him and walks away, but our table is immediately surrounded by other patrons who overheard the waitress and now want to talk to Will and get his autograph.

"Hey, Montgomery! Great to meet you!"

And for the next fifteen minutes, Will doesn't falter. He's charming and smooth, answers questions, poses for pictures – many of which I'm asked to snap – and works the crowd in his arrogant, I'm-a-football-star way.

And completely ignores me.

It pisses me the fuck off.

In the middle of all the hoopla, I slide out of the booth and leave. Will doesn't even look my way.

I wonder how long it'll take him to discover that I'm gone?

Ten minutes, and about two-cab-ride-miles away, my phone rings.

"Where the hell are you?" he growls.

"Heading home," I respond calmly.

"What the hell?"

"Look, Will, I'm not interested in the arrogant, cocky football hero. That's not who I agreed to go out with." I close my eyes and try to calm my pulse. Why does he make me so fucking nervous?

"Where are you?" he repeats, clearly pissed.

"In a cab. Maybe this wasn't a good idea."

"Meg, I can't change my job..."

"I'm not asking you to," I interrupt him. "But you had to know that you'd get a helluva lot of attention in a *sports bar*, Will. Showing off how famous you are is not the way to impress me. I'm not a woman who thinks that scoring a celebrity is sexy. I think *you're* sexy, without the football jersey." *Fuck, why did I say that?* "So, you go ahead and enjoy your photo op, but I have better things to do with my time than be ignored. Have a good night."

This date so did not count toward the three. And there probably won't be any more dates, either. I just don't need to date an arrogant ass.

Damn it.

Chapter Five

I'm sorry.

I stare down at the note that accompanied the dozens of chocolate cupcakes that were delivered to the hospital just a few minutes ago.

It's obvious who they're from.

He sent beautiful, intricately decorated, chocolate cupcakes for all of us, not just me. There's enough here for all of the patients, the staff... hell, even the kids' parents.

"What did he do?" Jill asks from behind me and I whirl around.

"Stop reading over my shoulder!"

She chuckles and picks up a cupcake, sniffs it, and takes a big bite. "What did he do?" she repeats.

"He pissed me off."

"When?"

"Last night." I pick up a cupcake and take a big bite. *Mmm... so good.*

"Wanna put these in the lounge?" Jill asks as she licks her fingertips.

"Yeah. People can graze on them all day, although I don't think they'll last that long." I smirk and wheel the cart full of the chocolate goodness down the hall.

"You know, he could have just sent *you* a cupcake," Jill murmurs beside me, examining her fingernails.

"I know." Damn him for being so sweet.

"Mmm hmm."

"Stop. I get it. He's nice, but he fucked up yesterday, so it's okay for me to be frustrated with him, okay?"

"Okay." Jill raises her hands in an "I surrender" motion and snags another treat. "These are delish."

"Yeah, I guess he listened the other day when the kids told him I like chocolate."

"I guess he did," she responds with a smile.

"You have chocolate in your teeth," I mutter and pick up another cupcake for myself.

I arrange the cupcakes on a long table in the lounge and then pull out my phone.

Delicious. I hit send and bite my lip. Maybe I should have said more, but he needs to earn it.

Yes, you are. He responds immediately, and I laugh. Suddenly my phone is ringing, *Football Star* displayed on the caller ID.

"Hey," I answer.

"Hey," he responds softly. "I wanted to hear your voice, and this is faster than texting. We're about to get on the plane to go to San Francisco for Sunday's game."

"Oh, it's an away game this week?" I ask, disappointment in my voice. He'll be out of town all weekend.

That's okay, I work all weekend.

"Yeah, we'll be back Sunday night. Look, Meg, I'm sorry for last night. I should have known that it would get crazy, but I really did just want to take you out for a good burger."

"Yeah, you should have known," I agree softly.

"Have I completely fucked up, or are you going to let me make it up to you?"

I bite my lip and clench my eyes shut. Damn it, what is it about this guy that I just can't seem to tell him no?

"Next time, I pick the spot," I reply and I hear him sigh in relief.

"Deal. So, where shall I take you for date number two?"

"Uh, let's worry about date number one first."

"We already went on date number one," he growls, making me grin.

"No, we didn't. You didn't take me home and you pissed me off. It doesn't count."

"Fuck," he mutters and I can imagine him running his hand through his shaggy hair in frustration. "You're killing me, honey."

"How is that?" I ask and peel the paper off another chocolate cupcake. *Jesus, I'm going to gain ten pounds today.*

"Hold on," he takes the phone away from his mouth and calls out to someone, "Hey! I'll be right back."

"What are you doing?" I ask.

"Finding a private spot," he mutters and I hear him walking. A door opens, then closes. "As I was saying, you're killing me because I want to taste you, everywhere."

I stop chewing the now-cardboard chocolate in my mouth and swallow hard.

"Excuse me?" I whisper.

"I want to slowly undress you and taste every delectable inch of you. I want you squirming and wet."

"Mission accomplished," I mutter and then slap my hand over my mouth as he laughs.

"I want to see you Sunday night."

"I work Sunday night. I'm on swings this weekend. I don't get off work until two am."

"Do you work that shift often?" he asks quietly and I frown at the change in his tone.

"It's a rotation. We all work all the shifts. But I only work three twelve hour days a week, so it's not so bad."

"So, let me get this straight. You go home in the middle of the night to a house in North Seattle with no alarm system?" His voice is steel, and my stomach clenches.

"It's no big deal, Will."

"I'm installing an alarm system in your townhouse on Monday." His voice is firm.

"No, you're not." *What the hell?*

"Yes, I am. Don't argue with me on this, Megan. I'm gone a lot; I need to know you're safe."

"Will, we've been out on one date…"

"A-ha! So it was a date," he exclaims triumphantly.

"Don't change the subject. You don't need to install anything in my house. I'm fine."

"We'll see."

"Is that a 'we'll see' so I shut up and you do it anyway?" I ask suspiciously.

"Yes. Your safety isn't something I'll fuck with. If you have to go home in the middle of the night alone, I need to know that you're safe."

"Will, I…"

"I have to go," he interrupts, and I'm instantly disappointed in not only the loss of his fun and carefree tone, but that I won't see him all weekend. "Are you going to watch the game on Sunday?" he asks, his tone softened.

"Is it a morning or afternoon game?" I ask.

"Afternoon."

"Yeah, I usually watch the games with the kids. I'll be watching in between work stuff."

"Okay, pay attention at half-time. I'll make sure I'm on camera as we head off the field, and I'll say hi."

"Seriously?"

"Yep, watch for me."

"Okay. Have a safe trip."

"*You* be safe, sweetheart. I'll text you when I can."

"Okay, bye."

"Later."

And he's gone.

* * *

"NO NO NO!!" Nick exclaims from his position on the leather couch in the lounge on Sunday afternoon. There are roughly a dozen patients, parents, a few staff on their breaks, all with their eyes glued to the enormous television watching the football game.

The kids are wearing the team gear that the guys gave them last week. Will had a spread of food delivered around noon of sandwiches, chips, popcorn and soda.

What is it with this man and food?

So everyone is munching and enjoying the game. Instead of a hospital lounge, it looks like someone's living room during the Super Bowl.

The kids love the sense of normalcy, and I can't wait to thank Will for it.

Everyone groans as Will is tackled on the field and I hold my breath until he gets back up and walks steadily to his teammates.

Dear God, I can't watch him get tackled again. How does he not get hurt?

The first half of the game comes to an end, and Will's team is winning, twenty-one to seven.

My eyes are glued to the television, watching intently for my message from Will, and sure enough, right before they go to commercial, he's on the screen. His hair is wet with sweat and plastered to his forehead, face is dirty, and he's breathing hard from exertion, but he grins at the camera and taps his nose with his forefinger, then points to the camera and mouths, "miss you."

Well, shit, he's sweet.

Without over-thinking it, I pull my phone out and text him.

Miss you, too, football star.

* * *

"Miss McBride?"

"Yeah." I croak and stare at the man through blurry eyes. He's standing on my porch, in a uniform of some kind, holding a clipboard. I run my hand through my hair and frown. "What time is it?"

"Ten in the morning, ma'am."

Fuck, it's early.

"What's up?" I ask and wish for coffee.

"I'm Doug from Home Security Systems. I have a work order to install a system in your home." He smiles politely and I scowl.

"I didn't order you."

"I know, Mr. Montgomery did."

"How do you know?" I ask.

"Because I own the company, ma'am. He asked me to do it personally."

I sigh deeply and lean my forehead against the door. I guess there's no getting out of this.

"How long will it take?" I ask, resigned to letting it happen.

"Most of the day. This is a full system."

"How much is my monthly bill going to be?" I ask and juggle some things around in my head. I could disconnect the cable.

"It's been paid in full for the next year," he replies as he makes notes on his clipboard.

"Seriously?"

"Yep. Can I get started?"

"Go ahead. I'll be in the shower, but then I'll be around if you have questions."

"That's fine, I'll start outside anyway."

I trudge back to my bedroom and flop down on the bed. I grab my phone and dial Will's number.

"Hey, gorgeous," he whispers.

"Why are you whispering?" I whisper back.

"Because we're watching tape from yesterday's game. Why are you whispering?" I hear the smile in his voice and it makes me grin.

"Because you're whispering."

"Did the alarm guy show up?"

"Yes, control freak, he did."

Will chuckles softly. "Good. I trust him, he's done all of my family's homes and businesses."

"Okay. Did you have to send him so early?"

"It's ten am, sweetheart."

"I didn't go to bed until four," I remind him.

"I'm sorry, I forgot."

"It's fine. I didn't want to sleep my whole day away anyway." I get up and start the shower. "I'll let you get back to your tape."

"Okay. Do you have tomorrow off?"

"Yeah."

"I have to train in the morning until about noon, but then I want to spend the rest of the day with you."

God, his whispery voice is sexy as fuck.

"Sure, what do you have in mind?"

"You'll find out tomorrow. I'll pick you up at noon."

He hangs up and I take a long, scalding hot shower. It wakes me up and invigorates me. I dress in a loose, floaty black tank dress and head into the kitchen, open my laptop on the countertop.

While it wakes up, I brew some coffee.

Thank God for coffee.

I hear drilling and see the security system guys bustling about the townhouse, one in the front and one in the back. So while they work, I decide to work a little too, catching up on email, Facebook and bills, while I bring up my favorite station on internet radio.

By the time the alarm workers are done at around six, I'm caught up with my virtual social life, emails, made a few calls and I'm broke. Well, I will be, anyway, when I send Sylvia her check.

I'm shown how to set my alarm, disable it, punch in my passcode, and call for help. It's incredibly scary.

Not the idea of being burgled, but how many damn steps I have to go through to arm this fucker.

When I'm finally alone, I slip on my flip-flops and head out for a walk through the neighborhood. I don't know why Will is so freaked out about my safety. My neighborhood isn't that bad. It's just an average, middle-class area of Seattle. In fact, the majority of my subdivision is townhomes. Some are condos, and most are single or childless couples who live there. Surrounding us are single family homes, all rather cookie-cutter, built in the last five years or so.

It's not the freaking ghetto.

But if it helps *him* sleep at night, whatever.

It's unseasonably warm for a late-summer day in Seattle. There's not a cloud hanging in the bright blue sky, and the trees are just barely starting to turn yellow. Before we know it, they'll turn red and then fall, leaving the trees bare.

I wave hello to my neighbor and cross the street to my house, to see Will sitting on my front steps, elbows braced on his jean-clad knees, wearing a black Nike t-shirt and black Oakley sunglasses. I can't see his eyes, but his mouth is tilted in a half smile and I can feel him watch me saunter up to him.

As I get closer I put a bit more swing in my hips, enjoying the way the dress floats around my thighs, and grin down at him.

"I thought you were picking me up tomorrow at noon." I plant my hands on my hips and try to look stern, but it so doesn't work. I'm happy to see him after his trip to San Francisco.

"I am. But I decided to drop by, make sure the alarm was installed okay." He reaches his hand out for mine and pulls me into his lap. I squeal in surprise and then giggle and wrap my arms around his neck.

"Is that the only reason?" I smile up at him and tug his Oakleys off. His blue eyes are happy and hot.

"I needed to see you," he whispers and hugs me hard, burying his face in my neck and breathing me in.

God he feels good.

"I missed you," he murmurs and kisses my cheek, then pulls back and looks me in the eye again. "How are you?"

"I'm good. It was a busy weekend at work, between football games and deliveries and those pesky things we call patients." I giggle and push my hand through his dark blonde hair. It's soft and feels so good, I do it again. "Seriously, thank you, for everything you did for the kids, and for me, this past week. It far surpassed anything any of us were expecting."

"So, you watched the game? Not just half-time?" He smiles, but I can tell he's hopeful that I did, that I watched him to support him and because I'm proud of him.

And I am.

"I watched most of it, yeah. I have to cover my eyes when you get tackled. I hate that part. And thank you for half time. That was cool." I grin.

"You're welcome." He brushes my hair behind my shoulder and looks so serious all of a sudden.

"What's wrong?"

"Nothing." He shakes his head and smiles down at me again. "I brought pizza."

"I will never turn down a man with pizza." I scramble out of his lap and unlock the door, then lead the way inside.

"Why the fuck isn't your alarm set?"

Chapter Six

I spin around and glare at him, and plant my hands on my hips. "I was gone for fifteen minutes, Will. In the sunlight. Why the fuck are you freaking out?"

"Will you please, for the love of God, set the damn alarm when you leave the house?" His words are measured, and it's obvious he's trying really, really hard to stay calm.

"Can I leave it off when I check the mail?" I ask sarcastically.

He purses his lips like he's thinking really hard, the smart ass. "Yes."

"Gee, thanks. Now, give me that pizza before I throw you out for being so bossy."

He grins, holds the pizza out of my reach, and shuts the door behind him and locks it. "What's your code?"

"What if you're the one I'm trying to keep out?" I ask with a sassy grin. He raises one eyebrow at me and waits for an answer. "That look doesn't work on me."

"I won't share my pizza if you don't tell me."

"Bribing me with pizza?" I scoff. He grins and shrugs, and he's so damn adorable in this moment, I'd tell him my blood type, social security and grandmother's maiden name, if I knew it. "Fine. One two three four."

"Your code is one two three four?" he asks with a laugh.

"I'll remember it."

He shakes his head and leads me to the kitchen, still holding the pizza over his head.

"Will you please explain to me why you're so adamant about the alarm? I've never had any issues in this neighborhood, Will. It's perfectly safe here." I follow him and pull down plates for our meal.

He takes a look around the small kitchen and grins. "It looks different in here in the light."

Ah yes, the last time he was here, I was drunk as fuck and he had to take care of me.

"I like this kitchen," he continues.

I look around the space and grin. This kitchen is what sold me on the townhouse. It's open to the living room, has light granite countertops and light wood cabinets, making it feel bright and cheerful.

"Thanks. Now spill it, Montgomery."

Will sighs and slides pizza on the two plates, and hands me mine.

"Beer?" he asks.

"Fridge."

He pulls out two beers, pops the tops and leads me to the living room. I sit on the couch and he folds himself onto the floor, leaning against the couch. I can feel the warmth of him against my leg.

"I know I sound really controlling about the alarm, Meg. But it's really important to me because as our relationship progresses, people will try to get to you. Press, weird fans, people with morbid curiosity. And like I said before, I'm gone a lot, and I don't live here with you, so I can't be here all the time to protect you." He pauses to eat and frowns as he thinks.

I'm just speechless. *As our relationship progresses?* I'm stuck like stupid on that one sentence.

"What relationship?" I ask, confused. "We've known each other for three minutes. We haven't even had a whole date."

Will's jaw drops and he blinks rapidly, then clenches his jaw and glares at me.

"What, exactly, do you think I'm trying to pursue here, Megan? If I just wanted to fuck you and bail, I would have backed off as soon as you told me no at my sister's party." He shakes his head and pushes his pizza away.

"I just..." I begin, but he interrupts me, not hearing me.

"Yes, it's early, but fuck Megan, all I do is think about you. You've gotten under my skin. I want to learn your body. I want to know what it feels like to sink inside of you." He swallows hard and so do I as I squeeze my thighs together and feel myself go wet.

"But I also want to know what makes you laugh. What pisses you off. What you're passionate about. I just want to learn everything about you. You're in my head, and I haven't felt this way in a long time. Jesus, I don't give shout-outs to women during every game for fuck sake."

He looks truly rattled and I soften, just a bit. Moving fast? A little. But he wants me safe, and I can appreciate that.

We have a relationship. Huh.

"I want to get to know you too," I murmur and smile happily.

"So," he continues and looks up at me with serious blue eyes. "Please be patient with me, and just set the damn alarm when you leave, and when you're alone inside."

"Okay," I shrug like it's no big, and continue eating my pizza.

"You're not going to argue?"

"No, why would I? It's just an alarm. But I don't like being bossed around, so just talk to me about stuff, okay?"

Will smirks and sets both of our empty plates aside. He lifts himself onto the couch, his arms flexing all sexy-like and I just sit back and watch him move.

He's just so… *hot.*

Suddenly, he's pulling me in his arms, settles me against him, kisses the top of my head and grabs the remote to my television.

"What are you doing?" I ask with a laugh.

"Watching TV."

"Why?"

"Because you won't let me make love to you, so I have to distract myself somehow."

Holy shit on a stick.

I gape up at him. "Unless you've changed your mind about the three date rule?"

"Are you turning this whole pizza and TV thing into a date?" I ask him, suddenly hopeful.

"You noticed." He kisses my nose and smiles proudly at me.

"Then no, I haven't changed my mind." I settle against him and watch him flip through the channels. When he gets to the movie channels, and finds them blocked out, he frowns down at me.

"No movie channels?"

"No."

"Why?"

"They charge an arm and a leg for them, and I wouldn't watch them often anyway. I just go to one of the kiosk things for movies when I'm in the mood."

"Hmm, okay." His hand is moving rhythmically up and down my side, gently caressing me through my dress. My arm is around his lean waist, and I really, really want to feel his smooth skin, so I lift the hem of his soft shirt and slide my hand under it against his ripped abs. He sucks in a breath and his stomach tightens, but as he gets used to my touch, he exhales and kisses the top of my head.

I smile smugly as I feel him lift the hem of my dress and slide his hand under it, caressing my skin along my thigh.

God, that feels good.

I sigh and continue to touch him, enjoying his skin, the way his breath hitches when I hit a ticklish spot. I feel him wince when I touch one of his ribs and I frown up at him.

"Does that hurt?"

"A little," his face is calm and he doesn't explain further. I move my hand lightly over the rib again and he grimaces.

"A little, my ass." I climb over him and pull his shirt up so I can see his ribs and sure enough, there is a deep purple bruise. "Sunday?" I ask.

"Yeah. No big deal."

I glare up at him and then down at the bruise again. "I don't like it."

"I'm not in love with it myself, sweetheart," he laughs and pulls me back to him.

"Does this happen a lot?"

"Meg, I have three hundred pound guys crashing into me. Of course I get bumped and bruised. I'll live."

I frown again and look down at his chest, not saying anything. I hate the thought of him getting hurt.

He tilts my head back with his fingers on my chin and smiles softly down at me. "I'm okay."

I run my fingers down his smooth cheek. His eyes close as he leans into my touch, then he kisses my palm, and pins me with those blue eyes.

"I'm going to kiss you," he whispers.

"It's about time," I whisper back. He grins and kisses my forehead, down to my nose, over to the dimple in my cheek, and then lays those lips on mine, resting them there, for just a second, and then he starts to move. Those amazing lips nibble mine, and finally his tongue licks my bottom lip and leisurely makes love to my own, dancing and twirling, gently exploring me.

This is so different from when he kissed me at the party. This is intimate and tender. I love both sides to him, and can't wait to learn more about him.

I push my fingers up into his hair and moan contentedly as he continues the soft assault on my mouth.

He pulls back slightly, breathing hard, his eyes on fire. "I wouldn't mind kissing your lips all fucking day."

"I wouldn't mind that either," I murmur and grin at him.

"I hate your rule, you know."

"I kind of hate it right now, too," I admit and chuckle.

"You're worth it." He runs his knuckles down my cheek. "Hey, what happened to the pink?"

I frown at the change of subject, not understanding what he means and then I remember; my hair. "It's not permanent. It's this hair chalk stuff that I can paint my hair with, and then it washes out."

"Oh, that's cool." His hand glides up my thigh again, under my dress and I sigh. When he gets up to my hip, his eyes widen in surprise. "You're not wearing any underwear?"

"I rarely do." I shrug.

"So, no pajamas and no underwear." He swallows hard, clenches his eyes shut, and swears under his breath. His hand has stilled on my hip like he's afraid to move it.

Maybe my rule is stupid.

Maybe it would be okay to break the rule, just this once. He's already told me that he wants to pursue something more than just sex with me, and isn't that the point of the rule anyway?

He opens his eyes and gazes down at me, and smiles gently. I brush my fingers through his hair, then cup the nape of his neck and pull him down to me. I nuzzle his nose and kiss him chastely.

"Touch me," I whisper.

He pushes a strand of hair behind my ear, and sighs deeply.

"I won't be able to stop."

"So don't stop." I grin at him and he glares at me, making me laugh.

"You can't change the rules, Meg."

"Why not? It was my rule."

"Because, you'll resent me for it later." His hand clenches on my hip for just a brief second, and then glides back down my thigh.

Okay, he's going to be all gentlemanly. Damn him.

"Will," I whisper and kiss him again.

"Yeah."

"I really need you to touch me." *God, please touch me.*

In one large, smooth move, his hand glides up my thigh, over my ass, to my back and back down again. I groan and push my hands under his shirt, running my hands over his smooth, warm skin.

"Can I take your dress off?" he asks.

"Yes, please."

It's dark in the living room now, the only light coming from the glow of the muted television. He sits up and pushes me to my feet before him, grips the hem of my dress and pulls it over my head and tosses it on the floor. He sucks in a loud breath and his deep blue eyes are hot as he looks me up and down from my hair, down my black-bra covered chest, my stomach, waxed pubis and legs, and then they travel back up again and find my own eyes.

"Take your bra off," he murmurs.

I comply and throw it on top of the dress.

"Dear God, Megan, you're beautiful."

I grin down at him and suddenly he pulls me down into his lap and cups a breast in his palm as he kisses me senseless. I trace the muscles in his shoulder with one hand and bury the other in his hair and hold him close to me while his hands roam over my sensitive body.

God, his hands feel so damn good!

Finally, he trails kisses along my jaw and over to my neck where he pays extra-special attention as his hand travels oh-so-slowly south.

"I knew you felt good, and I knew you'd look fantastic, but you surpass every fantasy I've had about you, sweetheart."

"Hmm. I want to see you," I mutter but he shakes his head and chuckles.

"Not yet. This is about you, honey."

I start to protest, but then those magical fingers slip down over my pubis and find my center and everything in Will, those fingers, his breath, even his heart, still.

"What is this?" He pulls back and stares down at me in awe.

Oh, that.

"It's a piercing," I respond and lean up to kiss him again but he pulls back and his eyes narrow.

"Your clit is pierced?" he asks incredulously.

"No, technically, my clitoral hood is pierced."

"Fuck, I have to see this." He stands abruptly with me in his arms, and just when I think he's finally going to take me up to my bedroom, he lays me gently down on the couch. He turns off the TV, but flips on a soft lamp and kneels on the floor next to my head.

"You're amazing, you know that, right?" He kisses me softly, gently teasing my tongue with his, and then nibbles his way down my jaw again to my ear and down my neck to my collar bones.

"Will," I grip his shirt in my fists and try to pull it over his head but he backs away.

"Honey, I can't get naked." He swallows and shakes his head. "I can't. We're going to respect your goddamn three date rule, but I want to explore you a bit. Is that okay?"

"Okay," I whisper and he smiles wickedly.

"Just lay back and enjoy." He captures a nipple in his mouth and suckles it gently at first and then a bit harder, making me moan. His hands are *everywhere*. Brushing up and down my ribs, down my thighs, and up again. Finally, after he pays special attention to the other nipple, he begins to gently bite, suck and nibble his way down my stomach as his hand glides up the inside of my thigh.

"Will…"

"Shh, it's okay."

He spreads my legs and sits there, just looking down at my center, and I suddenly become very shy.

"Turn the light off," I whisper.

His eyes find mine. His face is tight with lust, his eyes bright, and his jaw ticking from clenching his jaw shut.

"Not a chance," he growls. "I want to see you. Fuck, Meg, you're so sexy."

He settles on his elbows and gently brushes my piercing with his fingertip. It makes my back arch and catch my breath.

"Shit."

"How long have you had this?" he asks.

"Five years."

"Why?" he asks and brushes it with his thumb while his fingers slide through my wet lips and I gasp again. "God, you're so wet."

"I was in a band, people had piercings, I didn't want mine to show." The words come out super-fast because of what he's doing to me and he chuckles.

"Does it heighten pleasure?" he asks and I swear again as he barely brushes the little bar-bell and it sets my clit on fire.

"What do you think?" Fuck, I can't stop moving.

"It's tiny," he remarks.

"It's a tiny part of my body," I remind him ruefully and then squirm again as he brushes it one more time with his finger.

Will kisses my navel, and I push my hands into his hair. He moves down and gently wraps those amazing lips around my clit and metal and I come undone, pushing against his mouth, raising my hips up off the cushion. His hands are cupping my ass, holding me against him and I ride my orgasm, jerking and shuddering, and suddenly his lips move farther down and his tongue is inside me, then licking my labia, and inside me again. It's a full-on assault Will-style, and it's the most amazing fucking thing I've ever experienced in my life.

He sinks his tongue inside me again and pulls one hand around to worry my clit some more and I feel another orgasm building.

"Ah, hell, babe, I'm gonna…"

He growls against me and I lose it, this orgasm completely eclipsing the last one, if that's even possible.

When I surface, Will is nibbling his way back up my body, caressing my skin gently, and then he's kissing me softly and his fingers are running gently down my face.

"So sweet," he murmurs against my lips.

I can taste myself on him. I reach for the hem of his shirt again and push my hand under it so I can caress his back, his ribs. He sighs deeply and rests his forehead on mine, eyes closed.

"Your hands feel good," he whispers.

"So do yours. Take your clothes off."

He sighs again, kisses my forehead and sits back on his heels.

"I don't think so." He shakes his head and then chuckles ruefully while scrubbing his hands over his face. "I can't believe I'm going to say this, but I think I'd better go."

What??

He must see the alarm on my face because he chuckles again and kisses me swiftly.

"I'm picking you up for date number two tomorrow at noon." His eyes take one more leisurely stroll down my naked body and he curses under his breath.

"Okay," I respond, a bit unsure, and sit up, tug my dress over my head and stand as he also rises from the floor.

"You are incredible." He cups my face in his hands and leans down to kiss me softly.

I lead him to the front door, punch the code into the alarm system to disarm it and open the door for him.

"Noon tomorrow," he reminds me, as if I could ever forget.

"It's a date." I smile shyly at him.

"Set this alarm when I leave." He glares down at me, daring me to defy him and I giggle.

"Yes, sir."

Chapter Seven

"How many times have you been here?" Will asks me as we stand in line waiting to purchase tickets for *Seattle's Experience Music Project Museum.* It's a music museum, and so much more.

I love this place.

"Dozens," I smile up at him, *geez he's tall* and squeeze his hand. "It changes all the time, with new exhibits and stuff. Plus, I could just sit and stare at the guitars for days. Have you ever been?"

"No, I've just never taken the time." He winks down at me. "I'm a rookie."

"That's okay, I'll protect you."

He smirks and pays for our tickets, and I lead him into the museum.

We wander up to the second floor where the exhibits are and I get lost in Jimi Hendrix, Nirvana, The Stones, the guitar gallery. I point out interesting tid bits of information for Will and drag him from room to room.

I love sharing this with him, and I love how interested he seems. He's not just tagging along, trying to make me happy.

Best. Date. Ever.

We head up to the third floor and stand and stare at the enormous guitar sculpture. It's at least fifty feet tall and is made up of real guitars, of all different shapes and sizes and colors. My eyes travel up it, examining the instruments, and I feel Will's eyes on me.

"What?" I ask without looking at him.

"You look awesome in that outfit."

"This old thing?" I ask and smirk, still not looking away from the sculpture. I'm in a white v-neck t-shirt with a loose, brown cotton vest over skinny blue jeans.

After a few moments, he's still watching me.

"Do I have something on my face?" I ask dryly.

"No, you're just so beautiful, with your auburn hair spilling down your back and pink lips parted. I like watching you. You love this, don't you?"

"More than almost anything," I respond truthfully. Music saved me when I was taken from Sylvia. It was my whole life in college.

"I've heard there's a place here where you can get on stage," Will comments casually and I grin.

"There is. No, I'm not getting on it," I murmur before he can suggest it.

"Why?"

"Stage fright," I reply and start to lead him away from the sculpture.

"Bullshit." Will laughs and pulls me against him, his front to my back, and wraps his arms around my waist, kissing my head. "You're not shy, sweetheart."

"I just don't want to."

"I would love to hear you. Please?"

I sigh against him. I haven't sung for anyone other than my patients since college. Since the band broke up and Leo left town.

"Maybe," I mutter and he chuckles behind me.

"Let's go find it. Before you change your mind."

"It's not far."

We turn a corner, and sure enough, there it is. There's a room with a stage boasting instruments, lights, even a sound machine that will emit applause and crowd sounds if you really want to feel like a rock star.

Because it's the middle of the week, there aren't many people wandering through the museum today, and this room is empty, which is unusual because most people love interactive exhibits.

"Go ahead. I'm dying here."

I grin up at him and wrinkle up my nose, then gaze back at the stage.

"Why not?" I shrug and climb on stage. I grab an acoustic guitar, plug it into the amp and sit on a stool in the middle of the stage.

There's suddenly a spotlight on me, and one of the museum employees waves at me and speaks into a mic. "You're ready to go, miss."

I nod and strum the guitar, making sure it's in tune, and speak to Will through the mic.

"What do you want to hear, sir?"

Will laughs. "Whatever you know."

"I know a lot." I search through the library in my head and settle on one. "Okay, this one is called *I Never Told You.*"

I strum the guitar and clear my throat and murmur, "I can't believe I'm doing this."

Will laughs at me, his eyes happy and trained intently on me and I just smile and shake my head and continue playing the intro, and then start singing about a blue eyed boy whom I miss after all the things we'd been through. The song is sweet and a little sad, and reminds me a little of Leo, although I was never in love with Leo.

The song comes to an end. I open my eyes and look out at Will. His face is completely sober, his eyes unblinking and still trained on me. He's leaned his elbows on his knees and isn't moving.

Glancing around, it occurs to me that other patrons have filed in to listen to the song, and are now applauding, snapping me into the here and now. I smile and say thanks, put the guitar away and walk down the steps toward Will, who is now standing, waiting patiently for me.

"Come here," he crooks his finger at me and I comply, walking to him.

He pulls me into his arms and off my feet, buries his face in my neck and holds on tight. I have no choice but to wrap my arms tightly around his neck.

"That was beautiful. Meg, why did you ever stop?" he asks as he sets me down, takes my hand and leads me out of the theater. If he hears the other patrons murmur about him being 'Will Montgomery' and snapping our photo with their cell phones, he pays them no mind.

"Leo left." I shrug and feel a tug on my arm as Will stops dead in his tracks.

"Who the fuck is Leo?"

"He was my best friend since I was twelve, and band mate. He's five years older."

"And you were in a band together?" Will asks, his voice no softer and I sigh.

"Yes, through college. We got pretty good. He decided to pursue a career in music down in LA and I chose to stay here to pursue nursing." Of course, I leave out the part about Leo signing with a band behind my back and that he's now the lead singer of one of the hottest bands in the freaking world.

"Do you really prefer nursing? Honey, you're a fantastic musician."

"Thank you." I kiss his cheek as he holds my door open for me to climb into his car. When he joins me in the car I continue. "I love being a nurse, Will. I'm a damn good one."

"I know you are." He takes my hand in his and kisses my fingers before linking them with his and lays our hands in his lap. "I'm just surprised. With a voice like yours, you could go really far."

"I'm where I need to be," I say softly.

"Okay." He winks at me and grins. "Thank you for singing for me."

"You're welcome."

"Are you hungry?" he asks. I check the time, and gasp.

"We spent all afternoon there! It's almost dinner time. So, yeah, I'm hungry."

"Wanna try burgers again?" he asks with a grin and I smirk.

"Not in downtown Seattle."

"Nah, I know a place."

* * *

"I want to show you something," Will says out of the blue. We're in his car, having finished our burgers at Red Mill, the same place where we first met that day when I ran into him and

Jules.

"What?"

"Well, you shared a really important part of yourself with me today."

It thrills me that he understands how important music is to me. I smile at him and wait for him to continue.

"So, I want to share something important to me with you."

"I'm game," I reply happily.

"Ironic choice of words." Will chuckles and merges onto Interstate 5 heading south into the city center. I sit back into the plush leather seat and enjoy the ride in this sexy car of his. God, I love this car. It turns me on, big time.

I look over at Will and lick my lips.

He glances my way and then does a double take and gives me a confused smile.

"What?"

"Your car is sexy."

"Are we back at this again?" he asks and laughs as he changes lanes.

"You look sexy as hell in this car." I turn in my seat and face him.

His eyes find mine again. "This is only the second date."

As if I need a reminder.

"Yep."

"You keep fucking me with your eyes like that…"

"And what?" I interrupt him. "You had me naked and coming on my couch last night and didn't break the rule. I doubt me eye-fucking you will make you break it either."

"Jesus, keep talking like that, honey, and see how fast I break your rule. You have quite the dirty mouth you know."

"I know." I shrug and laugh. "I went to college with Jules and Natalie. Have you heard them talk lately?"

Will smirks and takes an exit off the freeway.

"Besides," I continue. "I hung out with a band full of guys. I was never destined to have a clean mouth."

Suddenly it occurs to me that maybe my language offends him.

"Does it bother you?" I ask.

"Does what bother me?" he asks and pulls into a private underground parking lot under the football stadium.

"My mouth."

"Your mouth is delicious."

"My language, smart ass," I mutter and smack his arm.

"Ouch! You like it rough, sweetheart?" He offers me a wolfish smile and I laugh.

"Sometimes, yeah."

This gives him pause. He parks the car, shuts it off and stares at me. "Seriously."

"Sure." I shrug. "You didn't answer my question."

He just stares at me, his mouth agape. I rub his thigh gently with my fingertips.

"Will?"

"Yeah?" He comes out of his trance and swallows.

"Does my language offend you?"

"No." He shakes his head and frowns. "You're not nearly as bad as Jules."

"Few are, Will." I laugh and climb out of his sexy car. He waits for me, takes my hand, and leads me to an elevator.

"So, obviously, we're at the football playing place," I comment casually in the elevator.

"Football playing place?" Will asks and doubles over in laughter.

"You know what I mean."

"Do you know anything about football?" he asks, delighted with me, and I glare at him.

"Of course I do."

"What position do I play?" he asks.

"Is this a quiz?"

"A little one."

"You're the quarterback."

"Who do I throw the ball to?" He ushers me out of the elevator and then leans against a wall and crosses his arms over his chest.

"Another guy in a blue and green uniform." I respond confidently. "Usually," I add, earning a glare from him.

"I'm going to torture you for that."

"I hope so, babe." I grin at him and his face sobers. "What?"

"Why can you call me babe, but I can't call you that?" he asks.

Good point. I frown and shrug. "I guess babe doesn't sound like baby to me. It sounds more grown up, maybe? I don't know. It doesn't weird me out, though."

"Okay, so noted. Come on."

He takes my hand again and pulls me down a long hall and through an enormous set of double doors that open up to a tunnel that leads up to the football field. All of the stadium lights are on. It's empty.

"How...?"

"I called ahead while you were in the restroom at the restaurant and asked someone to turn the lights on for me." He continues pulling me out on the field and stops, right in the center of the fifty-yard line.

"Wow," I whisper and look around the stadium. "How many people can this seat?" I ask.

"Sixty-seven thousand," he states like it's no big thing, and I stare at him with an open mouth and wide eyes.

"Holy shit."

"We sell out every weekend."

I knew that. Yet, being here, right here, in the middle of the field, looking around at the empty stadium seats, at the enormity of this place, just about knocks me on my ass.

In fact, I just sit, right there, on the turf.

"Are you okay?" he asks, his brow creasing with worry and joins me on the ground.

I'm speechless as I gaze around the stadium, and it occurs to me that this could have been me, on stage, singing in front of sixty-seven thousand people, rather than small little clubs around Seattle, or reception halls full of wedding guests. If Leo hadn't made the decision to go without me, I would have been singing in places just like this one.

"Meg?" Will's worried voice pulls me out of my trance and I shrug.

"You must not get stage fright either," I murmur.

"Only during the play-offs," he replies and pushes my hair back over my shoulder. I love how he's always touching me.

"You're a lot to take in, you know?" I ask him.

He smiles shyly, and frowns for a second, looking down at this hands. "I can be, yeah. But remember, this is just what I do. It's only part of who I am."

"It's important to you," I remind him and he nods.

"Very. I've played football for as long as I can remember." He takes one of my hands in his and plays with my fingers. "Football got me through school, Meg. I knew I had to get good grades and stay out of trouble if I wanted to stay on the team. And I did. I wanted the camaraderie with the guys. I had some really smart coaches who pushed me and taught me. It earned me a scholarship to college, and I worked my ass off there too."

He takes a deep breath and looks up, his eyes taking in the stadium, the scoreboard, the ads. "This is all I ever wanted, and I was lucky enough to get here."

"This isn't luck," I state firmly and his gaze whips to mine, surprised. "Will, this is the result of you working your ass off and earning it. I may not know everything there is to know about football, but I know that it's not easy, and I know that I'm so very proud of you. Not because of your contract, or the jersey you wear – which you look damn hot in, by the way – but because you're doing what you always dreamed of. How many of us can say that?"

His eyes soften as he cups my cheek in his big hand and rubs his thumb across my lower lip. He leans toward me and brushes his magical lips over mine, and then sinks into me, pushing me back to lie on the turf. He runs that hand down my face, over my breast, and rests it on my hip as he continues to make love to my mouth, his tongue searching and dancing. Our breathing quickens, and dear God, *I want him.*

He pulls back and gazes down at me. "Someone's probably watching us," he murmurs. He kisses my forehead and then lies on his back beside me. We just lay here, breathing hard.

"I should tell you something," I whisper.

"What?" I feel him look over at me, but I just look up at the black night sky above the brightly lit, empty stadium.

"I want to suck your dick in your car."

"What?!" He pushes up on his elbow, leans over me, and makes me look him in the eye. "I don't think I heard you right."

"Your car makes me crazy, Will." I lick my lips and grin. "All I've thought about since the other day is going down on you in your car."

I've never seen anyone spring to their feet so quickly in my life. He pulls me to my feet as well and starts stalking back the way we came.

"Slow down! Will, your legs are longer than mine!" I'm practically running behind him, and he stops abruptly and turns back to me. He looks pissed, his eyes narrowed and on fire, mouth tight, jaw clenched. I take an involuntary step back. "I'm sorry, I didn't mean to sound like such a whore, I just…"

"If you ever call yourself a whore again," he pushes his face into mine, his nose only centimeters from touching my own, "I will take you over my knee and spank the hell out of you. Do you understand me? You turn me inside out. I want to fuck you seven shades of Sunday, and I want to make long, slow, sweet love to you for days. I'm craving you, goddamn it, and you can't just say shit like that to me when I know what you taste like, and what you look like and I need desperately to know what the fuck you feel like."

I blink at him, completely thrown.

Well, okay then.

"Now, as much as I want to strip you naked and take you on the fifty-yard-line, I don't need those photos surfacing on the internet any more than you do."

And with that he bends down and in one swift move, lifts me onto his shoulder and begins carrying me off the field, just as quickly as he was before.

"I can walk," I remind him.

"Not fast enough," he mutters and slaps my ass.

"Hey!"

"You deserve that and more, now shut up, Megan."

Holy fuck.

We get to the car and he sets me on my feet, and then helps me into the passenger seat. He walks briskly around the car and folds himself easily behind the wheel, starts the car and pulls out of the garage, speeding toward the freeway.

His handsome face is scowling and he won't look at me.

I'm not sure what to think. Why is he so pissed off? Too much sexual tension? Well, join the club, sexy man.

"So…" I start but he interrupts me.

"Don't talk."

What?

We're back on Interstate 5, heading north this time, and he's driving way past the speed limit. He passes the exit for my place, and I frown over at him but he doesn't acknowledge me. Suddenly, he's pulling off the freeway, turns left, and follows the road to an exclusive part of Seattle. The homes are set back from the road with gates. He approaches the end of the street, pulls into a drive and enters a code for the gate.

"The code is 051877. Can you remember that?"

"Oh, so you're speaking to me," I mutter sarcastically.

He just looks over at me expectantly until I huff and say, "051877."

The gate opens and Will drives us down to a beautiful home that has an unbelievable view of the Puget Sound. From what I can see in the semi-darkness, the house is a traditional-style stone house, two stories, with a four car garage.

"Wow. This is beautiful."

"Thank you," he mutters and pulls the car into a garage, parks and cuts the engine. He unbuckles both of our belts and looks over at me, just stares at me for a long minute.

"What is it?" I whisper.

"I want you."

"I sort of figured that out, babe." I offer him a smile, but he doesn't return it. Maybe this is an invitation without actually asking me, to make good on what I said in the stadium?

"Are you wearing underwear?" I ask him.

He laughs ruefully – *finally!* – and shakes his head. "Of course. Most people do, Meg."

"Tilt your seat back," I tell him. He holds my gaze and does as I ask. I kick off my shoes and pull my legs under me in the seat, settling my butt on my heels. Bracing my hands on his shoulders, I lean in and kiss him hard and deep, earning a growl from deep in his throat. I reach down and unbutton and unzip his jeans and he helps me by raising his hips and shimmying his pants and *really sexy* white boxer briefs down his hips, letting his heavy, long, thick erection spring free.

Jesus H. Christ, the man is hung! Given his height, this shouldn't surprise me in the least, but it does intimidate me. I bite my lip and look into his gorgeous blue eyes uncertainly.

"What's wrong, babe?" he asks me and runs his knuckles down my cheek.

"When we do finally get to have sex, I'm not sure…" I can't complete the sentence and he chuckles.

"You'll stretch, Meg." His eyes are warm and happy, and he pulls me in for another long, slow kiss. I reach down and stroke him, loving the velvet-soft skin, the feel of the veins, and the smooth, round tip.

"Goddamn, honey." He throws his head back and sucks in a deep breath. "Your hands should come with a warning label."

I grin and lick the head of his cock, right across the top, lapping up the little bead of dew that already formed there. His hips buck up off the seat and I decide I've played nice long enough.

I want to drive him fucking mad.

I lick him from his balls to the tip, and then back down again, and then, cupping his scrotum in one hand, I sink down on him and suck.

"Holy, fuck!" He sinks his hands in my hair and gently starts to guide me up and down his hardness. I suck and lick, and suck and lick some more with each movement and continue the torture with my hands. I feel his balls tighten in my right hand, and I know it won't be long before he loses control.

So I sink down on him as far as I can, until I feel him deep in my throat, and slip my finger down past his scrotum to that sensitive skin just underneath and I rub gently, making him crazy.

"Megan, I'm going to come."

I hum in pleasure, but I feel him holding back, so I repeat the motions, move my mouth up and down his shaft, and rub that little spot below his scrotum.

"Ah, fuck!" Will comes violently, shoots his warmth into the back of my mouth and I swallow quickly. I continue to lick and tease him as droplets continue to flow out of his slit, and I smile as his body goes lax.

I look up into his deep blue eyes and offer him a shy grin. "Was that okay?"

"Sweetheart, if that had been any more okay, I would have died."

I laugh as he tucks himself back in, and then he leans over and kisses me hard and fast.

"Stay with me tonight."

Yes!

"Not for sex," he continues. "Although I'm about to kill some-one if I don't get inside you soon. I just don't want to be without you tonight. You can stay in my spare room if you want."

"Can I sleep with you?"

"If you wear one of my shirts, yes."

"Deal."

Chapter Eight

I wake with a start, sitting up in bed, disoriented. I'm swimming in a huge football jersey and boy boxer-briefs, which immediately throws me off. I take in the large room, bathed in moonlight, and remember I'm in Will's room.

In Will's bed.

The sexy man is sleeping soundly next to me, on his side, facing me. His handsome face is relaxed in sleep and there is stubble starting to grow on his firm, square chin. His hair is messier than usual, begging my fingers to run through it.

So I do.

He's also in a t-shirt and pajama pants, and when he brought me here, to his beautifully decorated bedroom, and bed the size of a small country, he'd been tender and sweet and the perfect gentleman.

I love it and I hate it.

I'm ready to give my body to him. Hell, I think I've already given him my heart, and that scares the hell out of me.

I lie like this for a long while, gently brushing his soft almost-brown hair with my fingers, memorizing his sleeping face. He shifts slightly and reaches up to take my hand in his, kisses my hand, and without opening his eyes, pulls me against his chest, wraps his arms around me and holds me close.

"Go back to sleep, sweetheart," he whispers and kisses my hair.

My eyes close, and I fall asleep to the sound of his heart against my ear.

* * *

"Do you know how to drive a stick?" Will asks me nervously as I adjust the driver's seat in his sexy Mustang.

"Of course I do. Don't insult me," I shoot him a mock glare and then smile widely, jumping up and down in the seat. "Gimme the keys."

"You're adorable." He's grinning at me, enjoying my enthusiasm. He's letting me drive his car to our date tonight.

"I'm ready to drive. Hand them over, Montgomery." I hold my hand out, palm up, waiting for the keys. He kisses my palm, and then drops the keys in it.

"Okay, let's go."

I press on the clutch and start the car. It purrs to life and I sigh in happiness.

"I might have an orgasm while I drive," I mention casually.

"I'd rather you didn't," Will laughs. "Let's get there in once piece, sweetheart."

"Where are we going, anyway?" I ask and start to pull into his driveway, but kill the car, making it jerk frantically.

"Holy shit!" Will exclaims, gripping onto the car door.

"Sorry. Just getting used to the clutch." I start the car again and pull into the drive, ignoring the glares coming at me from the passenger seat.

"Don't kill my transmission."

"Oh, calm down. It's just a car, right?" I bat my eyes at him and giggle when he twists my ear in his fingers. "Where are we going?"

"Bowling. The Alley not far from your place."

"A couples date?" I ask incredulously.

"No, a family date," Will clarifies.

I stare at his profile for a second and then look back to the road and can't help but laugh. "Is this your plan to keep your hands off me until the official end of the third date?" I ask.

He smirks and then rubs his hand down his face. "Fuck."

"We almost had sex with your family sitting twenty feet away before, Will."

He glares at me and then smirks again. "You were hot for me even then."

"Whatever, don't flatter yourself." I smother a happy smile and focus on the conversation at hand. "Why bowling?"

"Well, a few times a year we all like to get together and go."

I gape at him, trying to wrap my head around Luke Williams, movie-star, bowling.

"It's okay, sweetheart, I'll show you how."

This time I can't stop my smug smile. I bowl quite well, thank you very much, but I choose to let him think he'll be giving me instructions. Hmm… Will, pressed up against my back, showing me how to roll the ball down the lane… yes, this has possibilities.

"So, who's going to be there?" I ask and purposely swerve on the two-lane side street, just to get a rise out of Will.

"Hey! Stay in your lane!"

"You have insurance," I smirk at him, earning another glare. I laugh out loud, enjoying both him and the car.

This car is fucking amazing.

"Who's going with us?" I ask again.

"Jules and Nate, Luke and Nat, Brynna, Isaac and Stacy, although she'll just watch because she's miserably pregnant at this point." He offers me a wide smile. "And I think Matt and Caleb and Luke's sister Sam are even coming tonight, so we'll have everyone accounted for."

"I'm going to need some drinks," I mutter and Will scowls.

"No, no alcohol for either one of us tonight." He shakes his head adamantly.

"Why ever not?"

"Because when I get you back to my bed later, I'm going to make love to you for hours, and you will not only be awake for it, you'll have full use of your beautiful brain." He takes my hand in his, links our fingers and kisses my knuckles. "I mean it, Meg, no alcohol. Please."

How can I refuse that?

"Okay, no alcohol," I agree and my stomach twists and turns nervously. He smiles softly and kisses my hand again before I pull into the bowling alley parking lot. I find a parking spot and kill the engine and take a deep, deep breath.

"Thank you for letting me drive your car," I murmur over to him with a big smile on my face.

"You're welcome. You look hot driving this car."

"It's the car. Anyone would look hot while driving it."

"Can I have my keys back now?" he asks.

We find the whole gang already in the bowling alley, putting on their shoes and choosing balls. The alley is small, in an out-of-the-way neighborhood of Seattle, and I'm sure it was chosen on purpose to minimize the chance of Luke and Will being recognized. The lanes are dark, the pins and artwork lit up with black light and pop music is playing loudly. This is obviously techno-bowl night.

Will and I approach the counter.

"Rental shoes," He smiles down at me, and I grimace.

"And rental foot-disease."

He laughs loudly and kisses the top of my head. "They disinfect them, I think."

"With what, Aquanet?" I eye the spray can on the countertop and the guy behind the counter gives me the stink eye.

"Size?" the big guy asks.

"Eight," I mutter.

"Fourteen," Will responds and I giggle.

"What?" he asks.

"You know what they say about men with big feet…" I giggle again as he glares at me, and if I'm not mistaken, actually blushes.

"Behave."

"What did I say?" I ask innocently.

"Yeah, you're not innocent, babe. You just had to wear that outfit, didn't you?"

I look down at my red, thigh-length sun dress, and brown shrug and frown up at him.

"What's wrong with my dress?"

"Are you wearing underwear?" he murmurs into my ear so only I can hear.

"Of course not."

"That's what's wrong with your dress."

"Hey, let's get this game going!" Jules yells from our lane and we join them.

Natalie and Jules pull me into big hugs. I'm so excited to see them. I've really missed them over the past few years.

"Hey, guys." Will shakes hands with his brothers, kisses the girls on the cheek and puts his shoes on.

"Hey, Meg, how are you?" Stacy asks from her chair by the ball chute. Will wasn't kidding when he said she's incredibly pregnant.

"I'm good, thanks. How are you feeling, little mama?"

Stacy laughs and rubs her belly. "Oh! He's kicking! Here." She grabs my hand, jerks me down to squat in front of her and lays my hand over her belly, and sure enough, the baby is pushing against my palm.

"He's a strong little sucker." I smile up at her and she chuckles.

"My ribs would agree. He's going to be a soccer player."

"Football," all of the men correct her at once and we laugh.

"I'm Brynna," a pretty, brown-haired woman with the darkest eyes I've ever seen smiles at me from her seat next to Stacy. "We met at the party, but I didn't really get to talk to you."

"Hi, Brynna. Meg." I shake her hand and stand.

"Really? We just got here. God, you guys!" Jules exclaims. Nat and Luke are making out, again.

"Ignore them," Nate murmurs in her ear and Jules grins up at him. Wow, she loves him. The Jules I used to know never would have looked at a man like that.

Of course, Nate is a fine specimen of man. That tattoo he's sporting on his right arm is bad-ass.

"Stop ogling my soon-to-be brother-in-law," Will growls in my ear.

"I'm not. I'm appreciating the art on his arm."

"Speaking of art, what song is that on your arm, Meg?" Matt asks, referring to the tattoo on my inner bicep.

"Oh, just a song," I wave him off, and search my head for a conversation changer. I'd rather not discuss the song, or what it means to me.

Not yet.

"Okay, c'mere, sweetheart, I'll show you how to throw the ball."

"Oh, you don't have to…" Jules starts but I shake my head at her, halting her. She smiles sweetly at her brother. "You don't have to wait. Go ahead and show her."

"Are you the man for the job?" I ask him sarcastically.

"I know my way around balls, babe," he winks at me and all the guys snicker. "I work with balls for a living."

"Oh dear God, please don't talk about your balls all night. I'll be sick." Jules scowls at him and Will smirks.

Will chooses a ball and backs up onto the lane, crooking his finger at me with a knowing smile on his sexy lips.

"Oh, thank goodness you're here to show me how to handle the balls," I announce sarcastically, earning laughter from our friends.

"Come on, smart ass." I step up to him and he folds his large body behind me, wraps his arms around mine and places the ball in my hands. To torture him, just a little, I wiggle my butt against him and lean into him. He growls low in his throat and swears under his breath before he begins his instructions. "You have to be gentle with the ball. Respect the ball. Visualize in your head where you want the ball to land."

I giggle-snort and feel him scowl.

"Pay attention."

I clear my throat. "Sorry."

"Do you want to give it a try?" he asks.

"Sure."

"Okay, good luck."

He pats my ass and moves back and I have to bite my lip to keep from breaking down into hysterics. Taking my usual stance, I line the ball up with the arrow that will drive it home, take one, two, three steps and then roll the ball down the lane. It quickly moves over the arrow I aimed for and straight for the head pin and *crash*! Strike!

"Yes!" I clap my hands and turn around to applause and Will looking stupefied.

"You played me."

"You'll live." I shrug and wrap my arms around him to hug him.

"You bowl?" he asks.

"She is a crazy-good bowler. We used to go all the time back in the day." Natalie tells him and I smile smugly.

"Why didn't you say?" he asks.

"And spoil the fun of you showing me how to handle the balls? Never."

Will's eyes narrow and he glares down at me and I can't help the wide smile on my face. Have I ever enjoyed tormenting someone so much? No, I don't believe I have.

He leans in and whispers in my ear, "You're going to pay for that later."

"I can't wait." I respond and sashay past him to join the girls.

Caleb is up next and crashes all the pins into a strike. Jeez, he's so muscular and, well, a little scary. He's Will's Navy SEAL brother, and he's just as big as his brothers; tall, broad, muscular.

I'm surrounded by a whole lot of hotness. If I wasn't me, I'd be jealous of me.

That makes me chuckle to myself.

"What are you laughing at?" Luke asks me. He has kind eyes. I never noticed that before. Luke Williams is super-hot, and very sweet. And completely in love with his wife and daughter.

"Nothing, just wondering how I got here."

He smiles knowingly.

"This clan can be a lot to handle."

"Everyone is so nice, it's just…"

"I get it." He smiles reassuringly. "I haven't been a part of them for long, only about a year. It's pretty overwhelming at first."

"Oh, I'm not a part of them, I'm just hanging out with Will."

"Right." He smirks down at me and shakes his head. "Megan, I don't know you, but I've spent some time with Will. Trust me. He's not just hanging out with you."

I watch Will throw the ball down the lane and scowl and cuss when he only knocks eight pins down. My gaze finds Luke's again.

"You think?"

"I know. Be careful. Have fun. He's a good guy." And with that, he pats my knee and moves back over to his wife.

"What was that all about?" Will asks as he takes the seat Luke vacated.

"Nothing. He was just saying hi. Do you guys really do this regularly?" I ask, trying to distract both of us.

"We try to. It's not usually this many of us at once, though."

"It's fun. And cool that you all like to hang out together."

"Don't you like to hang out with your family?" Will asks.

Fuck, why did I bring up family?

"Uh…"

"Hey, Meg, have you heard from Sylvia lately?" Jules asks and takes a swig of her beer.

God, I wish I could drink some beer right now.

"No, not for about a year." I mumble and immediately begin to twist my fingers in my lap. *Please don't ask about Leo.*

Will frowns down at me. "Who's Sylvia?"

"Her mom," Jules states matter-of-factly.

"You haven't talked to your mom in a year?" he asks. Everyone has gone quiet now and are listening to this conversation and I just want to die.

"No. It's no big deal."

Jules snorts. Natalie shifts uncomfortably. Matt, the quiet, but no less attractive, one of the bunch, sits back in his chair and watches me thoughtfully.

"More margaritas?" Samantha asks brightly.

"I'll buy this round." Caleb and Samantha make a trip to the bar to order the drinks and everyone starts talking about other things, much to my relief.

"This subject isn't closed," Will whispers in my ear.

"Yes it is."

"I love this song!" Jules hops up and pulls Natalie with her, who then pulls me and Brynna up to join them in a spontaneous dance about the lane. Carly Rae Jepson is singing *Call Me Maybe*. I hate this song.

And yet, I can't help but love this song.

Sam and Caleb return with a fresh batch of drinks, and Sam joins us girls in our dancing frenzy, weaving and bobbing around us. Stacy grips her belly as she giggles at us and sings along to the fun song.

We are dancing about, being silly girls. I glance over at the guys and they are staring at us, with smirks on their faces.

"You all have the same taste in music as a thirteen-year-old girl," Nate taunts us.

"Every woman in this country loves this song," Brynna informs him. "It's a law, I think. Hey, Matt, isn't it a law?"

Matt laughs and then purses his lips like he's thinking really hard about it. "I don't pay attention to the girly laws," he finally responds, making Brynna scowl at him.

"Traitor."

When the song ends, another begins, and I cringe. It's *Lonely Soul* by Nash.

As in Leo Nash.

As in, *my Leo.*

He and I wrote this song together right before he left for LA. Leo had been over at my place, hanging out with me and listening to me bitch about school and this guy that I went out with twice and never called me again after I slept with him.

Hence, the three date rule.

I could tell that he wanted to track the idiot down and pummel him, but he listened and drank beer with me, made me laugh. It wasn't like I was crying over the asshole, but venting to the only brother I'd ever known helped to put things in perspective. And he gave me the best advice he'd ever given me that night.

"Meg-pie," he said seriously, "we teach people how to treat us. If you don't put up with shit, and don't settle for anything less than respect, that's what you'll get. But if you let the douchebags walk all over you and treat you like you're disposable, then that's what you'll always get. You're too good for that."

I miss him.

"I love *this* song!" Sam exclaims and sings along loudly.

"This is a great band," Jules agrees and winks at me.

I just shrug back at her and sing along in my head.

It really is a great song.

* * *

"Tell me about Sylvia."

Will and I are back in his car, heading to his house, and the nerves have kicked in. This is it. Tonight is the night.

I really, really wish I'd had something to drink.

"Sylvia doesn't matter."

"She's your mother."

"Trust me, genetics doesn't make someone a mother."

"Tell me." He looks over at me, his face unreadable and I sigh. "Why?"

"Because we have to talk about something or I'll pull this car over and take you on the hood. And the date isn't technically over until I get you inside the house. So talk."

"Okay." I clear my throat. "But can we do the fucking on the hood thing sometime soon?"

He glares at me and his hands tighten on the steering wheel. He's not touching me.

"Yes. Talk."

"I was taken away from her when I was twelve."

"Why?" he asks, deceptively softly.

"Because she sucked as a parent. Drugs. A revolving door of men."

"Did any of them…?" he can't finish the sentence.

"No. She made me go in my room and lock the door when the men were around. Mostly she just neglected me. Forgot to buy food, forgot to send me to school. Eventually a teacher took interest and I was taken away."

"What happened then?"

"I got shuffled around. Ten foster homes in four years."

"And then you found a family to stay with until you turned eighteen?" he asks.

"No, then I got cut loose. The system couldn't afford me anymore."

"You were on your own at sixteen years old?" he asks, shocked and angry.

"I had Leo. He had already come to Seattle to go to school, so I followed him and stayed with him. He made me get a job, finish school, enroll in college. He's really like a brother to me."

"How did you meet him?" Will's voice is softer, but he still doesn't sound happy.

"The first foster home. He was there too. We had music in common. He taught me to play the guitar, and he had a job, so he got me a cell phone so I could stay in contact with him."

"I'm glad you had him," he mutters. "Why do you even still talk to your mother?"

"I send her money every month." *Damn it. I hadn't meant to say that.*

"What?!" Now he's really, really angry. "Why the fuck do you send her money?"

"Because I feel guilty." I look down at my hands and feel ashamed. "Because she would probably starve without it."

"She would have let *you* starve, Megan."

"I don't need the money. She does." I shrug. "And if I send her money and keep her in Montana, maybe she won't ever come here to ask me for anything."

The last part is a whisper. I've never told anyone this before. Not ever.

We pull into Will's drive.

"What's the code?" he asks me with a smile.

"051877," I respond and he nods happily, inputs the code and drives us to the house and into the garage.

We climb out of the car and he leads me into the house. The garage enters into a mud room, and then into a gorgeous kitchen. It's open to a dining space and family living area, with floor-to-ceiling windows covering one whole wall, showing off the Sound.

"I really love this space," I murmur and walk over to the windows, taking in the view. It's dark out. Lights twinkle from homes and businesses on the island across the water.

"I really love having you in this space."

Will's voice is soft. He's standing a few feet behind me. I see his reflection in the dark window. His hands are in fists at his sides, and he's breathing quickly.

His eyes are running up and down my back. I slip the shrug off my shoulders and let it fall to the floor. The red sundress has spaghetti straps and flows down around my hips to my mid-thigh. His gaze meets mine in the glass and then he closes his eyes tightly and exhales roughly.

"Will?" I ask as I turn around to look at him. *God, he's so gorgeous.* He's wearing a gray button-down shirt with the sleeves rolled up his forearms. He's in black jeans, and he already took his shoes off, so he's just in black socks.

His blue eyes are hot on mine.

"Yes, sweetheart?"

"Is this date over?" I ask.

"I believe so, yes."

"Thank God."

Chapter Nine

I jump into Will's arms, wrap my arms around his neck, thrust my fingers into his hair and kiss him like I'm dying. He grips onto my ass as my legs circle his waist and groans.

"Let's do this right here, on the kitchen counter," I mumble and kiss his neck. He chuckles and carries me up the stairs toward his room.

"No way. My bed first, kitchen later."

"Okay," I agree. I lean back, completely confident that he won't drop me and unbutton his shirt. He sets me on my feet at the edge of the bed, turns on a sidelight and grabs the hem of my dress and pulls it over my head in one swift move.

I immediately reach for his shirt but he backs out of my grasp.

"Come here, I want you naked."

"Let me look at you," he murmurs, bringing me to a stop.

"No, you've seen me. Let me see you, babe. Seriously, I'm gonna die if you don't get naked like thirty seconds ago."

His eyes burn over my body as he quickly shucks off his jeans and shirt, leaving just his tight, white, short boxer briefs.

I allow myself the luxury of standing and staring at him. Dear God, he's physically perfect. The muscles in his arms, chest, abs and legs are defined. He's sporting that sexy V down his hips, disappearing into those sexy as fuck underwear. His body is so well taken care of, it's almost intimidating.

"So this is what you do when you're off training every day." I realize I must have said that out loud when Will smirks. "You're just… wow."

And cue the self-consciousness. I'm not too fat, not too thin, I'm just an average girl. I'm not terribly toned. I don't run. I work a demanding job that keeps me on the go, so I don't work out often.

I start to cover myself, but Will quickly lifts me in his arms and gently lays me down on his bed, covering me with his large, hard body.

"No covering up this amazing body, sweetheart."

I smirk and try to look away but he grips my chin and forces me to look him in the eye. "You. Are. Amazing. Meg, I love a woman who looks like a woman. I don't want to be worried that I'll snap you in half, and when I lay on your stomach, I don't want your ribs poking me in the face."

He braces himself on his elbows at the side of my head, buries his fingers in my hair and kisses the dimple in my cheek and then down to my neck.

"You smell good. Like fresh air." His lips travel down my neck to my collar bones and then down my sternum. I brush my hands over his arms and shoulders, up through his soft hair, and then down his shoulders again.

"Will…"

"Shh. Let me enjoy you."

"You've already enjoyed me. It's my turn," I whine and he smiles against my stomach.

"You'll get a turn, trust me, babe. But first I want to kiss this delicious body all over."

I wiggle beneath him, impatient.

"We've waited long enough. Can't we fuck fast first and then make love after?"

He moves up me quickly, lowers onto me so I'm cradling his pelvis in my own. His eyes are on fire and he's panting.

"We aren't going to fuck, Meg. Even when it's hard and fast or a little rough or a lot dirty, I'm not fucking you. In the kitchen, in the bedroom, on my car, or any damn where I want to take you, will not be fucking. Fucking is for strangers or people who don't give a shit about each other." He circles his hips, pushing his erection against me, and I bite my lip to stifle a moan.

"Okay," I whisper and close my eyes.

"Open your eyes." I comply. "You're not a fast fuck for me. Do you understand what I'm saying?"

"I think so."

"We haven't spent all this time together, getting to know each other, driving each other crazy, to have a quick fuck and go our separate ways. You need to understand, Megan, once I make love to you, you're mine."

I feel my eyes go wide and jaw drop and I can just stare up at him in shock. Did he just say that?

And why doesn't it scare the living hell out of me?

He's looking at me, waiting for a reaction, and suddenly, I feel... happy. This is who I want. This is where I'm supposed to be.

"Say something, darlin', 'cause I'm dying here."

I run my fingers through his hair and cup his face in my hands, drawing him down to me so I can kiss his lips gently. I brush over them once, twice, my eyes never leaving his.

"You are *so* mine." I whisper and watch with satisfaction as his eyes dilate and the breath he's holding escapes him.

"You bet your sweet ass I am," he growls and takes my mouth again, harder this time, as though he's branding me. He moves down my body again, paying close attention to each breast, down my stomach and then abruptly flips me over.

"Hey! I can't see you from here."

"This is an angle I haven't explored before." I hear the smile in his voice. "I see the dimple in your cheek isn't the only dimple you have, babe."

"It's impolite to mention my cellulite the first time we have sex, Will. You haven't even been inside me yet."

He slaps my ass firmly, making me yelp.

"Hey!"

"There is no cellulite back here. But you do have the cutest dimples right above your ass." He kisses and then nibbles each of them, making me raise my ass in the air. "You have the sweetest rear-end." He kisses each cheek, and the next thing I know, he's parted my cheeks, spreading my labia open, and his mouth is on me.

"Holy shit!" His large hands pin my hips to the bed and his mouth is going to town on me, sucking, lapping, nibbling, and when he sucks my clit and my metal into his mouth, I come unglued, pushing my pussy against his mouth and screaming into the pillow, my muscles pulsing.

Finally, he loosens his grip and I flip myself over beneath him, brush my hair off my face, and before I can say anything, he lifts my hips and puts his mouth on me again, harder this time, rhythmically pushing his tongue in and out of me while his nose pushes on my piercing.

It's too much.

"I can't," I murmur but he only grunts against me and speeds the movements of his amazing tongue.

"Will, damn it, I can't." He pulls his face away from me and replaces his mouth with fingers, two of them, slowly working my vagina, spreading the wetness around my lips and clit.

"Yes, you can. I need to get you good and ready, babe, so I don't hurt you."

"You won't hurt me."

"If you're not ready, I will."

"I'm fucking ready already!" I yell in frustration and he laughs.

"Almost. God, you're so tight, honey."

I look down at him, down his body that is now tense with lust and need, and see his large erection straining against his shorts.

"Take your underwear off."

His eyes narrow on me.

"Please." I offer him a sweet smile.

His hand leaves me long enough to pull the shorts off, and he's kneeling in front of me, completely naked.

Holy hell this man is gorgeous!

Seriously gorgeous.

"I love this," he whispers as he brushes his finger across my metal, making me squirm.

"I'm glad."

"It's fucking sexy." He leans down and swipes his tongue over it twice and just like that, I wrap his hair in my fingers and come against him.

Just as I am able to open my eyes again, Will climbs up my body, and nestles his long, hard cock against my center, and leans in and kisses me.

"Mmm," I moan and wrap my arms around him, keeping him close to me. "You feel so good."

"Meg, open your eyes," he whispers as he moves his hips in just that way that slides the head of his cock against my clit.

His deep blue eyes stare down into mine as he rears back and braces the impressive head of his cock against my lips.

"Are you sure?" he whispers.

"Will, in me. Now."

He smiles softly and pushes inside me, oh so slowly.

Sweet Jesus, he's so big. Maybe this isn't going to work. There's no way I can take all of him.

My eyes widen, but he kisses me softly. "It's okay. We'll take it slow and easy."

His hips retreat, and then he pushes in again, a bit farther this time.

"Just relax. I won't hurt you." He kisses my cheek and my neck, and then kisses my lips again as his hips find a long, slow rhythm. He ever so gently slides out and then in, going deeper and deeper each time until finally he's all the way inside me, and he stops and gazes down at me.

"You feel so fucking good," he whispers.

"You can move," I whisper back. I love how quiet the room is, as though we're writing our own song.

"I just love feeling you wrapped around me. I've never felt anything like you." He barely moves his hips, but it grinds his pubic bone against the metal above my clit and I gasp.

"Piercing?" he asks.

"Yeah, it hits my clit when you move your hips like that."

"Good to know," he mutters with a smug grin.

I rotate my hips and clench around him, wanting desperately for him to move.

"Ah, hell, don't do that."

I smile and do it again.

"Megan, this won't last long if you keep…" Before he can finish the sentence I rotate my hips again and squeeze my intimate muscles and he starts to really move, gliding out to the tip, and then back in to the hilt.

"Oh, yes."

"Is this what you want?"

"Yes."

"Tell me, babe." His voice is raw and sweat is beading on his forehead and I'm stunned at how much he wants me.

"I want you. Just you."

"Damn right, just me." And with that he picks up the pace, rocking in and out of me, thrusting harder and harder, so when he's pushed as far as he can go, it almost hurts. He's so big, there's no avoiding it.

"Goddamn it," his teeth are clenched. He grabs my hands, laces our fingers, and pulls them above my head, restraining me. "You're so fucking sweet."

Every touch of his pubis against my clit is setting me on fire, until finally I can't stand it anymore. I feel the orgasm building, my legs clench, I grip his hands harder.

"Come," he whispers in my ear and bites my neck, sending me over the edge, pulsing and bucking beneath him in the best damn orgasm of my life.

"Ah, hell," he shouts and follows me with his own release. He buries his face in my neck and unlocks our fingers. I wrap my arms around him and cradle him to me, still inside me, and know that I'm totally and completely lost to this beautiful man.

He rolls to the side and takes me with him, reversing our positions. He manages to stay inside me, and I'm in no hurry to kick him out.

"Well, I guess it's safe to say we're compatible in bed," I murmur against his chest. He laughs and kisses my head.

"True, but you might kill me."

"How so?"

"Now that I've had you, I won't be able to get enough of you. I think I'm addicted to how you feel, how you sound, and being buried deep inside you."

I don't really mind the sound of that at all.

And besides, it's totally mutual.

I sigh and rest my arm across his chest. Will traces the music inked on my arm with his finger.

"What song is it?" he asks softly.

"*I Dare You To Move* by Switchfoot."

"What part of the song is this?"

Startled, I gaze up at him. "You do know me pretty well already, don't you?"

"You wouldn't permanently put anything on your body unless it meant something. What lyrics go with this music?" He smiles down at me and kisses my forehead.

I've never shared this with anyone.

"*I dare you to lift yourself up off the floor.*" I whisper and feel Will sigh.

"It's beautiful," he murmurs and drops the subject.

"I like yours too." I grin up at him and then pinch him.

"Hey! What was that for?"

"You never told me you have a tattoo."

"You never asked." He hugs me tighter and sweeps his hand down my back to my ass and back up again.

I want to purr like a kitten.

"I get the number eight is your jersey number, but what does the rest mean?" I ask him and trace the number eight on his side. His tattoo is over his ribcage on his right side. It's the number eight surrounded by lots of little lines and squiggles that don't seem to make any sense.

"Look closely," he mutters and raises his arm so I can get a better look.

Holy shit.

"It's all the players' signatures?" I ask.

"Yep. It represents my team. I may be the center of it, but I'm surrounded by a whole team of great men and really good players. So I had a board made with the number in the middle and asked all the guys to sign around it, and there it is."

"Do you add names as teammates come and go?" I ask.

"Yeah. It started with college, and I've added the names as the years go by."

"What if your number changes?" I ask.

"It's not going to. They retired my number at UW and Seattle will probably do the same when I retire."

"Big shot football star," I murmur, earning a light slap on my ass and I grin. I continue tracing it with my fingertips and push up to kiss his chin.

"So you're not just a pretty face," I remark sarcastically.

"No, that's you, babe. You've got the pretty face."

"I'm so not your type." I roll off him and run my hands down my face.

"What the fuck does that mean?"

Will rolls on top of me and glares down at me, pissed off.

"It just means that I'm not what most athletes would go for. I'm not tall, blonde and leggy. I'm not arm candy. I'm a rocker chick-turned-nurse. I'm no one special."

With each word coming out of my mouth I'm pissing him off more.

Why? It's just the truth.

"Have you heard a word I've told you? You are exactly my type. Physically and emotionally. I love this sweet body of yours. I love your dirty mouth. Aside from your crazy hours, I'm proud as fuck of you for being an awesome nurse and friend to those kids of yours. I don't care what anyone says, you are who I want."

He cups my face in his hands. "You are what I want. Just you."

"I didn't mean to piss you off, I just…"

"You didn't just piss me off, honey. You put yourself down, and hurt my feelings. Trust me, if you didn't interest me, you wouldn't be here."

I run my fingers down his face and smile up at him gently. "Okay."

"Now, I'm hungry."

"Kitchen sex?" I ask excitedly as he pulls me to my feet and tosses one of his jerseys at me.

"Food first, then yes, if you're good, I'll let you have your way with me on the kitchen counter."

"Yes!"

* * *

"I never realized how messy kitchen sex is," I murmur and watch Will fiddle with the shower heads, lowering them so they don't hit me in the face.

His shower is massive. We could easily host the entire offensive line in here.

"That's better, come on." He takes my hand and pulls me gently into the shower. Oh, God, the hot water feels amazing. I glance down to see the remnants of ice cream and chocolate syrup get washed down the drain.

"Here, it's your fault that I'm sticky. You wash me." I hand him a washcloth and he lathers it up with my body wash. "Hey, when did my body wash show up here?"

"I bought it to keep here. I'm hoping you'll be staying here a lot, at least when I'm home." He smiles down at me and warmth spreads through me. "Of course, you're welcome here even when I'm not home."

"I'm happy to stay when you're home. It seems silly to stay here when you're gone, given that my place is less than twenty minutes from here. We'll have to put some of your things at my place too, in case we end up there."

He jerks me against him and kisses me roughly.

"Hey! I'm not clean. Let's get clean before we get dirty again."

He laughs down at me and finishes cleaning us both off, and then we take turns rinsing the suds off our bodies.

Will wraps me in a large bath sheet, warm from a towel warmer. "You're going to spoil me, Montgomery."

"Good." He kisses my forehead and wraps a towel around his waist. "Let's go back to bed."

"My hair is wet."

He frowns at my hair for a second. "Wait here."

He marches out of the bathroom and I hear cabinet doors banging and then he's back with a blow dryer. "Jules left this here a few months ago. She probably has ten of them."

He plugs the blow dryer in and motions for me to stand in front of him, and he systematically blows my hair dry.

Well, shit. No man has ever done that before.

I meet his eyes in the mirror and he smiles contentedly, then concentrates again on my hair. When it's dry, he turns off the dryer and lays it on the countertop to cool.

"Bed."

Chapter Ten

"Wake up, sweetheart."

Will brushes my hair off my face and kisses my cheek.

"Hmph."

"I have to go, babe, I need you to wake up."

Go?

I open my eyes and take in the pretty. God, he's a nice way to wake up. "Mornin," I murmur and stretch.

"Good morning."

I sit up and let the sheet drop to my lap and push my hair back over my shoulders. Will's eyes are on my breasts and I grin. "Like what you see?"

"You have no idea."

"Stay here and show me." I lay back and open my arms to him. He climbs across the bed and kisses me, hovering over me.

"I can't stay. I have to go train for a while. You can come with me if you want." He kisses my nose as I laugh up at him.

"Honey, I don't run. If you ever see me running, you'd better start running too 'cause that means that something is chasing me."

He chuckles down at me, kisses me again, and then sits up. "You're funny. Okay, then lazy bones, stay here and look gorgeous in my bed. I have to go get tortured for a while."

"I work tonight," I remind him and he frowns.

"What shift?"

"Swing. I have to be there at two and get off at two in the morning."

"How long does this shift go this week?"

"Just tonight, then I'm off three in a row." I snuggle down in the comfortable white sheets and hug Will's pillow to me as I talk to him. "This pillow smells like you."

"Come here tonight after work."

"I don't know…"

"Please." His hand glides from my knee, up my thigh and over my hip to my side. "I don't want to be without you tonight."

"Okay. No game this weekend? This is Sunday, isn't it?"

"It's Monday night this week. I was hoping you'd be off so you could come. I own one of the suites and the family usually comes and hangs out and watches the game."

"Oh, that's right. Jules and Natalie asked me to go out for a little shopping and happy hour with them Monday. They said the guys were going to the game and we should do the girl thing."

"That's cool too. We can meet up after the game." He kisses my forehead and climbs off the bed.

"Are you really cool with me not going to the game?" I ask uncertainly.

"It's fine. We're still early in the season, there will be plenty of games for you to see. Have fun with the girls."

This is so not the arrogant man that I thought he was, and the fact that I ever labeled him as an asshole shames me.

"What's wrong?"

"You're not an asshole."

His eyebrows climb into his hairline and he stares down at me. "That's a bad thing?"

"No, I'm saying I'm sorry for calling you an asshole before. You're not."

"Apology accepted."

"Okay, go, before I pull you back in this bed and give you a work out myself."

"I'll be back before you leave for work."

"I'll probably just head home and get ready from there. I don't have scrubs here. Shit!" I cover my face with my hands.

"What?"

"I don't have a car. You picked me up last night."

"Take the Rover. Keys are in the mudroom." He turns and leaves the room before I can argue.

"Have a good day, dear!" I call after him and hear him chuckle as he jogs down the stairs.

I climb out of Will's monstrous bed and wince at my sore muscles. Will is an attentive and inventive lover. I was in positions and used muscles last night that I didn't know were possible. The fact that he's so strong and can just move me where he wants me is sexy as hell.

I pull on my dress from last night and head downstairs to gather my purse and shrug and head home.

Will's house is simply stunning. There are large windows everywhere, letting in an abundance of light and a view of the beautiful water and landscape of the Sound. His furnishings are inviting and plush. I haven't seen the whole house yet, but it's definitely a home that's lived in, and is comfortable and welcoming.

Like the man who owns it.

The keys to his SUV are where he said they would be. I grab my purse and the keys and head home, and for the first time since I started my job, I'm already wishing my shift were over.

* * *

"He's not doing well, Meg."

Jill rubs her hand up and down my back consolingly as I read Nick's chart. I've only been gone for a few days, how could he have gotten so sick so quickly?

"What happened?"

"He caught pneumonia. He's been sleeping a lot, and his family is with him. He won't take that jersey that Montgomery gave him off. He's been asking for you, honey."

Shit. This is the part of my job that I absolutely hate. Nick could get better, but his cancer is aggressive, and to catch pneumonia with all the chemo in his body is not a good thing. I grab his chart and head for his room, schooling my features and straightening my shoulders. Nick doesn't need to see me sad; he needs me to be professional and upbeat. Reassuring.

I knock lightly on his door and poke my head inside. Nick's mom is sitting next to his bed, knitting. She looks exhausted.

"Hi, Meg. Come on in." She offers me a half smile.

"Hey, how's our guy?" I ask and come in the room. Nick's asleep, and just as Jill said, he's in his jersey. His breathing is labored and he's a bit sweaty. I take his temp and frown at the high number, then check his chart to see when he received meds for fever last.

"Not good," she whispers and blinks tears from her eyes.

"Hey, Meg." Nick's voice is nothing but a gravelly whisper.

"Hey, buddy." I take his hand in mine and smile down at him. "I hear you got sick on me while I was away."

"Yeah."

"Well, we're gonna get you better, okay? You just rest." I pat his thin shoulder and sigh as he falls back to sleep. "I'm going to go get him some more medicine for his fever and catch up with his doctor. I just got here and wanted to come see him when I heard the news."

"Thanks, Meg. I'm glad you're here today."

I leave his room and march straight to the nurses' station with Nick's chart.

"Who was assigned to Nick this morning?"

"Elena, why?" Jill asks with a frown.

"He's *two hours* late in getting fever meds, Jill. He's burning up. Did she leave for the day?"

"I think so."

"Well, she's getting written up for this. If she can't keep track of her patient's meds, she shouldn't be here." With that, I walk to the charge nurse office and pull my phone out, and text Will.

If you have any time available, at any point today, can you come to the hospital?

Will won't magically cure anything, but it might lift Nick's spirits to see him, and I'll try anything to get him better.

I know that we shouldn't have favorite patients, but Nick is special to me. He's been here for three months already, and we were hopeful that the treatments were working and we'd be able to send him home by the end of September. Now I'm not so sure.

My phone pings with a response from Will.

What's wrong?

I'm fine. I respond. *Nick's really sick.*

I probably shouldn't impose on him like this. My job isn't his problem. Just as I start to text him again to say never mind, he responds with *I'll bring you dinner and chat with Nick for a bit.*

7 ok?

I grin as I respond.

Perfect. Thank you. I owe you.

* * *

"He doesn't look good," Will remarks and takes a bite of his Chinese food.

"He's not," I reply. We're sitting in the charge nurse office, the door is closed, and an array of Chinese food choices is spread over the desk. Will arrived about thirty minutes ago, and after kissing me silly by the elevator, I took the bags of food and he said a quick hello to the sick teenager.

"I'm sorry, Meg. He's a great kid." His eyes are somber.

"Yeah, he is." I push my plate away and lean back in the chair, brushing my hands vigorously though my hair. "I hate this part of my job."

"You look tired."

"I'm okay." I shrug and gaze over at him. His eyes are worried, roaming over my face and I love him for being concerned about me and for just being here. "Thanks for coming. I needed to see you."

His eyes flare with happiness at my words and he grins over at me. "All you ever have to do is ask, babe. Come here."

He pushes his chair back from the desk as I stand and quickly walk around to him. He pulls me down in his lap and I curl up against him. He tucks my head under his chin and caresses my back soothingly.

God, it feels good to be in his arms.

* * *

It's been a long day. Nick is no better when I leave for the night, and I feel guilty because I won't be there for the next few days. So much can happen in that small amount of time. Maybe I should pick up a shift. I'll call the day nurse tomorrow and see if they need me over the next few days.

I'd love to go to Will's but I ended up working late. It's almost 4:00 a.m., and he has a game tonight, so I decide to just go home and not bother him. I'm still driving the Rover. It's much fancier than my Toyota sedan, and is fun to drive.

My phone suddenly starts ringing and I frown when I see *Football Star* flashing across the screen.

"Hello?"

"Where are you?" he sounds sleepy.

"In your car. I just left work; I got out late."

"Are you on your way here?" he asks and I hear the covers rustle as he moves in the bed.

"I think I'll just go home. You have a game tonight, you should get some sleep."

"I'm fine, babe. I'll sleep better if you're here. I kept waking up every few hours checking to see if you were here anyway."

I chew my bottom lip. Who am I kidding? I want to see him. Get naked with him. Thank him for earlier.

"I'm on my way," I murmur.

"Good." I hear the smile in his voice as he hangs up.

I drive through his gate and park in the garage. He's left a few lights on in the house for me, so I turn them off as I make my way upstairs. He's in bed, asleep, naked from the waist up with the white linens wrapped around his waist.

He looks tan and sexy and...*mine.*

I strip down to nothing and slide into the bed, over to him, and wrap myself around him. Head on his chest, arms and legs wrapped around him, clinging to him.

He wakes and holds me, kisses my hair, runs those magical hands down my back, and the next thing I know, he's rolled us so he's on top of me.

"I missed you," he whispers against my ear.

"I missed you, too."

He kisses my dimple, and then over to my lips and offers me soft, sweet kisses. He gently nibbles my lips, and then slides his tongue into my mouth, taunting and playing with me. I run my hands up his back and then down to his ass and smile against his mouth when I find him naked.

His ass is really spectacular.

He pushes my legs apart with his and settles himself between my legs, not moving, just resting there, kissing me, brushing my hair rhythmically with his fingertips. I continue caressing his back, his sides, his arms, and we are just content to love each other softly. Be together.

I raise my legs and hitch my thighs around his hips, opening myself to him. I feel my wetness against his sex, and he groans as he slides effortlessly against me.

"So wet," he whispers.

"Need you," I whisper in return. He pulls his face back and gazes down at me, runs the backs of his fingers down my cheeks and slowly, oh-so-damned-slowly, sinks inside me.

His eyes close as he reaches my cervix and is buried balls-deep inside me. He rests his forehead on mine and starts to gently move, letting me get used to him, allowing my body time to accommodate him.

"Your body is already learning mine," he murmurs. "It's easier this time, isn't it?"

"Mmm…" I moan and circle my hips, inviting him in further. I clench around him when his pubis rubs the metal against my clit.

"Fuck, that piercing is going to be the death of me," he mutters and I giggle. "You have the most beautiful smile."

He disarms me. With just a few words, or a touch, this man completely disarms me.

His hips begin to move a bit faster, a little harder. His lips circle around a nipple and he sucks greedily, making it harden even more. He pays the other the same attention and I writhe beneath him, as my body becomes just sensation. His beautiful cock is moving deliciously in me, his strong body is blanketing me, his hands still running through my hair, his mouth on mine… I am draped in him, and yet I can't get enough of him.

"I love the way you love me," I whisper. He grins against my mouth and pushes his cock all the way inside me, grinds his pubis against me, and holds himself there until I come apart around him, my muscles spasm, my hands clench onto his ass, pulling

"Ah, hell, honey." I feel his body tighten and he's coming with me, emptying himself inside me.

He kisses me softly and then pulls out of me and lowers his head to by belly. He rests there, his cheek against my navel, arms wrapped around my waist, and falls asleep.

I think I just fell in love with him.

* * *

"So," Jules flashes her sweet grin at me and I tense. Ah hell, she only uses that when she wants something. "What's going on with you and my brother?"

I take a long drink of my margarita and eye Jules. She's sitting across from me at the same sports bar where Will brought me on our it-doesn't-count-first-date. She, Natalie and I are enjoying late happy hour after having shopped all evening and getting pedicures.

These girls don't play when it comes to shopping.

"Leave her alone," Natalie mutters, then eyes me suspiciously. "On second thought, I want to know too. What's up? You guys seemed pretty cozy while bowling the other night."

I shrug and look down. "We're sleeping together."

"Duh." Jules rolls her eyes. "The way you were making the googly eyes at each other screamed sex. And I'm trying to ignore that he's my brother because otherwise, that's just... ew." She shudders.

"What we want to know is, what *else* is going on?" Natalie asks with a grin.

"I don't know. We just started sleeping together the other night."

"Your three date rule?" Jules asks.

"Yep," I smile smugly at her.

"Good girl." Nat fist-bumps me and I laugh.

"We're seeing each other, I guess." I shrug and take another sip of my margarita. "He's a great guy. Not the asshole I originally thought he was."

"He's arrogant as can be sometimes, but definitely not an asshole," Jules agrees.

"I'm not crazy about his arrogant public persona," I admit. "But I like how he is with me when we're alone. He's been great to the kids at the hospital, and he is fun to be with. I don't think I could afford to feed him for long. The man can pack away the food."

"You should have seen him as a teenager. This is nothing. I think mom and dad had to take out a second mortgage on the house just for Will's groceries."

"I'm not surprised," I laugh.

"So, you like him," Natalie grins knowingly.

"I like him," I agree.

"If he hurts you, I'll kill him." Jules' eyes are narrowed menacingly and I giggle.

"Aren't you supposed to be saying that to me? He's your brother."

"He's a man." She shrugs as if that explains it all.

"Hey! He's on TV! Turn up the volume!" Natalie yells over to the bartender. He turns up the volume on the TV in time to catch a post-game interview with Will.

He looks fantastic, all sweaty and dirty, panting.

Damn, that jersey does things to me.

"Great game, Montgomery. Congrats on another win." The shorter man turns the mic to Will, who smiles graciously.

"Thanks, man. We played a good game."

"Do you think Jennings will be out for the rest of the season with that knee injury in the third quarter?"

"Oh, man, I hope not. I don't know."

"Did you feel any pressure from the Green Bay defensive line tonight?"

Will frowns down at the guy like that is the stupidest question he's ever heard. "I feel pressure from every defensive line."

"Are you ready for Miami next week?"

"I think so. We're training hard, watching a lot of tape. We'll be as ready as we can be next Sunday."

"You've been seen around town with an auburn-haired woman. Is she your girlfriend?"

My heart stops. Literally stops. Natalie gasps and Jules frowns.

"This guy is an idiot." Jules mutters.

Will offers the guy a lazy, cocky grin. "Dude, does she look like someone that I would date?" He laughs mockingly. "She's a friend of the family. I don't have room in my life for a woman right now. Football is my priority."

"Good luck next week, man."

Will nods and then the screen turns back to the four guys at a table talking about the game.

"Meg, he didn't mean it to sound like that," Jules says quietly.

Does she look like someone that I would date?

I feel nauseous.

"Fuck, I'm stupid." I whisper.

"No, sweetie. Seriously, he didn't mean to sound like that."

"I think he meant exactly what he said, Jules." I shake my head to clear it and dig some cash out of my bag, toss it onto the table and stand. "I'm going home. Thanks for the fun night out, guys."

"Meg, don't go."

"I'm okay. I just need to think. When you meet up with the guys later, tell Will I didn't feel well, and I'll call him in a few days."

Yeah, like that's going to work.

"I'm gonna kill him," Jules fumes as I walk away.

Chapter Eleven

~Will~

Will

How could you? How could you start seeing someone when I know that you love me? That ugly bitch is nothing, and she will never love you like I do. Why won't you notice me? If you'll just stop seeing her, and love me the way I know you want to, I won't hurt her.

Your love.

Holy fuck. What kind of sick fuck would leave this in my locker and how in the hell did they get into our locker room? I need to talk to Mike, our head of security, now.

"Hey! Someone get Mike for me!" I yell out, confident that someone will fetch him.

We played a kick-ass game against the Packers tonight. Hell, I've been playing the best ball of my life the past few weeks, and I don't think its coincidence that it's since I've started seeing Meg. This dumb-ass stalker fan bullshit won't touch her. Thank God I put that alarm system on her house.

The thought of anything happening to her makes me sick.

"Hey, Montgomery, can I ask a few questions?" A new sports-cast guy is holding a mic in my face and I paste on my public smile and play the post-game game.

"Sure, man."

"Great game, Montgomery. Congrats on another win." The shorter man turns the mic to me.

"Thanks, man. We played a good game."

"Do you think Jennings will be out for the rest of the season with that knee injury in the third quarter?"

"Oh, man, I hope not. I don't know." *How the fuck would I know? Do I look like a fucking doctor?*

"Did you feel any pressure from the Green Bay defensive line tonight?"

I frown down at the idiot and want to ask him if he's ever watched football. Jesus, where did they find this asshole? "I feel pressure from every defensive line."

"Are you ready for Miami next week?"

"I think so. We're training hard, watching a lot of tape. We'll be as ready as we can be next Sunday."

"You've been seen around town with an auburn-haired woman. Is she your girlfriend?"

Fuck. *Please, babe, don't be watching this.* My stomach clenches and I'm glad I'm already sweaty from the game so no one can see the fresh sheen that's just broken out on my face.

I offer him my lazy, cocky grin. "Dude, does she look like someone that I would date?" I laugh down at him, like that's the most ridiculous thing I've ever heard. *Yes, she's my girlfriend! She's the best thing that's ever happened to me, and I plan to be buried deep inside her sweet body as soon as possible.* "She's a friend of the family. I don't have room in my life for a woman right now. Football is my priority."

"Good luck next week, man."

I nod at him, and he turns away from me, on to the next guy to interview.

Fuck. If Meg saw that interview, I'm so screwed. She's already got issues with my arrogant public persona, and this will be the nail in the coffin of our relationship if she sees it.

And that is not possible.

She's mine, goddamn it.

I quickly shower and get my shit together, ready to be out of here so I can meet up with my brothers up in the suite, then go meet up with our girls for a night out.

I need to see Megan.

"You wanted to see me?"

Mike, a former Army Ranger and current Seattle cop, is standing behind me.

"Yeah, man. Someone left this in my locker. I found it when I got in after the game." I hand him the fucked up note and scowl. "How the fuck did someone get in here?"

Mike frowns as he reads the note and then swears under his breath. "I don't know. She probably flashed someone her tits. I'll check the security cameras and we'll find her. Don't worry about it."

I narrow my eyes at him and cross my arms over my chest. I know Mike is good, he's been with us forever, and no one fucks with him. But some of the other guys come and go.

"I want whoever let her in here fired."

"Without question."

"And if one hair on Meg's head is touched…"

"It won't be. This is just some stupid girl with a crush, Montgomery. I'll handle it."

I nod once and turn my back, dismissing him.

The guys, Isaac, Luke, Nate, Matt and Caleb, are in the suite, still eating the spread of food laid out and drinking beer. I grab some chips and stuff my face. *Fuck, I'm hungry.*

"Good game, bro," Isaac salutes me with his beer and I nod back at him.

"Yeah, we kicked some ass. Felt good. Ready to go get the girls?" I ask and grab another handful of chips.

"Stacy stayed home tonight. She's just uncomfortable, so I'm going to head home and rub her feet and put Soph to bed." Isaac pulls out his keys and waves at us, then heads out.

"Okay, let's go get the girls and take them out for dinner." Nate leads us all down to the private parking garage. "But I'll just tell you all right now, we'll be leaving early. I've got plans for her tonight." He grins and all of us stop and frown at him. Luke laughs.

"Just because you put a ring on her finger doesn't mean we won't kill you, McKenna," Caleb warns him. I suppress a laugh. Nate may be smaller than us, but he could take any one of us. Not all at once, but in a one-on-one fight, I'd put my money on Nate.

"You kill me, Julianne kills you. I know you're afraid of her."

"I'm not afraid of my kid sister," Matt mutters, earning a sidelong look from Luke. "Okay, I'm afraid of her. She doesn't fight fair."

"That's my girl," Nate announces proudly. I like him. He's good for my sister.

Now I need to get my hands on *my* girl and make sure she didn't hear what an asshole I was on TV tonight.

* * *

"You are such an asshole!"

Jules storms at me across the parking lot of the restaurant we arranged to meet at earlier. She pushes me hard in the chest, knocking me back a step. Matt's right, she doesn't fight fair.

"Jules…"

"You know," she interrupts me. "I know that you can be an arrogant ass at times, but what you said on fucking *live television* tonight takes the cake. Who the fuck do you think you are to hurt someone like that?"

"*Fuck!*"

She takes a step back and her eyes widen a bit. The guys are all standing around, watching us. Natalie's hands are planted on her hips, and she's glaring at me too. Brynna stands next to Caleb, links her arm through his, and I frown.

What the fuck is that about?

"Seriously, Will, what the hell were you thinking?" Natalie asks.

"Where is she?"

"Not here." Jules raises her chin stubbornly. I turn to Natalie.

"Where is she, Nat?"

"I believe she went home. Why in the name of God would she be here, Will? You announced to the world that she's no one you would dare date. She's no one to you, remember?"

"Fuck, man, what the hell did you say?" Luke asks and I wince.

"You guys didn't see it?" Jules asks, her eyes still narrowed menacingly and on me. Part of me wants to cover my dick with my hands, but the man in me won't stoop to that.

"No, we didn't see any post-game interviews," Matt adds.

"Well, let me fill you in. When asked who the pretty girl is that he's been seen with recently, our stupid-as-fuck brother responded with, and I quote, 'Does she look like someone I would date? I don't have room in my life for a woman. I'm a selfish douchebag with a small dick."

"I did not say that last part!"

"Fuck, man, why didn't you just say no comment?" Luke asks, looking at me like I'm a moron. And I am.

Why didn't I?

"Because less than thirty seconds before that asshole pushed the mic in my face, I found a note in my locker from some fucked-up fan saying that if I don't stop seeing Meg she'll hurt her. I didn't have time to talk to security, or think it through. I had to play it off like I don't have a girlfriend because if anyone ever hurts Meg, I'll fucking kill them, and I can't go to prison."

Jules frowns at me, and my brothers both narrow their eyes menacingly.

"Does she have security at her house?" Caleb asks, his voice low and pissed.

"Yeah, I had it installed last week, thank God."

"Did you give the note to Mike?" Matt asks and pulls out his cell, dialing while he talks.

"Yes, he said he'll take care of it." I pace back and forth behind my car, and then move quickly to the driver's side. "I'm going to her place. I'll see you guys later."

"Will, she was pretty pissed off. You might want to give her a couple days to cool down." Nat's big green eyes are worried, but I offer her a half smile.

"I have to apologize and grovel a bit. Hopefully she'll understand when I explain."

"They caught the girl," Matt announces as he tucks his phone back in his pocket. "Some nineteen year old college student who offered one of the security guys a blow job if they'd let her in. She's been arrested."

"Thanks, man. Go have dinner, all of you. I'll text you tomorrow."

What the fuck did I do? I drive like a bat out of hell to Meg's place. I need to see her. I need to hold her and reassure her that everything I said in that goddamn interview was a lie.

I can't lose her.

I pull up to her house, slam the car door and stalk up to the front porch. I ring the bell.

No answer.

The lights are on. I can hear music coming from inside, but it's not so loud that she wouldn't be able to hear the doorbell.

I ring again.

No answer.

I try the knob on the door, and much to my surprise, it's unlocked. She didn't set the alarm or lock herself inside like I asked her to.

Goddamn stubborn woman!

"Meg?" I call out and let myself in. There's no sign of her in the living area or her cute kitchen. I make my way upstairs, calling out for her as I go.

"Meg? Where are you, babe?"

I can hear the shower running in her master bathroom, so I let myself in. "Meg?"

"Ack!" She yelps in surprise and I can't help but laugh.

"It's just me."

"You scared the shit out of me!" She turns off the water, whips back the shower curtain and at the sight of her soft, wet body my mouth goes dry.

Fucking hell, she's beautiful.

She's all soft, white skin, rosy pink nipples, soft curves. That hair of hers is some weird mixture of red and brown and blonde, and her hazel eyes undo me.

Of course, right now they're shooting daggers into me.

"I'm sorry, but you left your front door unlocked and you didn't set the alarm like I asked you to."

She shrugs and reaches for a big bath towel and wraps it around herself, covering her body from my view. I want to rip it off her and take her right here against the bathroom wall, but I don't think I'd be welcome at the moment.

"It's not any of your business if I set the alarm, Will." She stalks past me into the master bedroom and starts looking through her dresser for clothes.

"Of course it is. I need to know that you're safe."

"I'm safe."

"You're safer when you turn on the alarm."

She just shrugs again, as if it's no big deal, and pulls on a tank top and yoga pants. Jesus, even in yoga pants her ass makes me hard.

"Look, you made it quite clear tonight that the only thing you give a rats ass about is football. So stop it with the crazy I-want-you-safe-bullshit and leave. I don't want you here."

My stomach flips and my heart makes a beeline straight for my throat.

"Meg," I reach out for her but she pulls back out of my reach, and panic sets in. "Meg, let me explain."

"No need." She shakes her head and moves past me and down the stairs to the kitchen. "I think I get it. You said what you needed to say to get through the three dates so I'd fuck you, and I was stupid enough to believe you. I won't make the same mistake twice."

"No." I grip her shoulders in my hands and turn her toward me and make her look up at me. God, she's such a tiny little thing. "No, Megan. I told you before, I've never fucked you. Every time I've been inside you has been the best damn moment of my life."

"You announced on television that I'm nobody." Her hazel eyes are hurt and sad, and I feel like such a fucking asshole. "Will, I won't be your dirty little secret. I'm not someone you get to hang out with, take around your family, sleep with, but you deny my existence to the press. If you're ashamed of me, you shouldn't be with me. I'm pretty ashamed of you right now."

I swallow hard and clench my eyes closed, and then stare down at her. How did she become my whole world in such a short amount of time? My God, I'd do anything for her.

Even lose her.

"Megan, someone threatened you tonight." Her eyes widen, and I see I've got her attention. "I found a note in my locker from a stalker fan. She said that she'd seen us together, and if I didn't stop seeing you, she'd hurt you. Then the next thing I know that asshat is pushing a mic in my face asking me about you. I couldn't tell the truth and risk your safety."

She frowns in confusion, and her eyes are still hurt, and it's killing me.

"Babe, I'm so sorry that you got hurt. I don't ever want to hurt you. But I panicked, and I didn't know what else to do."

"You embarrassed me, Will. I know I'm not anyone special. I know that you shouldn't be interested in someone like me. We are from two totally different worlds. Maybe it's just best if we take a step back and stop seeing each other now before you completely break my heart later."

"Stop putting yourself down like that! I'm more than interested in you. For the love of Jesus, I can't stop touching you. I'm not going to break your heart, Megan." *Goddamn it! She's breaking my heart right now!*

"Oh yeah, you will." She shakes her head slightly and backs out of my grasp. "It's inevitable. People don't stick, Will. Everyone leaves eventually, and I think that I'd rather you left now rather than later, because I don't think I could survive it later." The last part is whispered, and I take a step toward her to hold her and reassure her that I'll do everything in my power to never hurt her again, but she evades me.

"Please," she whispers. "Just go."

Well, I'll be damned if I'm going to stand here and beg. I take a moment to look at her. Really look at her. God, she's so strong and sweet and gorgeous and she is *mine.*

"I'll go, Meg, if that's what you want." I take her face in my hands and kiss her forehead, breathing in her sweet smell, her wet hair against my nose. "You are not a dirty secret," I murmur into her ear. "You are everything."

Before I make an ass of myself and beg her to forgive me, I walk out of her house, gently close the door behind me, and climb in the car to drive home. *Fuck.*

Chapter Twelve

You are everything.

It just plays over and over in my head all day. *You are every-thing.*

I picked up the swing-shift at work today. I needed to occupy my mind and I wanted to check in on Nick. He's worse. Much worse. His family has chosen to honor his wishes of no extreme life-saving measures, so we just keep him as comfortable as we can and pray that his body is strong enough to fight the infection. Unfortunately, because of the amount of chemo in his system, he's not strong enough to fight much.

I've spent the majority of my evening watching his vitals like a hawk and standing vigil. I don't want him left alone for long. He's so fragile, anything could happen so quickly, we need to be with him pretty much every second.

"Meg, there's a call for you." Jill pokes her head into Nick's room and offers me a sad smile. Nick's turn for the worse is affecting us all. "I'll relieve you for a bit."

We all invest ourselves into these kids, whether we want to or not. They're all so great, how could we not?

I quietly leave the room and cross to the nurses' station.

"Hello?"

"Hey, Meg, this is Lyle with security. I have a delivery for you."

I frown. "Okay, bring it up."

"I can't, I'm the only one in the office right now. Do you mind coming down?"

"Sure, I'll be right there."

God, I'm tired. Bone tired. I didn't sleep much at all last night after Will left. I kept replaying the conversation in my head over and over again. Asking him to leave was for the best. I need to put some space between us. I meant what I said, he'll eventually come to his senses and break it off, or I'll get sick of his arrogance and break it off, and why waste time on something that will end, most likely sooner rather than later?

Lyle is indeed the only guard in the security booth right now. The others must be on foot patrol. I walk up to the plexi-glass window and offer him a smile.

"Hey, Lyle. You have something for me?"

"Yeah, I'll bring them out to you."

Them?

Flowers. I should have known. Lyle comes walking out of the glass office with both his arms loaded down with gorgeous red flowers. Roses, peonies, poppies, calla lilies. All beautifully red.

Damn him.

I pull the white card out of the bouquet and rip it open. There is only one word:

Everything.

I take the flowers and ride the elevator back up to my floor and set the flowers in my office. I read the card again and then tuck it into the pocket of my scrub top and pat it in place. I'll carry him with me tonight.

I pull out my phone and text him, one word: *Beautiful.*

Before I can put my phone back in my pocket, there is a response. *Not as beautiful as you. Forgive me.*

"Meg, come quick, something's wrong." One of the techs, Brandi, pokes her head in my office, her face ashen.

"Nick?" I ask, my stomach clenching in fear. She nods yes, and we run to his room. The monitors are beeping frantically, and his parents are huddled together in the corner of the room, crying.

"His lungs are failing," Dr. Lee, a young and handsome doctor is urgently checking monitors and listening to Nick's chest. He looks over at his parents, his eyes worried. "We need to intubate him."

"No," Nick's father chokes out. "No life support. We promised Nick we wouldn't make him suffer."

"He's suffering now. He's suffocating." Dr. Lee loops his stethoscope around his neck and sighs deeply. "I understand." He runs his hands down his face and looks down at Nick with sadness. He's worked with the boy since he was first diagnosed with the bone cancer.

"Meg," he murmurs to me. "Keep his morphine up, and his head elevated so he's getting as much oxygen in his lungs as possible. We're going to keep him sedated, and comfortable." He walks over to Nick's parents and hugs them both. "Sit with him. Talk to him. I don't think you'll have long with him now."

I gaze down at this boy, this sweet boy, who had his whole life ahead of him. He was an athlete, he had a girlfriend, and the promise of going to college and living a long, happy life. He'll never have the chance to experience so many things. Fall in love, dance at his wedding, hold his children.

He's only seventeen fucking years old.

I arrange Nick to a comfortable position in his bed, check the drip on his IV and step back to let his family gather by him and say goodbye.

* * *

Six hours later, I'm wrung out. Nick passed away two hours ago. We all comforted his parents and did our job of comforting the other kids who were so sad and scared and mourning. I hate the days that we lose a patient. It just sucks all around, for every single person on the floor.

I should stay here tonight. Find an empty bed and catch a few hours' sleep, then get up and put in another shift. But I push my hand in my pocket and run my fingers over the note that came with Will's flowers, and I know that I don't want to stay.

I need him.

I need to be in his arms. I want to feel his warmth, and hear him tell me that everything will be okay.

Even if it won't.

I don't know if I'd be welcome. I haven't replied to his last text. But if I've learned anything at all in the last twelve hours, it's that life can be cut so incredibly short. I don't want to waste a minute that I could spend with Will.

If he leaves me and breaks my heart later, I'll deal with it then.

I drive to his house, let myself in through his gate, and because I still have the Rover, I park in the garage and let myself into the house. It's dark and quiet, Will is no doubt in bed and went to sleep long ago.

I climb the stairs, two at a time. I can't get to him fast enough. Sure enough, there he is, sleeping peacefully. His face is relaxed, hair a mess from his fingers. I slip out of my shoes, and don't even take the time to strip out of my clothes.

I need him *now.*

I climb into the bed and wrap myself around him, startling him awake.

"Hey," he mumbles and wraps his arms around me.

"I'm sorry," I whisper and nuzzle in deeper, burying my face into his neck, clinging to him.

"Babe, what's wrong? You're trembling."

I am just so *cold.*

He tries to pull back, but I cling tighter. "Don't go." I hear the desperation in my voice.

"Sweetheart, I'm not going anywhere. Talk to me. You're scaring me. Are you hurt?"

I shake my head. God, there's just so much running through me. So much in my head. I'm so sad about Nick, and afraid of losing Will, yet afraid of loving him too. And I'm so fucking tired of being afraid of losing something, someone, important to me.

"Need you," I murmur and suddenly feel the tears leaking out of my eyes.

"Megan," he's awake now, and worried.

"I'm not hurt," I mutter and lean my forehead on his shoulder, still clinging to him, relishing the feel of his impossibly strong arms around me. "We lost Nick tonight. I miss you. I just want to be here with you, okay?"

"Oh, baby."

I don't even care that he calls me baby. It's comforting and loving, and I need it. I need him.

"You are always welcome here, Meg. Always."

I finally lean my head back and look into his soft blue eyes. He's so kind. How did I ever think that he was trying to hurt me?

"I'm so sorry about Nick. He was a really good kid. He was completely smitten with you, but I can't blame him." He grins down at me and kisses my nose, and I relax again. He just soothes me.

"Will, you scare the fuck out of me." His eyes widen briefly, and then he exhales and closes them. He chuckles softly as he leans in and rests his lips against my own.

"Megan, you exasperate me, and turn me on, and make me crazy." He kisses me softly, brushing his lips across mine, and gently combs his fingers through my hair.

"Don't you see what I feel for you? Can't you feel it when I make love to you? The way I look at you? Jesus, Meg, you're all I see. You're all I want."

I close my eyes and try to pull away from him but he holds on tight.

"No, you won't back away again. Now that you're here, I'm keeping you here, damn it. You're mine, Meg, just as much as I'm yours."

"Thank you," I whisper.

"For what?"

"For this. For being here. For the flowers, and being with me all night, even though you didn't know you were." I shake my head and close my eyes. "You scare me, but I don't want to lose you."

He pulls me in to him tightly and kisses my hair, rubbing his hands up and down my back soothingly. "Go to sleep, babe."

Laying here, in the quiet, I let my eyes drift closed and fall asleep to the sound of Will's steady breathing and heartbeat against my cheek.

* * *

I wake to an empty bed and sunshine pouring in through the windows, reflecting off the stark-white linens, making the room bright and cheerful. Will's bedroom is stunning. The walls are

120

robins-egg blue and all the trim and linens are white. His bed is the size of my living room, and faces the floor to ceiling windows that face the water.

I could get used to waking up in here.

Holy shit, it's noon! I haven't slept this late in I don't know how long, even if I've worked a night shift. I frown down at my scrubs and remember coming to Will's after work, attacking him in his bed, and the most terrifying part of all: falling apart on him.

Before I can dwell on that, I climb out of bed and strip naked and it occurs to me that the shower in the master bath is running. I would have thought he'd be at the training center today.

I pad into the bathroom, pull my hair up into a messy bun on the top of my head and watch him through the clear glass shower door. The shower itself is massive. All white and blue tile. And a very tall and tanned and muscular Will is standing beneath the tallest of the four shower heads, his hands braced on the wall and head bowed forward, letting the hot water run down the back of his head and back.

Good God, he's hot.

I haven't had him inside me in days.

I silently enter the shower and wrap my arms around his wet waist. I press myself against his back, take a deep breath and let the water run over me.

"Good morning," Will murmurs and turns around to have a look at me.

"It's actually afternoon now," I reply and smile widely at him. He's examining my face, cupping it in his big hands. He must be satisfied with what he sees because he smirks down at me and his shoulders visibly relax.

"Lazy bones," he mutters and kisses me softly.

"Hey, I worked late. I'm surprised you're home."

"I just got back. I had an early morning meeting and then trained for a bit." He grabs my body wash and lathers up a washcloth, turns me around to face the wall. "Brace your hands on the wall."

Oh, I love it when he's bossy!

I comply and lower my head, close my eyes, and enjoy Will pampering me, gliding the washcloth over my back and shoulders, arms, butt, down my legs. It's just heaven. On his way back up my legs, he pushes the cloth between them, washing my folds and I can't hold back a moan.

I've never had anyone wash me there before.

"Turn around," he murmurs.

I brace my hands on his lean, wet hips, my thumbs tracing that spectacular V, and watch his face as he washes my chest, breasts, stomach. His eyes follow his hand, taking in my body and they heat with lust.

"I love your skin," his eyes find mine and he smiles. "You're so soft."

"I love this spot, right here," I tap his hips with my thumbs and smile sassily at him. "Let's keep this."

He chuckles at me. "I'll do my best. Let's rinse you."

He shifts me under the water, and watches with fascination as the suds slide down my body. He's stopped touching me, and is just watching my body's reaction to the water and to him.

My eyes trail down his firm body, his flat stomach, a small patch of dark hair, and the most impressive, fully erect penis I've ever seen. I take him in my hand and move up and down the length in two long, slow strokes.

"Shit," he sucks air in through his clenched teeth and I grin as I sink to my knees, and lick the tip of him, slowly, softly, teasingly. I cup his balls in my hand, and hold the base of his cock in the other and sink down onto him, sucking and licking as I go. When he hits the back of my throat, I pull up and repeat the motion, slightly speeding up.

His fingers tangle in my hair and I speed up, jacking him with my hand.

"Fuck, I love your mouth," he mutters. He's panting, slightly thrusting his hips against me. "Don't make me come in your mouth."

I smile to myself. *Hell, yes, I'll make you come in my mouth!*

I move faster, harder. Suddenly, Will lifts me to my feet and kisses me hard and deep. He's gripping my shoulders hard, his kiss is desperate.

"I haven't been inside you in seventy-two hours, Megan. I'm not coming in your sweet mouth." He spins me to face the shower wall. "Hands on the wall."

He pulls my hips back and pushes his fingers through my folds to my clit. I gasp when he brushes my metal.

"Oh, Will."

"That's right. This is mine, Megan. Do you understand me?"

"Yes."

He pushes two fingers inside me and twists them, then pulls them out to wet my already swollen lips.

"So wet," he mutters.

"Will?"

"Yes, love."

A chill runs up my spine at that word and I grin.

"I really need you inside me."

"I'll get there, babe. God, you feel good."

"I'll feel better when you're inside me."

I hear him chuckle, and then we both gasp when the head of his cock brushes my sex. He gently pushes in, all the way.

"Are you okay?"

"Oh God, yes. More than okay."

"This is going to be rough, honey." His voice is tight as he starts to move, really move, frantically. He grabs my hair in one fist and slaps my ass with the other, startling me. "God, you're so fucking good."

"Oh my God, Will!"

He pulls out suddenly and spins me to face him, plants his hands on my ass and lifts me against the wall. I wrap my arms and legs around him, but he takes my hands and holds them both above my head with one of his, leans into me, and buries himself inside me again.

"So good," he mutters and pins me with his bright blue eyes. "Mine," he repeats and then buries his face in my neck, kissing and biting and I feel my orgasm pushing up through me.

My legs tense and I push against Will's hands, but he holds strong.

"That's right, let go," he commands, and I do, hard and fast, spasming around his beautiful cock.

"Ah fuck!" His jaw is clenched and he throws his head back and falls over the edge with me.

He rests his forehead against mine as we recover. "Do you work today?"

"No."

"Good. You're staying here with me, all day and night."

"Good plan."

Chapter Thirteen

"Is this really what you want to do all day?" I ask, lounging at the end of his couch. I'm in one of his old team jerseys and his boxer-briefs, since I don't have any clothes here, and my hair is up in a knot on my head, no makeup.

Dear God, I must look horrific.

I glance over at Will, on the opposite side of the long, plush black leather couch. It's really unfair that he looks so good in just basketball shorts and an old t-shirt.

"Why, is there somewhere you wanted to go?" he asks and flips through channels on his uber-huge television. We are in his media room, full of plush furniture, the outrageously enormous television – *dear God, is he blind? Who needs a TV this big?* – football memorabilia, a wet bar, a pool table. Basically a big ol' man cave where boys can hang out and do boy things.

"No, I'm just surprised." I lean back and plop my feet in his lap, getting more comfortable. He immediately wraps one big hand around the arch of my foot and rubs with his thumb and I sigh in contentment.

"It's nice to relax once in a while. We haven't really just hung out together much." He offers me a soft smile, and my stomach flips, just a little. Gosh, he's pretty to look at.

And he's right. It feels good to be lazy. I'm still super tired from last night at work, and just lounging in Will's extraordinary home with him all day is relaxing and perfect.

"Are we okay," he murmurs, drawing my attention. His eyes are sober, and he's watching me closely.

I turn my head to the side and offer him a half smile. "Yeah, we're okay."

He just nods and flips the channels to a show about whales on the Discovery channel.

"I'm hungry," he announces.

"You're always hungry," I laugh and kick his thigh gently. "You just had a huge sandwich an hour ago."

"Let's order in pizza."

"Let's go get the pizza and bring it back," I suggest.

"I like having you here, in my jersey, in my house, where I don't have to share you and you don't have to share me and we can just be."

"Be what?" I ask.

"Us." He pulls me into his lap and kisses me senseless, plunging his fingers into my hair and moving those amazing lips over mine. Then, just as suddenly as he started, he pushes me back onto the couch and reaches for his phone. "I'm calling for pizza."

* * *

"You are such a fucking cheater!" Will is glaring at me from his position on the floor, his back against the couch, xBox controller in his hands. God, he's adorable when he's irritated with me.

"I am not!"

"All you're doing is pushing all the buttons at once and waving the controller all about," he accuses me. He's right. I have no idea how to play this shit, and making him crazy is hilarious.

"It's called strategy, Mr. Football Star." I bat my eyelashes at him and laugh as his scowl deepens.

"You've never played this, have you?"

"*Madden Two Thousand Thirty-Four*? No."

"It's *Madden 2013*, smart ass." Now he's laughing at me. God, he's fun.

"I'm still kicking your Seattle ass. The guy with your name on the jersey looks nothing like you, by the way." I pick up my soda and sip from the straw. We are surrounded by junk food. Pizza boxes, chip bags, cookie containers, you name it. It looks like a twelve-year-old's birthday party exploded in here.

It's fucking fun as hell.

"It's a video game, babe, not a music video."

I throw a chip at him, hitting him in the head, and he turns to glare at me. "Did you just hit me in the head with a freaking Dorito?"

"No." I shake my head innocently and back up on the couch as he lays the controller on the coffee table and turns to me.

"Liar."

"You deserved it, *smart ass*."

"I know what you deserve." He kneels in front of me, grabs my hands and pulls me toward him and then in one swift move, pulls his jersey up over my head. "I don't think you can borrow this anymore."

"Fine." I lean back against the couch again and cross my arms over my naked chest, covering up my breasts. Will's lips twitch but he holds his smile back and gives me a mock-glare and grips his black shorts at my hips and yanks them down my legs and throws them over his left shoulder.

I think they land in the salsa.

"Those are mine, too," he murmurs, his eyes glassing over as he sweeps his gaze from my face down my body.

I move to cross my legs, but he holds them still, hands on my thighs, and pushes himself up between them so his pelvis rests against my own and his lips are inches from my face.

"Do you know how beautiful you are?" he asks softly.

I shrug, my smart mouth having suddenly left me, and just stare up into Will's sea-blue eyes.

"So beautiful," he murmurs and kisses my forehead, my nose, over to my dimple. "I love this dimple. Makes you look so innocent." He smiles against my cheek and kisses it again. "Of course, I know differently."

I chuckle and slide my hands up under his t-shirt, over the smooth muscles of his back. "Get naked."

"I will." He kisses his way over to my neck and runs his hand down my face to my breast to tease my nipple. I suck in a breath and squirm beneath him.

"Naked," I repeat but he just chuckles and keeps up the torment, running those hands over my body, those lips down my throat to continue the torture of my nipples. Oh dear God, that feels good.

"Your skin is so damn soft." He's on his knees again, kissing down my stomach to my navel where he pays special attention. He grips my hips in his hands, holding onto me, and bites and kisses my stomach, brushes his nose over it, and then kisses it some more.

Jesus, when did my stomach become an erogenous zone?

He suddenly jerks me to the edge of the couch and pushes my thighs wider apart and sits back on his heels, just looking at me.

"So damn beautiful," he repeats. He raises his hand to my face, his eyes on mine, and runs the backs of his fingers down my cheek, brushes my lower lip with his thumb, and then traces the pad of his index finger down the hollow of my throat, down my sternum, my stomach, over my navel and my pubis.

I can't move. I'm completely in his trance. For Godsake, we went from me playfully cheating my ass off on a video game to intense sexual tension in the matter of seconds.

Suddenly, he turns around and fishes an ice cube out of an empty soda glass and pushes it into his mouth. His eyes smile up at me before he lowers his head, and very gently, places a kiss right on my metal. His cold lips send a zing through my core and I raise my hips in response.

"Holy shit, that's cold!"

He chuckles and does it again, but this time he slides down, hollows his cheeks and sucks my lips into his mouth with the cold ice and I about come apart. I grip his hair in my fists and hold him to me but he backs out of my grasp and shakes his head.

"Grip the back of the couch with your hands, babe."

Huh?

"Why?"

"This is going to get intense for you, and it'll be even more so if you can't touch me." He gently caresses my thigh with his hand. "Trust me."

I do.

So I grab the couch above my head and watch him. He smiles reassuringly and kisses my thigh, then fishes out another ice cube, but instead of pushing it into his mouth, he spreads my labia with one hand and, eyes on mine, guides the ice from my anus, through my folds, and up to my clit.

"Watch this, Megan."

When he reaches my piercing, he hangs out there, circling the metal over and over, making it so damn fucking cold, and then pushes it down against my already over-stimulated nub and my hips come up off the couch. He pushes me back down firmly and gives my clit a reprieve, guiding the ice back down through my lips.

"I love this pink pussy," he murmurs, his eyes full of longing and lust.

"It's rather fond of you, too," I respond, panting.

"Well, that's good to hear," he replies sarcastically and reaches for another ice cube.

"Jesus, Will, I can't do it anymore." I shake my head from side to side.

"Hey, it's okay." He kisses my thigh again, twice, and places a soft kiss against my pussy. God, it's fucking hot to watch him kiss me down there.

He pops the ice in his mouth and kisses my labia deeply, brushing his nose over my clit, and suddenly I feel a finger brushing my anus. My hips jerk against him and I can't hold the orgasm in, I come violently against him, crying out his name.

He pushes that ice deep into me with his tongue and then quickly pulls his shirt off, pushes his shorts down around his hips, unleashing his impressive erection, and moves up my body. As his cold lips meet mine, he pushes his cock inside me.

"Holy shit, it's cold," he laughs and kisses me again.

"Can I touch you now?" I ask, raising my hips to meet him.

"Fuck, baby, yes, touch me." I wrap my arms around his neck, and am stunned when he suddenly stands with me in his arms, still inside me, and sits on the couch. I plant my knees on either side of his hips, and cup his gorgeous face in my hands.

"I love how you feel when you're inside me," I whisper against his lips. His hands are caressing my back, from my shoulders to my ass, and back up again. "I love the way you touch me."

My eyes never leave his as I start to move my hips, clenching down on him with every downward motion. His jaw clenches as he watches me, his eyes sober and hot. I run my hands through his hair and kiss him deeply, and he wraps those strong, muscular arms around my waist, and pulls me down harder, rolling his hips, making his pubic bone hit my metal, and it's too much. Before I can stop it, I fall over the edge again, spasming around him.

He buries his face in my neck and growls.

"Fuck, Megan." And suddenly he's falling with me, spilling himself inside me.

* * *

I wake alone in Will's bed, again. I have a feeling that with his early morning training and meetings, I'll be waking alone a lot when we stay together.

But, given that he woke me up with delicious kisses to let me know he was leaving, he's forgiven.

Yesterday was the best day I've had in I don't know how long. We literally spent all day being lazy gluttons. Except when we were making love, which was also often.

He's a freaking animal.

The more I get to know him, the more I genuinely like him. He's definitely not the arrogant asshole I originally thought he was. He's considerate and kind and funny.

And for some reason that I'm not going to examine too closely, he seems to be smitten with me.

I gather my things and head home. Today is Nick's memorial service, and I will be going. Nick was a special kid, and I need to say goodbye.

I take my time in the shower, letting the scalding water loosen sore muscles and soothe me. I smile as I remember the two showers Will and I shared yesterday, and how we ended up getting dirty again, before we ever even left the water.

The man likes water sports.

After buffing and shaving and scrubbing, I dry quickly and dress in a simple black dress. I twist my hair up and pin it at the back of my head, add minimal makeup and satisfied with how I look I head downstairs to eat something light before heading to the service.

As I descend the stairs, the doorbell rings.

Who the hell could that be?

I pull the door open to find a dark suit-covered Will standing on my doorstep.

God, he looks good in a suit.

It's tailored to his tall, lean body. He's wearing a blue dress shirt and deep blue tie with it, setting off those incredible eyes.

"Your alarm isn't set."

And he's pissed.

"What are you doing here?" I ask.

"Your alarm isn't set," he repeats stubbornly and walks past me into the living room.

"Will, I've been home less than an hour. What are you doing here?"

He pulls me to him, wraps his arms around me and just hugs me close. "Do you really think I'd let you go alone today?"

I rest my cheek against his chest and breathe him in. He smells clean and safe. He smells like Will.

"You don't have to go with me," I murmur.

He pulls back and cups my face in his hands. "Yeah, babe. I do. Then you're coming home with me."

"Aren't you getting sick of me yet?" I ask lightly, wrinkling my nose.

"Yes, I'm terribly sick of you. You eat too much, hog the bed, and cheat at video games. Not to mention, you require way too much sex. But, I'm muddling my way through."

"You know, you could use some work on your people skills."

He laughs down at me. "Haven't you noticed, Megan? I can't seem to get enough of you. I have to leave for Miami tomorrow, and I want you with me tonight. Is that okay?"

"Yeah, that's okay."

Chapter Fourteen

"How's your day going, sweetheart?"

God, it's good to hear his voice. I lean back in the plush desk chair behind my desk and grin.

"It's been a pretty smooth day so far. How about you?"

"The usual. We watched some film this morning, went to the field for a while. Now we're waiting to do some interviews and call it a day." He sounds tired.

"I hear Miami is fun. Gonna go party it up tonight?" I ask with a smile and systematically dismantle a paperclip.

He chuckles, and I clench my thighs together. Even from three thousand miles away, his voice does things to me. He's only been gone for roughly thirty-six hours and I'm itching to get my hands on him.

"No, we have a curfew when we're out of town, babe. We'll probably all just go to the hotel, order in room-service, and call it a night. I wish you were here." The last sentence is whispered, and I clutch my phone even more tightly in my hand.

"Me too," I murmur.

"Good. Get on a plane tonight."

I laugh loudly. Yeah, right. "Will, that's not possible."

"Why not? I'll book you something right now."

"I work a job, remember?"

"Call out sick."

"No." I shake my head and laugh again. "You'll be home to-morrow night."

"I want to see you tonight. Fuck the distance, Meg, you should be here. I want you at the game tomorrow. In fact, take the whole week off. We have a bye-week next weekend, and Coach is giving us the week off. Let's just go somewhere together for a few days."

I sit in stunned silence. Is he serious? Just pick up and leave?

"Will, I have to ask for vacation time months in advance."

I hear him sigh on the other end and feel like shit for raining on his parade.

"I want to see you too," I tell him firmly. "But I can't just leave town without any notice."

"You need a vacation, Meg. You're exhausted. We need time together."

"I'm with you every day." I remind him.

"I miss you."

Damn, we have it bad.

"I miss you too, babe. I'll call you tonight when I get off work."

"Okay. Later."

I hang up and rub my forehead. He's right, I do need a vacation. Being whisked away at a moment's notice sounds fantastic, but I'm not a rich superstar. I have a job, and a mortgage, and a crazy biological mother who seems to think I have to send her money on a regular basis.

I dig back into the charts in front of me and try to forget about a certain sexy football player and what he might be doing right now in sunny Florida.

"Can I come in?" My boss, Loretta, asks.

"Sure."

She sits in the shabby chair opposite me and sets a manila envelope on the desk.

"How's it going?" she asks.

"Fine, thanks. You?"

"Oh, fine," she waves my question off, and looks at me for a long minute. "It's been a rough week."

"Most weeks are rough around here, Loretta," I remind her. She nods thoughtfully.

"I saw that your football player was with you at the funeral the other day," she mentions causally, a knowing smile on her kind face.

"Yes, he was," I confirm. "He liked Nick."

"We all liked Nick," she sighs heavily. "Losing him was tough on all of us."

I not in agreement and watch her, wondering where she's going with this.

"You know, I was looking through your attendance records, and was reminded that you haven't had a vacation in two years."

Will Montgomery, I'm going to kick your ass. Right after I kiss you senseless.

"Okay," I reply.

"You have almost two hundred hours of vacation time saved up in your bank, Megan."

I nod, watching her.

Loretta shakes her head and sighs, then chuckles. "I appreciate your dedication. Trust me, I do. But Meg, this job will burn you out fast if you don't take care of yourself. Your football player called me earlier and asked me to give you this, along with the next ten days off work."

She slides the envelope to me and I open it, my jaw drops as I read the paper inside. It's a flight itinerary to Miami, leaving in four hours. Behind that is an email sent from Will.

Loretta,

Thanks for taking care of this. I owe you.

Will Montgomery

I shake my head and look up at Loretta. "Seriously?"

"Seriously. I don't want to see you for ten days, girlfriend. Go have fun. Get some sun. Have some sex. Spend time with that fine specimen of man of yours." She rises and heads for the door, but turns back to me when she reaches the doorframe.

"Oh, by the way. You've got the rest of the day off as well. Have a good vacation."

I sit for a long minute and stare at the itinerary, then pull out my phone and shoot Will a text.

Do you always get your way?

After I pull out my purse and gather my things, he responds.

I need you.

Well, how do I argue with that?

* * *

It's late when I arrive in Miami, but Will has a car waiting for me at the airport. I expect him to be asleep when I arrive at the hotel. The front desk concierge doesn't even blink when I give him my name and whom I'm with. He just hands me the key to Will's room and gives me directions on how to find it.

Pulling my large suitcase behind me, I head for the elevator. I probably over-packed, but what in the hell does a girl bring on a week-long vacation when she doesn't know where she's going and her man has more money that common sense? Jesus, we could end up in Iceland for all I know.

I use my key to let myself into his room, and about swallow my tongue. 'Room' is too tame of a word. It's the size of my townhouse, with trendy décor and large windows that show off the city. All of the lights are off except for the light by the bedside. Will is propped on pillows, with a playbook in his lap, and he's fast asleep.

I leave my bag near the bathroom, slip out of my shoes and jacket, and walk over to his side of the bed. I take the playbook off his lap, set it aside and push my fingers through his soft dark blonde hair, waking him up.

"You're here."

He wraps his arms around my waist and pulls me into him, buries his face in my neck, and just clings to me.

"Hey, are you okay?" I wrap my arms around his shoulders, caressing him, reveling in how strong and warm and *good* he feels under my hands.

"I'm fine. I missed you." He pulls back and brushes his fingers down my cheek. "Thank you for coming."

"Thank you for sending for me. Bossy man." I kiss his lips gently and brush my nose over his. "You need to go to sleep."

Instead of responding, he takes the kiss deeper. Plunging his hands in my hair, he holds my mouth to his and completely consumes me, kissing me like he hasn't seen me in years. He nibbles the sides of my lips, kisses my dimple, and then sinks into me again, tangling his tongue with mine.

Finally, he pulls back and growls, "I need to get you naked."

I chuckle and pull the loose dress I wore on the plane over my head and toss it on the floor.

"You're wearing panties," he murmurs, his eyes surprised and searching mine.

"I was on a plane, Will. Of course I wore panties."

His thumbs brush the lace over my pubis and I close my eyes on a sigh. I do love the way he touches me.

"Black lace looks good on you." He pushes me onto my back, kneels between my thighs, and runs that large, talented hand up and down my torso, skimming my breasts and stomach, my ribs and sides, and I arch into his touch. He peels my panties down my legs and tosses them aside, grinning down at me.

"God, I love your hands."

"I love touching your sweet body." He leans down and kisses my breast through the matching black lace. "So sweet."

I pull at his t-shirt, and he helps me get it over his head, strips out of his basketball shorts and boxer briefs, and tosses them with my dress on the floor. His shoulders are smooth and warm beneath my hands, his muscles firm and bunching as he moves over me, kissing and nibbling my skin.

"Will," I whisper. He pushes up and braces himself above me, looking down at me with hot blue eyes.

"Yeah, babe."

God, I want to tell him. I so want to tell him how I love him. How much he means to me. But I just can't bring myself to do it. I'm just too scared that I'll lose him. I close my eyes and bite my lip.

"Hey." He rests his elbows at either side of my head and threads his long fingers in my hair. His body is flush against mine, skin on skin, his pelvis pressed to mine. He is completely surrounding me, and I've never felt so safe.

So cherished.

"Meg," he whispers and kisses my lips gently. "Everything about you is so fucking addicting." He moves his hips slightly, slipping against the wetness of my core, and pushes into me slowly, effortlessly. He rests his forehead against mine and stills. "I can never get enough of you, sweetheart."

He kisses me again, softly, hands moving rhythmically in my hair. He is making love to me, body and soul.

"You are amazing." He begins to move, a slow, hypnotizing rhythm. I raise my hips to meet him, pull my knees up so he's able to push even deeper and clutch onto his biceps and show him how deeply I care for him in the only way I can.

I clench down onto his hard, pulsating cock, and gasp when his pubic bone pushes against my piercing.

"Damn, Will."

"Yes, baby, feel it." He rocks against me again, and when I squeeze once more, he clenches his eyes shut. "Fuck, Meg, you're so tight."

His voice is raw. Suddenly, he grips onto my shoulders and pushes into me one last time, hard, and spills himself into me.

"So fucking sweet," he growls as he rocks against me and takes me over with him.

* * *

How in the hell did I get here?

"Yes! Run, run, run, baby, run!" Tasha, the woman sitting next to me screams, jumping up and down. "That's my man!" She turns to me and hugs me tightly, her excitement palpable.

I am sitting with a small group of family members of the team players, in a box near the fifty yard line. We have the best seats in the house. Will made sure that I was welcomed and shown the ropes when I got to the Miami Stadium this morning.

We find our seats, watching the guys regroup for the next play and Tasha, a beautiful, and sweet woman with mocha-colored skin and long dark hair, smiles over at me. "Is this your first away game?"

"Yeah, pretty obvious, huh?"

She laughs and shrugs. "We've all been the newbie at some point. Don't worry, you'll get used to it."

"Do you come to all the away games?" I ask her and watch intently as Will throws the ball and is immediately sacked. I cringe and pray. *Please, God, don't let him get hurt.*

"No, only a couple a year. Most of us choose one or two games to travel to. We're lucky with this sport; the guys are home a lot, and away games only take them away from home for a few days."

Nodding thoughtfully, I turn my attention back to the game. Will has the ball and is looking for somewhere to pass, but there just isn't anywhere, so he runs. "Oh, shit. Go, Will!" I stand and scream, and then hold my fingers over my mouth as I watch him run, my stomach clenching in fear that he'll get tackled and hurt, but he runs through the defense and another thirty yards into the end-zone.

"Yes!" I jump and scream and laugh. "Touchdown, babe!"

Will throws the ball to the ref and jogs back toward the side-line, his teammates high-five and slap his helmet in congratulations, and I just can't stop smiling.

I'm so fucking proud of him!

Tasha smiles over at me as I sit next to her. "He's good."

"Yeah, he is."

"He's a really great guy too," she mentions casually.

"He's the best man I've ever met," I reply immediately. And I mean it.

I feel Tasha's gaze on me, and I meet hers straight on.

"He's a lucky guy."

"No," I shake my head and watch him take his helmet off and talk with a coach. "I'm the lucky one." Will is nodding at what the coach is saying, his hands propped on his lean hips, panting with exertion from the last play. He looks up into the stands and finds us, his eyes lock onto mine and he winks and taps his nose, just like he did that first weekend, when he told me to watch at half-time. *I am so fucking lucky.*

I smile widely and can't help but sigh as he turns away to talk to some of the other guys.

"You have it bad, girl." Tasha nudges my shoulder with hers. "And it looks like it's mutual."

I shrug smugly and take a sip of my diet soda. "I'm surprised how many fans travel this far."

Tasha follows my gaze up into the crowd. There are thousands of fans in blue and green gear, cheering loudly.

"Oh yeah, the die-hards follow the team all season. And the groupies, of course." She smirks and takes a sip of her soda.

"Groupies? Like rock star groupies?" I ask in surprise.

"Oh, honey, you haven't had to deal with the groupies yet?"

I just frown and shake my head.

"Girls be trippin'," she mutters and snorts. "It's disgusting how far they'll go to try to score with the team, pun intended."

"Do some of the guys… um…"

"Sure, some do, most likely. Especially the rookies." Tasha rolls her eyes. "But most of the guys are smart enough to steer clear of those women. They're just bad news."

"I had no idea."

"Well, honey, they're famous. Not to mention, hot, athletic and rich. Of course women are gonna wanna fuck them, and hopefully catch a ring on her finger."

"Gross."

"And dumb," she nods in agreement. "Which our guys aren't. Will's never gone in for that scene, Meg."

Surprised, I look over at her. "I didn't think he would."

"I'm just sayin'." She applauds as we get another first down. "Are you guys coming out with us tonight?"

"I don't know, I just got to town last night. I'm not sure what the plan is."

"Well, the guys usually have to travel back with the team, but since they have the week off for the bye-week, they can do what they want. A bunch of us were gonna go to dinner and maybe if they're not too sore, do some dancing."

"That sounds fun."

* * *

We won, 21 to 7.

I just can't stop smiling. God, what a rush, to be there in that stadium, watching Will lead his team. He's so commanding and strong.

Just the way he is with me.

We are waiting in the hotel lobby for our guys. They had to go back to the locker room to shower, deal with the press, and because they're off for the week, have a short meeting before being turned loose.

I'm texting with Jules when I hear someone shout, "There they are!"

Unfortunately, the press followed us back to the hotel, so photographers are snapping photos of the guys as they push their way into the lobby. There are also fans standing around, hoping for autographs and photos with their favorite players.

Will comes through the doors, looking fantastically delicious in a grey button down shirt and black slacks, his hair still damp from his shower. Flashes are going off all around him, and fans are pushing their way toward him, and to my surprise, he has about four security guards flanking him, holding people back.

His bright blue eyes are searching the crowd for me. When he sees me, hanging back from the crowd, his shoulders relax and he offers me his cocky grin and shrugs. I just nod and wait as he signs some autographs and poses for a few pictures. After pleasing everyone, he stalks toward me, wraps his arms around my middle and lifts me off my feet in a huge hug.

"You're a sight for sore eyes, babe."

"Congratulations!" I bury my face in his neck and breathe him in. "You did so great! I am so proud of you!"

"The best part was having you there." He sets me on my feet and gently tugs the sleeve of the jersey I'm wearing.

"Nice shirt."

"Thanks." I smile shyly. "I bought it last week, for just such an occasion."

Will grins and leans down to murmur, "I especially love that you're wearing my name on your back."

"Hey, Montgomery, who's your lady?"

We pull apart and glance over at the photographer taking our photo. I cringe up at Will and try to slink away, but he holds me tightly against his side and smiles confidently down at me.

"This is my girlfriend, Megan."

"What's your last name, sugar?" the photographer asks, but I shake my head.

"Just Megan."

"Thanks, man." The guy nods at Will and heads off to snap more photos of the other players.

"I'm sorry," I murmur up to Will. He frowns down at me, and cups my face in his hand.

"For what?"

"For you being cornered into calling me your girlfriend."

"You are my girlfriend, Meg." He laughs down at me and tucks a strand of my hair behind my ear.

"But last week, you said,,,"

"Stop." Now he's holding my face in both of his hands, and I grip his wrists in mine. It's as if we're the only two people in the room. Will's eyes are sober as he stares intently at me. "I made a stupid judgment call last week. I don't care who knows that you're mine. In fact, I want everyone to know you're mine."

"But…"

He leans down and kisses me softly, stopping the words, and then whispers against my ear so only I can hear, "You are mine, sweetheart. Get used to it."

"Ditto," I whisper back. I feel him smile against my cheek before he kisses my dimple and pulls away, takes my hand, and pulls me toward the elevator.

"I'm hungry. Let's order room service."

Chapter Fifteen

"Tiny donuts!" I exclaim as we pass Café Du Monde, a famous place for beignets and coffee. In fact, that's all they serve.

Will and I are exploring New Orleans. This is where he decided he wanted to bring me for our short vacation. For the past two days, we've been exploring the city; the rich history of music and food and culture.

It's freaking awesome.

"Hell, yes, let's get some." Will leads me inside, his hand linked with mine. "Coffee too?" He looks back at me with a smile on his lips.

"Yes, please." I nod and wait while he orders. "Three orders?" I ask dryly.

"They're really good," he answers simply and leads me to a table outside in the shade. Even in the fall, it's hot here. And humid. But I don't care.

"So," I sit across from him at a tiny bistro table and perch my sunglasses on top of my head. "What do you want to do today?"

"I thought we could just wander around, shop, listen to the street musicians." He shrugs as the waitress sets three baskets of square, fried dough with powdered sugar liberally dumped on the top on the table, along with our chickaree coffee. "I just want to hang out with you, everything else is gravy."

I smirk at him. "Getting laid is a given, Will. You don't have to be cheeky."

"Cheeky?"

"Cheeky," I mouth at him.

"I don't know anyone who says cheeky."

"I do." I smirk again and pick up a warm, fragrant beignet, shake a bit of the excess sugar off, and take a bite. "Holy sweet mother of God."

He laughs at the mess I make with the white powder and takes a big bite of his own treat. "Good?"

"Dear Lord, I think I need to change my panties."

"You're not wearing any." His eyes heat as he narrows them at me playfully.

"Well, if I were, I'd have to change them because I think I just had an orgasm." The old woman at the table next to us gasps, but I ignore her and take another bite and throw my head back as I chew, my eyes closed, savoring the deliciousness. The chickaree coffee compliments the beignets perfectly. "I might have to move here."

"Why?" Will's voice is quiet and strained, and I find his eyes with mine.

"What's wrong?"

He looks around, making sure that no one is listening, but one of the things we've come to love about N'Awlins is, no one cares who he is. "Watching you enjoy food turns me on," he whispers.

I grin slowly and brush my foot up and down his calf as I take another bite, making sure I lick the excess sugar off my lips. "Mmm."

He quirks up an eyebrow and chuckles. "Do you want to play this game?"

"Why, Will? Don't you want to play with me?" I smile sweetly and take a sip of my coffee, then another bite. "God, these are good. We might need more. I hope you don't care that I'm about to sit here and get really fat off of this fried goodness."

He laughs and takes another bite. "I have some physical activity planned later, or maybe sooner, that should burn quite a few of these calories."

"Thank God." I surprise both of us and eat more than half the beignets. I can't stop. It's like crack. "Seriously, these are crazy good."

"I'm glad you like them." He sits back and sips his coffee, looking at me speculatively, suddenly sober.

"What?"

"Just thinking." He shakes his head and watches me devour the last two small donuts. "You look beautiful today."

I look down at my orange v-neck sundress and brown cowboy boots. It's just a typical summer outfit, which seemed to be appropriate for fall in the south.

"Thank you."

"I love your hair up off your neck like that."

I tilt my head to the side and stare at him. He's looking at me like he could eat me alive. Like he's seeing me for the first time.

Like he loves me.

Holy shit!

He shakes his head, like he's pulling himself out of a trance and smiles softly at me. "Are you ready to go, or do you want more?"

"I'm done."

"Let's go." He holds a hand out for me and pulls me to my feet, and I follow him back out onto the sidewalk, pulling my sunglasses down onto my face. He's wearing his own black Oakleys, tight white t-shirt, khaki shorts. He's just so... big. Tall and muscular and strong.

He does crazy things to my insides.

As we walk up the street, I can hear a saxophone, its sultry notes filling the air. The song is slow and sweet. We turn the corner, and there is a young man, maybe about twenty-two, playing his sax, sitting on a stool, his case open for donations.

The kid is good. Amazingly good. I stop, pulling on Will's hand so he stops too, and listen. The sax player has dyed black hair, his ears both sporting gauges and his fingernails are black. He's dressed every inch the rock star.

But the bluesy notes coming out of that sax make him sound like a legend. If he keeps his head on straight, this kid is going places.

Suddenly, Will pulls me against him, curls his arm around the small of my back, pulls our linked fingers up between our chests, and tucks me against him, slowly swaying back and forth, dancing to the sweet song.

I smile up into his blue eyes, surprised. I'm seeing a whole new romantic side to Will this week.

144

He grins down at me and begins to move more, pushing and pulling us around the wide sidewalk. People are stopping to watch, the old lady from the table next to us at Café Du Monde smiling at us, but we ignore them all and just watch each other.

Damn, he can dance.

Figures.

The kid starts the song over again, not interrupting our dance and I silently thank him. I'm not ready for Will to let go of me; for the look in his eyes to stop.

It's like it was at the café. His blue eyes are intense on mine, full of happiness. His lips are curved in a soft smile, and I can't help but lift up on my toes and rest my own on them, breathing him in.

He smells of coffee and sweet, fried dough.

The arm around my back tightens, pulling me closer to him, practically lifting me off the ground, still swaying back and forth in time with the music, kissing me softly, his lips gently sweeping over mine, nibbling the corners of my mouth. He kisses over my cheek and to my ear, and whispers, "I love you, Megan."

I freeze, and thank the Lord above that he's not looking me in the face because I know my eyes have bulged and I break out in a light sweat, and it has nothing at all to do with the heat. Every muscle in my body contracts. But Will doesn't stop moving, he just wraps both arms around my waist and hugs me to him, and I rest my forehead against his chest as I process what he just said to me.

He loves me.

I want so badly to say the words back, but I can't. Loving means leaving.

Finally, I murmur, "Will…"

"Shh," he tilts my chin with his fingertips and his eyes are soft and kind and I bite my lip so I don't make an ass of myself in front of all these people and cry. "It's okay, sweetheart. I know."

"You do?"

He nods and kisses my forehead. "I do."

"Okay."

He pulls back and smiles down at me, pulls out his wallet, throws a twenty into the sax case, links his fingers with mine, and we wave at the crowd as they applaud and we walk down the sidewalk. My heart is still pounding. I feel… awkward, but Will looks completely relaxed and happy, looking around at the people walking by and the shops we're passing, and I begin to relax too.

I see a sign in a window for ghosts tours and point it out. "We should take a ghost tour!"

"Why?" he asks with a scowl.

"New Orleans is supposed to be one of the most haunted cities in the country." I don't really believe in that stuff, but it could be fun.

"I don't believe in that shit," he scoffs and leads me across the street toward another street musician, this one with a guitar, as I feel my phone vibrate in my handbag, slung across my body and resting on my hip.

"Well, then, it shouldn't bother you to go on a tour with me. You can hold me when I get scared." I laugh and answer my phone without looking at the caller ID. "Hello?"

"So you snagged a rich one."

I stop dead in the street and my stomach falls to the ground. *Fuck fuck fuck!*

"What do you want?" I whisper.

"Who is it?" Will is frowning down at me and suddenly horns are honking at us, telling us to clear the street. He pulls on my elbow and leads me to the sidewalk, watching my face. I can't look away from his eyes.

"What do you want?" I ask more clearly.

"Well, honey, what do you think I want? You have a new rich boyfriend. I want money." Sylvia's voice is raspy from too many cigarettes and heavy with bitterness and just plain mean.

"I just sent you money," I murmur to her and Will's scowl deepens.

"Yeah, well, you can afford to start sending me more. What you send me barely covers my bills."

I close my eyes and run a hand down my face.

"I'm not sending you more money, Sylvia."

"The fuck you're not, you ungrateful little bi-" I hang up on her, turn my ringer off and throw my phone back in my bag.

"Your mom?" Will asks, hands on his hips, watching my face.

"Yeah."

"Wants money?"

"That's all she ever wants." I start to walk away from him, but he grabs my arm and holds me in place.

"So, we'll send her money."

"Hold up." I face him, square on, and refuse to back down on this. "*We* aren't giving her shit. Ever. She found out that we're seeing each other and thinks she can milk it, but I'll be fucking damned if she'll ever get a dime out of you, do you understand?"

His eyes are narrowed stubbornly, and I grip his upper arms in my hands, trying to get my point across. "Will, seriously, I don't want you to give her money."

He exhales, his mouth set in a grim line. "Okay."

"Promise me."

"No, I can't promise you that. But I hear you, Meg."

"Will…"

"I fucking hear you. Trust me to respect you and do my best to protect you."

His face is fierce, and I know he won't bend on this.

"Okay."

"So, what's her deal?" he asks as he takes my hand in his and leads me back in the direction we were heading.

"She's a junkie, and she thinks I owe her."

"Why in the hell do you owe her anything?"

"Because she gave birth to me." I shrug and try to think of something else to talk about. "You know, I'm not wearing any underwear." Desperate times call for desperate measures.

"Yeah, we'll get to that. Why do you owe her, Meg?"

"Because after I was taken away from her, I told the cops that she did drugs and sold herself for money and she was arrested and went to jail for a while, and she's never let me forget that it's my fault. She's always been able to find me. Always. So, I give her the money each month and it keeps her in Montana and away from me."

"Fuck," Will whispers.

"Look, it's no biggie. It's not a lot of money. I don't need it."

"That's not the point. She's a fucking bully, babe. Tell her to kiss your ass."

"It's just easier this way." I shrug again and stop him when he tries to argue. "I don't want to fight about her. She's not worth any of our time."

He takes a deep breath in frustration and pushes his fingers through his hair. "Fine."

"Let's go check out one of the above ground cemeteries." I bounce up and down in excitement and he can't help but laugh at me.

"What is it with you and the dead? And why am I just now learning this about you?"

"It's N'Awlins, Will. Don't be a spoil-sport."

* * *

"Damn, you can pack away the food. Where do you put it all?" I ask as we enter our hotel suite. More accurately, the penthouse of an old, gorgeous hotel. The furnishings are grand and sturdy and the tapestries are thick and old.

I feel like we've stepped back in time each time we walk inside this vast room. It's beautiful, and way more space than we need, but I know that Will wanted to make this week special.

And he has.

"Meg, as a football athlete, I have to consume almost four-thousand calories a day to maintain enough energy to train the way we do."

"All the time?" I ask, stunned.

"During the season. In the off season, it's closer to three-thousand."

"Holy shit," I murmur and feel a little bad for constantly tormenting him about the volume of food he eats.

But then I look at him and remember how he laughs when I tease him, and I don't feel bad anymore. Teasing him is fun.

"There's something I want to show you," he murmurs and pulls me to him.

"I've seen that before, stud muffin." I grin up at him and glide my hands up and down his chest as he throws his head back and laughs.

"Not that. Well, not yet, anyway. Come on."

He leads me out of the room and to the elevator, but instead of pushing the button for the lobby, we go up to the roof. I look up at him in surprise, but he just smiles smugly down at me.

"What are we doing?" I ask.

"You'll see."

The doors open to reveal a beautiful rooftop patio, full of plush furniture, large, ornate gold planters boasting cut-leaf rhododendrons, Spanish moss falling down ledges of the balcony, and the tops of banana trees from the courtyard below. We can see across to similar patios on similar hotels, although it's small enough up here, and the foliage is plush enough that it feels private.

White lights are strung over-head, lanterns are lit on the side of the building, and on table tops, sending a soft glow over the space in the darkness of evening.

There is a sign that reads *closed for private party.*

"Oh, we're not supposed to be up here." I try to pull him back to the elevator, but he chuckles and easily pulls me back to his side.

"We are the private party, sweetheart."

"Oh." I smile ruefully as he leads me to a corner of the patio that has champagne chilling in a silver bucket and two silver plates covered with silver domes sitting on a small table before a gorgeous red and gold couch.

"What's all this?" I ask, my eyes wide, taking in this beautiful scene.

"Just dessert on the rooftop," Will murmurs and shrugs shyly, like it's no big thing.

But it is a big thing.

"Thank you." I raise on my tip-toes and kiss him. "It's lovely."

"You're lovely. Here, have a seat." He leads me to the couch and pours us each a flute of sparking, gold champagne. "To spontaneous vacations."

"I'll drink to that." We clink glasses and take a sip, Will's blue eyes are watching me over his flute.

"Did you have fun at the cemetery today?" I ask with a grin.

"It was interesting. Definitely a new experience."

"I thought it was fun. I still think you should let me talk you into the ghost tour."

"I can think of better things to do in the dark," he replies with a half-grin.

"Really? Like what?"

"Are you wearing any underwear under that dress?" he asks instead of answering my question.

"You know I'm not." I tilt my head and study him. "Why do you ask?"

"Just making sure." He pours more of the sweet champagne into our flutes and leans against the back of the couch, watching me. "Would you like some dessert?"

"Sure. What do we have?"

He pulls the lids off the plates and reveals little dishes of beautiful crème brule. "Looks like crème brule."

"Delish," I murmur and grin as he scoops up a spoonful and feeds it to me. "Mmm."

"Good?"

"Mmm hmm." I reach for it, but he pulls it out of my grasp and takes a bite himself.

"Mmm," he nods. "Good." He takes another bite and I frown at him and reach for the other dessert, but he blocks me. "I got this."

"Well then gimme!"

"Impatient little thing, aren't you?" he chuckles and feeds me another bite, then takes a bite himself. I crawl over and climb in his lap, and he feeds both of us, grabbing the other ramekin when the first one is empty.

"Did you get enough?" he asks as he pushes the dishes aside and wraps his arms around me.

"More than enough. Thank you."

He smiles against my hair and kisses me, while running his hands up and down my back. "You're welcome, babe."

His hand glides down my hip to my thigh and under my dress, and heads back up again. I grin against his chest as my pulse accelerates and I cup his face in my hand. "You know, someone could see us out here."

"They could," he mutters and kisses my forehead, that talented hand still exploring under my dress.

"We should behave," I whisper and kiss his lips gently.

"That's no fun," he whispers back, making me giggle.

"What do you want to do?" I ask as I nibble down his neck.

"You," he whispers and I grin again, spread my legs slightly and guide his hand between them.

"Feel how wet you make me when you say stuff like that?" I whisper against his lips. His eyes flare, his fingers find my clit and rub gently, then slip down and slide easily into my wetness. "Oh, God, honey."

Finally, he takes my mouth possessively with his own, kissing me deeply and madly, while his fingers continue to wreak havoc on my core. Dear God, he makes me crazy with just two fingers.

Who am I kidding, he makes me crazy by just looking at me.

"Want you," I mutter between kisses and he groans deep in his throat, lifts me to straddle him, and I reach between us to unfasten his shorts and unleash the hard cock that has been pressing into my hip.

"God, I love your hands," he mutters, looking down at me pumping his length. Finally I can't take it anymore, and I raise up and slowly guide him inside me. "Oh fucking hell, babe."

His eyes are clenched shut, jaw tight, hands gripping my hips like vices and I've never felt more sexy.

The skirt of my dress falls around our laps, so even if someone did see us, it just looks like I'm sitting on his lap, and I begin to rock. Not fast, and not so that it really even looks like we're having sex. I just rock slowly and clench around him tightly.

"Meg, you're gonna make me come like this, sweetheart."

"That's the point, babe," I lean down and kiss him, bury my hands in his hair and continue the assault on his cock, clenching and rocking, and as I do, it puts pressure on my metal, against my clit and I find myself getting close too, shivering and convulsing around him. "I'm going with you."

His eyes open and he watches me with hooded eyes and his mouth open, gasping. He cups my face in his hands and pulls me down to him, kisses me tenderly and then whispers, "I love you," as he surges up and empties himself inside me, growling. The words, the pressure of his orgasm, what he's doing to my body, sends me over with him, but before I can cry out, he covers my mouth with his to hold the sound down, and I explode in wonder and complete surrender.

I love you too.

Why am I so fucking afraid to say it?

Chapter Sixteen

~Will~

I could lie here all day and watch her sleep. God, she's so fucking beautiful. She is all gold skin and auburn hair against crisp white sheets. Her delicate face is soft in sleep, and little pink lips are slightly parted.

This week has been the best of my life. Hell, the month or so we've been together has been the best of my life, and that's saying a lot because I know that I am one lucky son of a bitch.

But Meg makes everything incredible. She's funny and smart and so damn talented.

And she's asleep, in this bed, with me. It's our last morning in New Orleans, and I must admit I regret that it's over so quickly. I'll be sure to take her away again as soon as the season ends. We'll go to Europe, or Hawaii.

Fuck, anywhere she wants.

It's been fun to watch her enjoy the amazing music of this city, the sounds and smells, the uniqueness that is New Orleans.

And I think it's effing adorable to watch her eat beignets. Speaking of, I check the clock. I'm expecting a delivery in about ten minutes.

Meg stirs in her sleep, raises one arm up over her head, causing the sheet to slide down her body and expose one perfect breast, the nipple tight from being exposed to the cool air. Her beautiful auburn and blonde hair is fanned around her on her white pillow, and one knee is bent, laying against the bed.

Which means I could slip my hand between her thighs and wake her with my fingers inside her, but I wait. I want to watch her for a few more minutes.

I knew that I'd fall in love eventually. That I'd end up meeting a nice girl and we'd get married and have a few kids and a good life together.

But I had no idea that I could love someone so much that it absolutely consumes me. That being away from her for merely hours makes me want to punch someone in the face and the thought of anyone ever hurting her in any way just makes me completely nuts.

I would kill for this woman.

Or die.

I wasn't kidding when I said she's everything. She is.

At the light knock on the door I roll out of bed, pull on yesterday's shorts and answer the door. I tip the delivery kid from Café Du Monde and carry the big bag of beignets and carrier of coffee to the bedside table, set it down, strip out of my shorts and climb back onto the bed.

She hasn't moved a muscle.

My little lazy bones. Funny thing is, she's the least lazy person I've ever known. She works tirelessly, and is always moving.

I love it when she's moving beneath me.

With this in mind, I lean on my elbow near her head and lean down to kiss her cheek.

"Megan, wake up," I croon softly to her and brush little wisps of hair off her neck.

"Hmph," she answers with a moan and turns away from me.

"C'mon, lazy bones, wake up." I plant little kisses on her bare shoulder and upper arm and slide my hand over her stomach and up to her breast, cupping it in my hand while I worry the nipple between my fingers.

I can't get enough of her soft skin.

"I'm sleepy," she murmurs and turns toward me, burrowing against me and settle in to sleep with her forehead pressed to my chest.

Fuck, she's adorable.

"I have a surprise for you."

"You do?" she asks, not moving.

"Yep, but you have to wake up to get it."

"I don't want it."

Stubborn woman.

KRISTEN PROBY

"Okay." I back away and open the paper bag full of fresh, hot donuts, take one out and turn back to her. Her eyes are still closed.

I shake it over her shoulder, dropping powdered sugar on her skin and lean down and lick it off.

"Mmm," I groan. "Good stuff."

No response.

So I shake some more over her neck and dive after it, lapping it up.

She opens one eye, briefly, then snaps it shut quickly. I grin and pull the sheet down to her waist, exposing her perfect little body, and shake more sugar over her breasts.

I lick it up and then take a big bite of the beignet. "Open your mouth," I instruct her, and she complies readily. I chuckle as I feed her the remaining portion of the fried dough, then dive in the bag for another and continue to shake the sugar on her delectable body, then eat the beignet, sharing pieces with her.

"I think you'll need to be my plate more often, babe. You make everything taste sweeter."

"Cheeky bastard," she mumbles sleepily and I laugh out loud.

Grabbing a fresh donut, I move between her legs, shoulder her thighs wide apart and settle in for some fun.

Fuck, she's already wet. Sleepy my ass. She's playing with me.

God, I love her.

I shake some sugar over her pussy and watch it fall like snow on her pink flesh. Her clit is hard, that silver piercing just begging for my tongue. So I lean forward and lick her, from her soft folds to that warm metal, and all around, licking up every last bit of sugar, then take a bite of donut. I look up at her face and her eyes are open now, watching me, her gorgeous hazel eyes shining in lust, hands fisting the sheets. I offer her the donut, and she takes it from me and flings it over the side of the bed, licks her fingers and plunges them into my hair with a huge grin on her gorgeous face.

"Didn't want anymore?" I ask sarcastically.

"I've had enough of those."

"Me too. But I haven't had enough of this." I spread her with my thumbs, opening her up to me and kiss her, plunging my tongue inside her and licking all around. Her hips buck up against my face, but I hold her firmly, not letting her twist away.

She goes fucking crazy when I eat her out. It's the sexiest damn shit I've ever seen.

Replacing my mouth with my hands, I move up to tease her clit, not flicking at it, but lapping at it, pushing it, and tugging, ever so gently, that silver with my teeth.

"Will!" she cries and bucks again. I push my fingers down, then pull them out and lick them.

"Yes, love?"

"Need you in me."

"I've been in you sweetheart." I push my fingers back in to prove my point, making her moan.

"Come up here," she pants.

"What do you need?" I ask and brush her clit with my nose, making her squirm and me smile.

"You. Always you."

"Fuck yes, me." I climb up her body and lay over her. She cradles me against her, her strong legs wrapped around my waist, arms around my shoulders and fingers in my hair and I just lean on my elbows and gaze down at her.

"You are so fucking incredible, Megan."

Her eyelids droop, and she blushes like she does when she's happy. I brush my lips over hers and slide my cock through her wetness, pushing her piercing with the tip and she bites my lower lip.

"Like that?"

"Mmm." She nods slightly and cups my ass with her hands, tugging me closer to her. God, I want to be inside her.

I need to be inside her.

I rear back and slowly push through the wetness, through her swollen folds, and sink in until I feel her resistence.

She's so damn tight.

"This is my favorite place to be," I whisper to her and feel her smile against my neck.

156

"It's the top of my list too," she whispers back.

And slowly, we begin to move. Everything in me is telling me to fuck the shit out of her, to pound her and mark her until I'm all she sees, and all she knows. All she remembers.

But on this sticky, sweet morning, all I want is to go slow. To be gentle with her. To memorize every sigh, every moan, every tightening of her muscles as she holds me to her.

I just want to make love to my girl.

And so I do, until she's writhing and shuddering, and I feel those sweet muscles around my cock tighten like a fucking vice.

"Let go, babe," I whisper and watch avidly as she tightens, every muscle in her delectable body clenching and pulsing around me, and cries out my name as she explodes.

I can't hold it in any longer, and I empty myself into her as she continues to move and shudder, my face pressed to her neck, telling her how much I love her.

It hurts, just a little, that she can't say it back yet. But she will.

Chapter Seventeen

~Meg~

"I had a great time this week." I am snuggled up to Will's side in our cab on the way to my place from the airport. The Seattle evening is rainy and dark. "Thank you."

"No need to thank me, babe." He kisses my hair and tightens the arm around my shoulders. "I had fun too. We'll go again soon."

"It's a date."

"Why don't you just come back to my place with me?" he asks for the third time, making me chuckle.

"Because I need to unpack, do some laundry and get ready to go back to work. And so do you."

"I could stay at your place with you. If you don't mind my dirty underwear being washed with yours." I hear the humor in his voice and lean back to look up into his handsome face.

"You're always welcome at my place." I plant a kiss on his cheek and lean my head on his shoulder again. "I need to make you a key."

He smiles against my hair and kisses me again as I see my townhouse come into view.

And the woman sitting on my steps.

Fuck me!

"Shit."

"Who is that?" Will asks as I pull out of his arms.

"Sylvia."

"Fuck," he whispers.

"Exactly."

I jump out of the car as Will throws bills at the cab driver and stalk angrily up to the beaten down, trashy woman smirking at me on the stairs.

"What the hell are you doing here?"

"You hung up on me, so I thought I'd just come talk to you in person. What, you're not happy to see mommy dearest?"

"Get the fuck off my property."

"That's no way to speak to your mother." Her eyes flash as she stands and the sight of her makes me sick. She's too thin, about my height. Her auburn hair is full of gray, hazel eyes are dull and her skin is ashy. Her old clothes hang on her slight frame. At one time, she'd been really pretty.

Now she just looks old and worn. And she's not even fifty yet. My stomach rolls.

"You know you're not welcome here." I tell her, my voice strong, arms crossed over my chest, ignoring the rain falling on me.

"So this is your new young man." Her lips spread in what she considers her flirty smile, but her teeth are yellow, and she just looks... pathetic. "Hi there."

Will is standing behind me now, his hands on my shoulders, showing me his support and I've never been more thankful for him.

"I believe Megan asked you to leave." His voice is hard and firm.

Her smile disappears and is replaced with a cold sneer. "I'm not leaving until I get more money out of this ungrateful little bitch."

"I told you…"

"I don't give a fuck what you told me. You owe me! I want what's mine!" She marches down the stairs to get in my face, but Will pulls me aside and steps in front of me, looking down at Sylvia with fire in his eyes.

"She doesn't owe you anything. She asked you to leave. Don't make me call the cops." His voice is low and pissed, and Sylvia takes a step back, her eyes wide and stunned.

Did she really think she could just show up here and leave with a pocket full of money?

Yes.

Because I always give in to her. No matter how ashamed I feel later, I always give in.

No more.

"Go back to Montana, Sylvia. You wasted your time coming here." I mutter angrily as I link my hand with Will's. He squeezes my hand reassuringly.

"I don't have any money!" she whines.

"Not my problem. I sent you money."

"Not enough," she spits out.

"It's the last you'll get from me." My voice is low now, and firm. Her eyes register surprise again, and then they narrow on my face with such hatred I take a step backward. Will frowns down at me and squeezes my hand again.

"You'll send it. You know what will happen if you don't. I'll go to the press and tell them all about the big football star's new girlfriend. What a piece of trash she is. Where she comes from." Sylvia sneers at me. "Won't that be great publicity for him?"

"Call the police," Will states calmly and Sylvia's jaw drops.

"I'll go to the press…"

"Go to the press. Go anywhere you want, as long as it's not here. I don't give a shit what you say. Megan is not trash, she just comes from it." I gape up at him, as Sylvia gasps at the insult. "You can't hurt her. She's told you to leave, now leave."

She looks at me, her mouth set in a grim line. "Fine."

She marches down to the ancient Honda parked at the curb and then looks back at me. "You always were a worthless piece of shit."

"Get the fuck out!" Will yells, cutting her off. She jumps in her car and speeds away.

I can't move. I just stand here, in the rain, hugging myself and watch her car disappear down the street.

"Look at me."

I'm too ashamed. Jesus, what must he think of me now? I bury my face in my hands and will the tears back.

Crying won't solve anything.

"Just go, Will."

"Look at me," he repeats, his hands on my shoulders now. "Megan, stop. Look at me."

I look up into his eyes, still so embarrassed.

"I'm so sorry…"

"Shh." He shakes his head and hugs me to him, wrapping his arms around my shoulders, pinning my arms against his chest, and I've never felt so safe. "I'm sorry she's so horrible."

"I meant it," I mumble against him. "I'm not sending her any more money."

"No, you're not."

"You're not either. She will ask you."

"Hmm," he murmurs, non-committally.

"I mean it."

"Okay. Let's go inside." He picks up our bags and leads me in the house, disarming the alarm.

"I'm surprised she didn't try to break in and wait for me in the house," I comment. That's her usual M.O.

"She must have seen the alarm. See? I told you you needed an alarm." He offers me a smug smile and my chest loosens. I don't want to think about Sylvia anymore. She can't hurt me.

I snicker as he turns his back to me to pick our bags up and take them upstairs. "Yes, you were right."

"What did you say?" he asks sarcastically.

"You're handsome," I reply with a grin.

"No, that's not what you said,"

"I like your shirt?"

"Nope." He sets the bags down and slowly saunters to me, his eyes narrowed and a smile tickling his lips. "Tell me."

"Um… I think we should order dinner in?"

He laughs now, full-out, and the knot in my stomach from seeing Sylvia on my doorstep is gone.

"I think you said something about me being right."

"Did not," I scoff.

"Did too."

"I wouldn't do that," I reply and shake my head. "You must be thinking of someone else."

"No, you're the only beautiful, smart-mouthed woman on my mind these days."

"Gee, that's so good to hear," I reply sarcastically and he sweeps in and throws me over his shoulder, heading for the stairs.

"Hey! Our luggage!"

"We'll get it later. I think I need to teach you a lesson."

"What kind of lesson?" I look down at his firm, tight ass and give it a little smack, just because I can.

He smacks mine back, making me yelp.

"The fun kind."

I smile and brace myself on his lean hips as he easily climbs the stairs.

God, I love him.

* * *

"So, you're playing Arizona next Sunday?" I ask from my spot on the couch. Will taught me my lesson. I think I may need more lessons like that in the future. I'm a slow learner. Then we ordered in dinner, and now we're on the couch, watching football.

Well, Will is watching football. I'm about to paint my toenails.

"Yes."

"At home?" I ask casually.

"Yes," he smiles at me. "And after the game, the whole family is going to my mom and dad's for dinner. It'll probably be the last weekend this year that we can still enjoy their backyard."

"Okay."

"I want you there."

It isn't a request, and makes me smile. I want to be there.

"Okay," I say again. Will nods and goes back to watching his game, that being settled.

I shake my red nail polish and pull my right foot up onto the couch, my heel tucked against my ass, and buff my toenails, then open the polish. Before I can swipe the brush down my toenail, Will interrupts me.

"Can I do that?"

My head whips up to meet his eyes, surprised. "What?"

"I want to do that."

"Why?"

162

He just shrugs and smiles as he slides across the couch, pulls my foot into his lap, causing me to turn so my back is against the armrest, and holds his hand out, waiting for me to hand over the polish.

"Are you sure?"

He just raises an eyebrow at me, that cocky smile still on his lips, and I hand the polish to him.

"It's not as easy as it looks, you know."

"I'm quite sure I can do it."

"I thought you were watching football."

"I'm listening."

I shake my head and settle back against the soft cushion, arms folded over my belly and watch his dark blonde head bow over my foot, his big hand holding the polish wand over the toes, and methodically paints each toe.

Miraculously, he doesn't end up painting my skin.

"You shouldn't be doing your own toes," he murmurs under his breath.

"Excuse me?"

"You shouldn't be doing your own toes," he repeats, raising his head to look me in the eye.

"Why ever not?"

"Because, you should pamper yourself and go get pedicures."

"Oh please," I wave him off. "Who has time for that?"

"You only work three days a week, babe."

"Well, now that I'm not sending every last dime to Sylvia any more, I'll splurge," I comment with a smile but the look he sends me is feral.

"That's why you do your own feet? Why you barely have basic cable? How much have you been sending her?"

"None of your business." I try to pull my foot away, but he grabs my ankle and holds strong.

"It is my business."

"No, it's not."

"Megan, don't fight me on this. I'm in love with you, damn it, and you're sending money you need to that piece of shit of a human being. Now tell me, how much do you send her?"

"Anything that's left over."

"What does that mean?"

"What I said. I pay the bills, buy groceries and keep a little for incidentals and send her the rest."

"Fuck, Meg."

"I already said I'm done. I meant it."

"Damn straight you meant it."

"Why does this bother you so much? It's not your money."

"It's not about the money. It's about that woman taking advantage of you, and you letting her, and it kills me that you've been going without when you didn't need to be."

"I don't go without." I shake my head and push my hands though my hair in frustration. "Trust me, Will, I know what it is to go without. This isn't it. I have everything I need. I'm fine."

"You're fine."

"I'm fine," I repeat. "I don't need to be rich. I'm happy with what I have. You do know that I'm not with you because of your fat contract, right?"

He laughs like I've just said the most absurd thing he's ever heard. "Trust me, babe, you're no gold digger."

"Well, there you go then." I shrug.

He goes back to my toes, and we sit in silence, the game playing in the background, as he carefully paints each little toe. When he's done with the second coat, he replaces the wand, tightens the bottle and then blows on my toes to help them dry.

It tickles.

"Your toes are so small," he comments softly.

I sigh as I just watch him pamper my feet. This big, strong man, gently painting my tiny toes. It's adorable.

And sweet.

He loves me.

"Thanks for painting them," I murmur.

"You're welcome," he replies with a grin. "It wasn't so hard."

"Maybe I'll let you paint them from now on," I wink at him and he chuckles, sending shivers through me. I love his voice. I love making him laugh.

"I think I'll just send you to the spa with Jules and Nat."

164

"You're not sending me…"

"Shut up, Megan." He pulls me into his lap, careful not to mess up my fresh paint, and kisses me hard, until we're both breathless. "Just let me spoil you a little, okay?"

"You do spoil me."

He brushes a strand of hair off my cheek and kisses my forehead, then settles me against him so we can finish the football game.

"Get used to it," he whispers.

* * *

"How was vacation?" Jill asks as she leans on the counter next to me where I'm charting and passes me a Starbucks.

"Fantastic," I reply with a smug grin.

"I hate you. You know that, right?"

"You love me." I laugh at her and give her a hug. "It's good to be back. Thanks for this."

It's Tuesday, and we are working the morning shift.

"How's your man?"

"Good. Working." I shrug and dive back into my chart.

"How long does he work anyway? I know nothing about what those guys do during the week."

"Well, it varies. Yesterday they trained in the morning and then watched films and had meetings the rest of the day. He didn't get home until about eight last night."

"Wow, long days."

"Yeah, it'll be the same today. They're working extra hard since they all took last week off."

"Cool." She smiles encouragingly.

The phone at my elbow rings, and I pick it up. "Pediatric Oncology, this is Megan."

"Hey, Meg this is Lyle in security. Just wanted to give you the heads up that Mr. Montgomery is on his way up to you."

I frown and turn toward the elevators as I hear them ding and see Will walk off, grinning from ear to ear, heading straight for me.

"Thanks, Lyle." I hang up and cross to him. "What's up?"

He just hugs me, pulling me off my feet and spins me in a circle, and then kisses me like crazy, in front of everyone.

Every. One.

"Uh, Will, I'm working." I laugh and pull back, confused, but pleased with how excited he looks. "What is going on with you?"

"Stacy had the baby this morning. I just came from there." He's so proud.

"Oh! That's awesome! How are they?"

"Perfect. Stace is tired, but she did great. The baby is tiny and adorable, and Isaac can't stop staring at him. I'd call him a pussy, but I can't blame him. The little guy is great."

"I'm so happy, for all of you." I run my hands down his chest, but I catch the quick frown between his eyes before it's gone, replaced by his handsome smile.

"Thank you. So, I was in the neighborhood and wanted to stop by."

"I'm so glad you did. I can't wait to congratulate them."

"They'll all be at mom and dad's on Sunday, but you're welcome to stop in and see them later today. I think they'll be in the hospital until Thursday."

"Okay, I will. For sure. I got them some gifts I can't wait to give them."

"You did?" He grins again, delighted with me.

"Of course." I shrug shyly. "New babies need new things. Plus, you'll approve of what I got."

"What is it?"

"Baby football gear. He'll be all decked out on Sunday to cheer on his uncle Will."

Will's eyes go soft and he pulls me to him and kisses me again, softly, brushing his lips over mine, and I don't care who sees. He buries his fingers in my hair and holds on tight as he devours me with his lips.

He smells good. Musky and clean.

He smells of Will.

"I love you," he whispers against my lips.

"I know," I respond, and he smiles again.

"I have to get back to the team for meetings the rest of the day. I'll see you tonight?" He raises a brow in question and I smile.

"I'll be there."

"Great." He kisses me, one last time, hard, and then turns to walk back to the elevator. "Later."

"Later." I wave and watch him disappear into the elevator.

"Oh yeah," Jill murmurs with humor behind me. "He's good. Damn, girl."

I just sigh and nod in agreement. "Yeah, he's good."

Chapter Eighteen

Apparently, losing a game makes Will a wee bit grumpy.

Or a lot grumpy.

We're driving to his parents' home after the game this morning, and he's unusually quiet.

I was at the game today, in his private sky box with Nat and Jules and the guys. It was fun. Until the end of the fourth quarter. We were up by three points against Arizona, but in the last two minutes, Will threw an interception, and the guy ran it in for a touchdown.

We lost.

Will was off his game most of the day. I could see it. He just wasn't himself.

The others went on ahead to the Montgomery's house and I hung back to wait for Will to give a couple interviews and take a shower. He'd hugged me when he saw me, but he hasn't said much.

What the hell am I supposed to say?

I don't know.

So I just reach over and take his hand in mine, link our fingers and kiss his hand, then rest them in my lap.

That earned me a half smile.

He pulls into his parents' drive, parks and opens the door for me. It's an unseasonably warm fall day.

"I smell rain," I say casually.

"I hope not. Grilling in the rain sucks."

"You live in Seattle. Grilling in the rain is the norm."

He smirks and leads me around his parents' house to the back yard, and I gasp. Holy shit, his dad must put in hours and hours each week into this yard. Even in the fall, when most of the flowers have died, and the leaves are turning, it's a sight to behold with paths and benches and fruit trees.

"This is gorgeous."

He looks back and grins. *There he is.*

"Yeah, Dad works hard on it."

"I can tell."

"They're here!" A little girl of about five years old shrieks and jumps up and down. She's in a Seattle football jersey and jeans, her long raven hair braided down her back. And suddenly her mirror image is standing next to her.

"Well, hello there," I smile down at the sweet little girls.

"Hi," they say in unison, smiling widely at us.

"Meg, this is Josie and Maddie. They're Brynna's daughters."

Everyone looks up from what they're doing and waves and I just stand here and look about the back yard in awe.

It looks like some sort of beautiful people convention.

Seriously.

"Come help me grill, son! Grab a beer." Will's dad is manning the grill, wearing a *Chillin' and Grillin'* apron and wielding a long metal spatula. Most of the guys are near the grill, either standing with Steven, or sitting at a nearby table.

What is it with men and grilling?

The women are scattered on the covered patio, in small groups chatting and laughing, holding babies, sipping drinks.

Holy shit, I didn't know that family gatherings like this existed.

"Sure, dad, let me just introduce Meg around." He grins down at me and links his fingers with mine reassuringly.

"I don't think I should be here," I whisper up to him. He scowls and leans down to kiss my dimple.

"You definitely should be here," he whispers in my ear. He straightens and leads me to the patio. "You know most everyone. My ugly brothers are over there," he points to his brothers, including Luke and Nate, who all grin and wave. Fuck, they're all hot.

"You know my mom and dad, and the girls," again with more smiles and waving. "And that's Luke's mom and dad, Neil and Lucy. That couple wandering through the trees is Stacy's parents, and Brynna's parents are sitting with my mom. And that big guy that looks like Nate with my dad at the grill is Nate's dad, Rich."

I'm completely overwhelmed.

"Hi everyone," I smile and wave at the group as a whole, and they all smile and wave back. They are a sea of green and blue, clearly dressed to support Will and his team.

Except Nate, who's just wearing a black t-shirt and faded blue jeans, his hair down, tattooed arm wrapped around Jules' waist, and he's whispering in her ear, making her laugh.

"I think Meg could use a drink," Caleb steps forward and hands me a beer. He has kind blue eyes and an effing killer body.

Of course, he's a SEAL.

"Yes, Meg could," I agree and take the beer from him. "Thanks."

"Come sit with us," Natalie calls, her daughter Olivia on her shoulder. She is sitting with Brynna, Samantha and Stacy in plush outdoor couches at the far end of the patio.

"I'll be over there," I wink at Will and turn to go, but he holds onto my hand and pulls me against him, swinging our linked hands behind my back and kisses me, long and slow, in front of all of these people.

"Get a fucking room!" Caleb calls out.

"Watch your damn mouth!" Will's mom, Gail, yells at him, making us all laugh.

"What was that for?" I ask him.

"Because I can." He winks and walks over to his dad. "That's no way to grill a steak, old man."

"Here," Brynna scoots over on the couch making room for me, and hands me the newest Montgomery, Liam. "He's wearing your outfit, you hold him."

I glance up at Stacy, who is lounging comfortably next to Natalie. "Do you mind?"

"Of course not. Babies are passed around this family all day. Get used to it." She grins at her son lovingly as I take him from Brynna and cradle him in my arms. He has a Seattle football beanie on his little head, matching the adorable onesie that looks like a jersey with the number eight on the front, tucked into the tiniest blue jeans I'd ever seen, and all wrapped up in a blue and green blanket. "That is the most adorable baby outfit, Meg. Thank you."

"Oh you're welcome. I couldn't resist it. But the girls are absolutely precious." Sophie, Isaac and Stacy's older daughter, and Olivia are in matching green and blue tulle tu-tus and green and blue hair bows almost as big as their heads.

"Stacy made the tu-tus," Natalie grins and pats her daughter's back.

"There's not much you can do when you're a thousand months pregnant," Stacy remarks with a frown. "I was bored out of my mind.

"That must have been a challenge with a one year old," I pull Liam up onto my chest, and he nestles down under my chin, sighs, and goes right back to sleep.

"It was, but Isaac was great. He was able to work mostly from home, and I had my mom and Brynna, and Nat and Jules, so I was never alone for long."

Luke joins us, kisses his daughter's cheek and then his wife's lips. "Want me to take her?"

"Sure," Nat hands the sleepy, dark haired baby to Luke and grins as he murmurs to the baby and walks back over with the guys.

"He's hot with a baby," Brynna remarks with a sigh.

"He's just hot," Stacy replies. "Sorry, Nat."

"Puke," Samantha remarks and makes a gagging noise. "That's my brother, girls. And why does he always get to hold the baby? He hogs her."

"Because she comes from my loins," Luke calls back, having heard Sam.

"Oh God, don't talk about your loins. I'm going to throw up."

"Don't be sorry, Stace. You're right," Natalie laughs. "Although, I think all the guys here are pretty hot."

I nod and look over at Will. He's frowning, hanging back from the others, deep in thought. He's beating himself up about today. How do I get him out of this mood? I purse my lips, rubbing Liam's little back, and then it hits me.

With a grin, I balance Liam on my chest and pull my phone out of my pocket, and send him a text.

Would the thought of me sucking your cock in the car on the way home cheer you up?

I hit send and kiss the baby's head, half listening to the girls chatting around me. My eyes are on Will when he pulls his phone out of his pocket to check his phone. His lips twitch and his eyes meet mine from across the patio, and then his thumbs are moving across the screen.

My phone vibrates with his response. *Are you wearing pant-ies?*

It makes me smile. I love how it turns him on that I don't wear underwear often.

No.

He raises an eyebrow and pins me with a hot look, then focuses on his phone again.

"Meg, how was New Orleans?" Jules asks as she joins us, Sophie on her hip. The baby is playing with Jules' phone.

"It was so great," I respond and feel my phone vibrate.

Can I bury my fingers deep in your pussy while you suck me off?

"What did you guys do while you were there?" Brynna asks as one of her daughters, I'm not sure which one, climbs onto her lap. We are surrounded by children and I'm sending x-rated texts to my boyfriend.

Yes please.

"Ate a ton of food, took in a bunch of music, wandered around the city. I wanted to go on a ghost tour, but Will was chicken."

"I heard that," he calls from across the patio.

"I wasn't trying to hide it," I call back, and everyone laughs.

"I've always wanted to go there," Stacy remarks. "Isaac and I will have to go sometime."

"You should," I nod. "It's a lot of fun. And warm, which was fantastic."

Just for that last remark, I'm going to spank your ass when I'm inside you tonight.

"You got a nice tan," Jules sets Sophie on her feet and she toddles over to me before I can respond to Will's text. I look up at him and nod. *Hell yes!* He just laughs and takes a pull on his beer.

"Baby!" Sophie points a tiny finger up at her little brother.

"Is this your baby brother, sweet girl?" I ask her, earning a big, slobbery smile, showing off four front teeth.

"Baby." She holds her hands up, trusting that I'll pick her up, so I cradle Liam in my left arm and lift Sophie up to sit on my right leg. "Baby." She points at him again and then sticks her tiny finger in her mouth.

"Yes, this is baby Liam. Isn't he sweet?" I kiss her smooth cheek, then blow a raspberry on her neck, making her laugh.

"Meg, look up and smile." I raise my head at Nat's voice and smile for her camera. The woman doesn't go far without that thing. Even Sophie is so used to seeing a lens that she poses for the camera too.

"Dinner's ready, everyone," Gail calls. The guys help her set bowls of salads and fruits on the long buffet table next to the house, while Steven piles steak and chicken on platters.

The food is abundant and delicious.

"This is the last time this year we'll grill. Until next summer, we'll have family gatherings catered. It's a lot of work to feed all of us," Natalie tells me as she stands and takes Sophie from me, planting her on her curvy hip.

"I can see that," I respond and kiss Liam's head again.

"Meg, you look good wearing a baby," Luke remarks as he joins his wife, Olivia asleep against his muscular chest.

"So do you," I wink at him, and he laughs.

"Stop flirting with my brother-in-law," Will scowls as he joins me. I stand and hand him the baby.

"I'm not flirting. I'm just paying extra attention to someone who's very attractive." I reply seriously, my eyes wide and earnest, trying to hold the grin in. Luke smirks and kisses his wife as Will's scowl deepens.

"He's not attractive. He's family."

I laugh, hard, grab my stomach and practically double over. "Will," I gasp. "Have you seen your family? You all look like you stepped out of an Abercrombie ad."

"Do not," he mutters and kisses Liam's tiny head.

"Yeah, you do," Natalie nods. "It's a nice family to be a part of."

"See?"

"So getting spanked later," he whispers to me as we join the others to eat.

"Dude, give me my kid." Isaac holds his hands out for the baby. "And I know he's the size of a football, but don't pass him off to the wrong guy. You seem to have issues with that today."

"Fuck you, Isaac," Will growls as he hands the baby gingerly to his oldest brother.

"Mouth!" Gail snaps.

"You're an asshole," Will mutters at Isaac so their mother can't hear them.

"I was just giving you a hard time. Too soon?"

"Too soon."

"What was the issue today, man?" Matt asks, now that the subject has been brought up, and Will sighs, runs his hands down his face and sits heavily a chair, staring down at his full plate of food.

"It was just an off day," he mumbles. "I think we took too long off last week."

I bite my lip. We were on vacation last week.

"Stop it," he catches my attention, his eyes fierce. "This is not your fault. I just should have taken advantage of the hotel gym when we were gone."

"It's okay, bro. Next week," Caleb claps him on the shoulder and sits next to him with a full plate.

And just like that, the subject is dropped. Conversation continues around us, the twins run and play in the yard, babies fuss.

It's loving, amazing, wonderful chaos.

And I can't believe I'm here.

"Hey," Jules nudges my leg under the table and leans in to chat with me so only I can hear. "Have you heard from Leo?"

"No," I whisper to her.

"Not at all?" She whispers back.

I shake my head and keep my eyes on my food.

"How long?"

"Three years," I whisper.

"I'm sure his number hasn't changed." I meet her worried blue eyes with my own.

"Neither has mine."

She nods and takes a bite of potato salad. "Good point."

I look up in time to see Brynna and Caleb share a look, then quickly turn away from each other. What's going on there? They're obviously attracted to each other, but they don't really interact with each other. They just watch each other.

I'll have to ask Will later.

"So, let's talk wedding," Jules claps her hands and bounces a bit in her chair while the guys all groan.

"Can't you and the girls talk about the wedding later, when we can escape to watch football or something?" Caleb asks, earning a glare from Jules.

"No. We're less than a month away. Besides, I don't have much, Alecia is handling most of it all anyway." She takes a drink of wine and pulls out a list, causing the guys to all groan again and I can't help but giggle.

"The date, as you all know, is October twelfth. Six in the evening. You have invitations with the address and all that crap." She takes another drink as we all listen, the guys fidgeting. "Since it's just Luke and Nat in the wedding, this is going to be easy on all of you. Dress nice, don't give us any gifts, and come ready to party."

She tucks the note back in her pocket and resumes eating.

"That's it?" Matt asks.

"Yep," she replies with a smile.

"You didn't tell us anything we didn't know."

"I know, I just wanted to talk about my wedding for a minute." She's smug as she takes a bite of steak and smacks her mouth as she chews. "Oh! And the bachelorette party is next Sunday night."

"Why on a Sunday?" Sam asks with a frown.

"Because we have some stupid business thing on Saturday." Jules rolls her eyes and Nate chuckles. "So, it has to be on Sunday. Every other weekend is full of wedding and football crap."

"I love you too, sis," Will throws a roll at her, and she blows him a kiss.

"So, everyone just take Monday off work to recover."

I giggle to myself. Jules is so not a selfish woman, she just thinks that things are simple. Like, everyone in the world should have no problem taking a day off work to recover from a hangover.

"You're coming," she pins me with a glare, daring me to say otherwise. I quickly run through my schedule in my head, aware that Will's eyes are on me.

"I believe I have next Sunday night off. I'll let them know I'm not available for on-call that night."

"Good," Natalie grins. "It's going to be a lot of fun."

Steven stands, holding his beer in the air. "I want to propose a toast. To my family, which has grown by leaps and bounds this past year. I am a blessed man, to be surrounded by good men, beautiful women, and the most amazing babies ever born."

"To family!" Luke's dad agrees, and everyone drinks, and then breaks off into conversation again.

As we're finishing dessert, the sky opens up. I knew I smelled rain earlier. We are, thankfully, under a covered patio, and most of the food has been cleared away. The four brothers work together to cover the now-cool grill, and we take the babies inside out of the humidity. For the rest of the afternoon, a football game plays on the television and adults play card games with the twins. The babies are fed, rocked, changed and fussed over.

Luke, Stacy and Brynna's parents all leave.

Will and I are lounging at one end of a large leather sectional couch, watching football, my head in his lap. I yawn and feel my eyelids droop.

"Hey, lazy bones, are you ready to go home?"

"When you are. I'm in no hurry."

He smiles gently down at me, his eyes soft. "I love you," he mouths.

I grin up at him, happily, and run my hand down his smooth cheek. "You're so handsome."

He grabs my hand and kisses my palm. "Let's get out of here."

176

He helps me out of the couch and we say our goodbyes, which takes another half hour. Will's mom, Gail, hugs me close.

"Please, come back soon, Meg. We enjoyed you."

"Thank you," I murmur shyly.

"She'll be back," Will comments as he kisses his mom on the cheek.

I tilt my head back as we step outside and enjoy the rain. It's dark now, and the rain is heavy, but not cold. It's that warm, late summer rain that feels like tap water.

"I love the rain this time of year."

"Great. Get in the car, babe."

I laugh over at him. "You don't like the rain?"

"It's fine, but you'll get sick if you don't get out of it."

"No I won't, that's a myth." I wave him off and stand in the rain for a minute longer, then join him in his car.

"Are you always this stubborn?" he asks.

"How long have we been seeing each other?" I ask.

"A while. More than a month." He responds and pulls away from his parents' house.

"Then you should know by now that I'm always this stubborn." I grin sweetly as he chuckles.

"So, about those texts you sent me…" He turns hot blue eyes on me and offers me a half smile.

"Yes?"

"Gonna make good on them?"

"I don't know your mood seems to have improved without me needing to resort to oral sex." I feel my phone vibe in my pocket and I pull it out as I laugh at Will's scowl.

Tell your bf thx for the $250k.

"Pull over."

"What?"

"Pull the fuck over."

Chapter Nineteen

"What's wrong?" His voice is panicked but I can't look at him. I have to get out of this car.

Now.

"Just pull over, Will."

"Are you sick?"

"Yes! Pull over!"

We're in a remote part of Seattle, mostly deserted, and dark. The sky has opened up even more, pouring rain as if someone has turned on a faucet.

He skids to a stop at the side of the road, and before he even puts it in park, I barrel out of the car, slam the door and start walking, fast, in the headlights.

"Meg!" he calls from behind me. "Megan, stop!"

"Leave me alone, Will."

"What the fuck has gotten in to you?" I hear him gaining on me, his feet shuffling in the gravel on the side of the road, so I twirl and confront him.

"How dare you?"

He stops in his tracks, his eyes wide with fear and worry and holds his hands up like he's being robbed.

"What?"

"I told you not to give her any money."

"Fuck." He hangs his head and props his hands on his hips, both of us ignoring the rain falling in sheets around us. "Meg…"

I spin on my heel and start to stomp away from him again, but he grabs my arm and spins me back to him. "You're not walking home."

"Fuck off, Will."

"Megan, stop this." He takes both of my shoulders in his hands and holds me in front of him, and all I can do is glare at him, panting. My anger is palpable.

"I told you, Will. You saw how it was last week. Why in the hell would you do this? She'll just keep coming back for more. She would have gone away if you would have just left it alone." I can't stand the break in my voice as I feel the tears mix with the rain on my face.

"She never would have gone away, sweetheart." His voice is calm now, but firm. I shake my head back and forth and bury my face in my hands.

"I don't need you to clean up my life!" I step back out of his grasp and look up into his face illuminated by his headlights, water running down the sides, his hair soaked and plastered to his head. "I can handle this myself."

"Megan, that woman is toxic. She drains you, financially and emotionally. You don't need her."

"I know that! You think I don't know that?" I throw my hands in the air and march in a frustrated circle.

"I'm trying to help you."

I stop, my back to him, and shake my head, hands on my hips. "I asked you not to help me like this."

"Look at me."

I stay where I am.

"Look at me, Megan."

"Will, you betrayed me."

"I did not fucking betray you!" He yells, and I whirl to look at him. His eyes are feral now, and his hands are in fists at his sides, every muscle taut with anger and frustration. "I paid off a woman who hates you for existing so she'll never bother you again. She signed a contract, Megan. She can never ask you for another dime."

"What?"

"Let me finish. That woman is the reason you can't tell me you love me. That. Fucking. Woman." He shakes his head in frustration and turns away from me, then turns back. "If I have the opportunity to remove her from you, why wouldn't I do it? The money is nothing to me. She is the reason you have trust issues. She is the reason it's so hard for you to show people you love them."

"What are you now, a shrink?" I ask with a smirk, and then hate myself for it when I see the hurt in his eyes.

"I know you," he murmurs quietly. His chest is heaving. "I love you, Megan."

I love you too.

I can't make the words come out.

"I love you, Megan." The words are stronger now, louder, and he's willing me to say them back.

I turn and start to blindly walk again, my steps quick, away from him, from his car, from all these fucked up feelings that I just don't know how to trust.

Suddenly I'm in his arms, and he's carrying me back to the car. He sets me down, ass on the hood and pins me, his hands on the hood at my hips, his face level with mine, nose millimeters from brushing the tip of mine, his eyes on fire. He's glaring at me with love and hurt.

"I. Love. You. Megan."

"Will." It's a sob. I take his face in my hands and brush his cheeks with my thumbs. "Will."

"I love you," he whispers, his lips so close to touching mine I can feel them move. I close my eyes and feel the tears on my face. I can feel the hot tears on his face, running into my hands, mixing with the warm rain.

I'm hurting him. And it's killing me.

"You can't say it." It's not a question.

"I can show you," I whisper.

He closes his eyes for a heartbeat, tips his forehead down to mine, and then suddenly grips my hips and pulls me to the side of the hood of the car and peels my sopping wet jeans roughly over my hips and down my legs, throwing them on the ground in a wet heap. My eyes are wide and on his, mouth gaping open.

"Someone could drive by."

"I don't give a fuck," he growls and sinks to his knees, pushing my thighs apart and burying his face in my core. He licks and kisses and sucks on my lips, my clit, pushes my metal against my nub, making me plant my feet on his shoulders, grip his soaked hair in my hands and lift my hips off the car, coming apart at the seams, crying out, not caring who can see or hear us.

He stands and shoves two fingers inside me roughly, pushing and pulling them quickly, teasing my clit with his thumb, and he's kissing me in the same way, with frustration and anger and I grip onto his shoulders, holding on for dear life.

"Will."

"You are mine, damn it. I will protect you from anyone and anything, do you understand?" His eyes are narrowed, on mine. "I don't need your permission to make you safe."

Before I can answer, he's kissing me again, and pushing me over into another orgasm.

He's claiming me, branding me in a way he never has before.

It's fucking hot as hell, and I want him. I want to be his. I love him more than I ever thought possible, and that scares the living hell out of me.

He pushes the hem of my jersey up under my armpits, dragging my bra along with it, unveiling my breasts and feasts on them, pulling and biting the nipples roughly. I let my head fall back and cry out in pain and pleasure, loving his mouth and hands as they assault me.

He's never been this rough.

Suddenly, he unzips his pants and unleashes his massive erection and I instinctively scoot even closer to the edge of the car, needing him inside me.

"I can't wait," he mutters against my mouth and slams himself inside me, hard. He grips my hips and jerks me down on him, over and over, fucking me with all he has, his eyes still pinned to mine.

"You are so beautiful. You are everything, Megan. When are you going to believe that?" He moves faster and harder until I feel him explode inside me, his muscles tensing, and growling deep into my neck.

He stays here, on me, in me, panting, for what feels like forever, before he slides out of me, and steps back. "Stay here."

He zips himself up, straightens my shirt, and scoops my pants up off the ground, walking briskly to the back of the car. He rummages around in the trunk and walks back to me, a blanket in his hands. "Scoot off the car."

I obey immediately, and he wraps me in the blanket, plants a soft, sweet kiss on my forehead, and suddenly the tears start again.

I love him so much.

"Don't cry." He lifts me in his arms and carries me over to the passenger side, and gently lowers me down into the low seat.

Instead of taking me back to my place, he drives us to his house, pulls into the garage, and lifts me back out of the car, carries me inside, and up the stairs through his bedroom and into the bathroom. He sets me carefully on the toilet and turns on the hot water, then kneels in front of me, takes my face gently in his hands and wipes the tears off my cheeks with his thumbs.

"Did I hurt you?" he whispers.

I shake my head no and bite my lip, looking into his soft blue eyes. He's tender now, the anger gone out of him.

"I'm sorry," I whisper.

"For what, honey?"

I shrug and look down but he tips my chin up to look at him. "For what?"

"For hurting you. I don't want to do that. You mean the world to me, Will."

He sighs deeply, relief written all over his face, and kisses me softly, then sits back on his heels and smiles softly. "I know."

I nod, still feeling shitty.

I want to give him the words. So much.

He strips me out of the blanket and the remaining wet clothes, and does the same with his own, takes me by the hand, and leads me into the hot shower. The shower heads are still adjusted for me.

He takes his time washing me, lathering up my body and my hair, and then rinsing me thoroughly, before doing the same for himself.

"I love your body," he murmurs with a smile as he leads me out of the shower and begins to dry me with a large, warm towel.

"Back at you, football star," I remark and offer him a half smile. He blows my hair dry, and leads me to bed. "It's a bit early for bed, isn't it?" I ask dryly.

"I have to be at the training center at six," he frowns and pulls the covers back on the bed, grabs the remote for the small TV mounted to the wall, and we climb into the soft bed, snuggle up together, and watch a bad action movie from the 90's.

"Thank you," I whisper without looking at him.

"For what?"

"You know." I tighten my arms around his waist and drop a kiss on his chest. "Just thank you."

He sighs and kisses the top of my head.

Chapter Twenty

It's been two days since we fought in the rain. Since the best damn car sex of my life. Since Will practically begged me to give him the words he needs to hear and I couldn't.

I wonder how long he'll wait before he decides I'm not worth his time and he cuts out. I hope I can give him the words he wants before that happens.

I sit across from him in a little diner in North Seattle known for their twelve-egg omelets. Even Will can't eat that much at once, but he's decimating the six-egg version, which makes me slightly queasy just to watch.

The man can eat.

"You look beautiful today." He smiles softly at me, and I grin back. I'm just in my usual; a loose t-shirt and jeans, hair down around my face.

"Thank you." I let my eyes travel over his dark blonde hair, startling blue eyes, blue t-shirt and strong arms. "So do you."

I take a bite of a waffle and sigh. "I love the food here."

"I know, it's awesome. You have to draw a picture for the wall." He points at the artwork with his fork and I giggle as I look around. There are hundreds of drawings done in crayon covering the walls, some really good, some just plain funny.

"Why don't you do a drawing?" I ask.

"I did. It's up there somewhere."

"Excuse me, aren't you Will Montgomery?" Two young girls are standing at the end of our booth, grinning, twirling their hair. They're young and cute and flirty and I can't help but roll my eyes.

"I am," he replies with a sigh and looks over to me, begging me with his eyes to not get mad. I just shrug and smile.

He can't help that he's a super-hot football star.

"Wow, can we get your autograph?"

"Yeah, and maybe your photo? We're big fans," the other one adds and they giggle.

"I'm sorry, I'm having lunch with my girlfriend. I'd really appreciate it if you'd just respect our privacy."

They stop and frown down at him, but he holds their gaze firmly.

Holy shit! This is new.

They both look at me for the first time, then back at Will.

"We saw in the paper that you had a new girlfriend, but we thought they were lying because you never have girlfriends."

Will smiles coldly, and I can hear his inner dialogue. *You don't know anything about me.*

"I do have a girlfriend, and I'm enjoying her company. Have a good day." He turns back to me, effectively cutting off anything they were about to say when the waitress comes over with a carafe of coffee.

"You heard the man. Either sit at a table and place an order or leave." She scowls at the girls as they leave the diner. "Sorry about that. They slipped by me."

"No worries." Will smiles up at her as she refills our coffee.

"That surprised me."

"Why?" he asks me and takes a sip of coffee.

"You usually like being the center of attention." I shrug and push my mostly empty plate away.

"Not always," he shakes his head. "As long as I'm your center of attention, I'm good."

"Needy much?" I ask sarcastically and laugh when he pins me with a glare.

"I am not needy."

"Okay." I sit back and grin at him.

"I'm not."

"I just agreed with you."

"Uh huh." He takes another sip of coffee and takes my hand in his, running his thumb across my knuckles. "What do you have going on today?"

"I have to work the swing shift tonight," I reply and check my watch. "You?"

"I have to go to the training center to watch some film this afternoon."

"Did you train this morning?" I ask.

"Yeah, early this morning."

"I slept through it." I smile over at him and he shakes his head, his eyes happy.

"So lazy."

"How do you get up so early?"

"I'm used to it. Been doing it for years." He shrugs and examines my hands. "You have tiny hands."

"I'm a girl. They're supposed to be small."

He kisses my knuckles softly and then pulls something out of his back pocket. "I need to talk to you about this."

"What?"

"I've been invited to a charity ball thing. It's formal, and I usually don't go, but I thought that you might like to go to this one." He shifts uncomfortably, and looks almost nervous, piquing my interest.

"What's the charity?"

"Seattle Children's," he replies, his eyes on mine.

A slow smile spreads across my face. He wants to take me to a formal ball in honor of what I'm passionate about. Because he knows what it means to me.

Because he loves me.

"Will, this would be amazing."

He smiles and looks down at the silver embossed invitation and then passes it over to me.

"It's next weekend?" I ask in a panic. *Shit! I don't have anything to wear!*

And no money to buy anything.

"Yeah, is that a problem?" He's watching me closely, so I gather myself and smile reassuringly.

"No."

"Bad liar. What is it?" He asks and takes my hand again.

"Nothing, really."

"What are you worried about?"

Damn it, he knows me too well already.

186

"I'll just have to figure out what to wear." I shrug, like it's no big deal. "It'll be okay."

Will narrows his eyes at me in thought but then just smiles at me. "Are you ready?"

"Yeah, I have to work in a little while."

"Let's get you home then."

* * *

~Will~

I drop into the Shelby and pull my phone out of my pocket before even leaving Meg's house. I just walked her to her door so she can get ready for work tonight. I hate that she works nights.

She works too fucking hard.

But then, I suppose most nurses do. It never occurred to me before I met her that patients need around the clock care. Of course, it makes sense, but not really something most people think about.

She works too fucking hard. And I hate that she drives home alone in the middle of the night in that piece of shit car of hers.

I told her to keep the Rover, but she refused.

Damn stubborn woman.

I dial Jules' number and wait impatiently for her to answer.

"This is Jules."

"Hey, it's Will. Do you have time to meet up with me tonight?"

"Um…" I can hear her shuffling papers and typing on her keyboard. "Yeah. I should be done here around seven. Why?"

"I just want to take you and Natalie out to eat," I answer innocently.

"Where's Meg?" she asks.

"She works tonight."

"Have you talked to Nat?"

"Not yet, I called you first." I run my hand down my face and sigh. "I just need to talk to you guys and I haven't seen much of you over the past few months."

"Hey, I'm not complaining. Sure, I'll pick Nat up and meet you. Where are we going?"

"Just come to my place, I'll order in."

* * *

"So," Natalie begins, taking a bite of an eggroll. She's adorable, and looks happy, which is all any of us have ever wanted for her. She's as much my sister as Jules is. "what's up with you and Meg?"

They're both fucking nosy as hell. But this is why they're here.

"I'm completely in love with her," I reply calmly and load my plate full of lo mein and chicken and egg rolls and dig in. I pause and look up at the girls. They're frozen. Jules' chopsticks are paused half-way to her gaping mouth and both sets of eyes are wide.

"What?" I ask.

"Did you just say you're in love with her?" Jules asks and sets her chopsticks down.

"Yes."

"Okay." They look at each other and then back at me. "Have you told her that?" Natalie asks.

"Yep."

"What did she say?" Jules asks.

I squirm. I really don't want to admit to these two that Meg hasn't said it back. They'll never let me live it down.

"Has she said it back?" Natalie asks softly, her eyes full of sympathy and all I can do is shake my head.

"No."

"Fuck," Jules whispers. "Will, Meg has trust issues…"

"I'm aware," I interrupt her. *Do they think I don't know this shit? Of course I know.* "I didn't ask you here for this."

"Well, I think we should talk about it," Jules answers stubbornly. "Meg is fantastic, and I'm so glad that you guys are doing well."

Natalie nods in agreement. "Definitely. Meg is awesome, and I'm glad that she's back in our lives. I've missed her."

"Look guys, I know you like her. That just makes a relationship with her that much easier. She's great." I shrug and smile at my sisters.

"Don't hurt her," Jules whispers, her pretty face completely serious. "Honestly, Will. Meg is strong, but she has already had enough shit thrown at her in this life."

"I know, Jules. Seriously. I've met Sylvia up close and personal, and have removed her from Megan's life."

Their eyes bug out again.

"How did you manage that?" Natalie asks.

"I paid her." I shake my head as I remember the look on that bitch's face as she signed the contract severing all ties with her only child. "She got a shit load of money to disappear. She signed a contract. She won't bother Meg again. If she does, I'll sue the shit out of her."

"Wow." Natalie swallows and laughs ruefully. "I wish I had thought of that."

"You wouldn't have been able to afford it back then," I answer softly.

"How much did you pay her?" Jules asks.

I just shake my head again. "More than she expected. Look, this isn't why I asked you here. I need a favor."

"Okay, shoot," Jules stuffs half an eggroll in her mouth and chews with her mouth open.

"You're so fucking classy," I mutter.

"Thanks." She smiles and stuffs the other half in her mouth.

"I'm taking Meg to the Children's Hospital Charity Ball next Saturday and she needs a dress. I need you to buy one for her. I'll give you my card, and then I need you to tell her you're lending it to her."

"Why?" Nat asks with a frown. "Just take her shopping."

"She wouldn't let me," I shake my head in frustration and sigh. "I know her. There's no way she'll let me take her out and spend a bunch of money on her."

"You're right. At least you didn't land a gold digger," Jules shrugs and then keeps eating, ignoring my scowl. "Okay, we can buy her something. What should we get?"

"Oh!" Nat jumps in her seat and takes a drink of water. "There's a local designer who makes the most beautiful gowns that are totally Meg's style. Rocker-ish, but elegant. Here." She pulls up her iPhone and starts tapping it, and when she finds what she's looking for she turns it so Jules and I can see. "See? Look at this one."

It's perfect. The dress is flesh-colored with red and orange flowers beaded in small patches. It's gathered lightly at the stomach, giving it definition. There are cap-sleeves, and a low v-neck so it'll show off her amazing cleavage.

It's Meg.

"That's perfect. I want that dress."

"Will, I don't know if that exact dress is available."

"I don't care how much it costs. That's the dress." I shake my head and glare at them. How hard can it be? "Just call her and tell her I want it."

They look at each other and then at me and start laughing their little asses off.

"Oh, Will, you're funny." Jules wipes a tear from the corner of her eye. "I'll see what I can do."

"Good." I sit back, satisfied that Meg will have the perfect dress for the ball and grin. "Thanks, guys."

"You're welcome," Natalie grins at Jules. "You know, she's going to need shoes too."

"And lingerie."

"Lingerie?" I ask. "What kind?"

Oh, God, this might kill me.

"Don't worry about it," Jules waves me off and I can see the wheels turning in her head. She's up to something.

"This is going to be fun." Nat grins.

* * *

~Megan~

I'm exhausted. It's been a long, long day. It's three am when I leave work, only an hour past my official time off.

Thankfully, I'm off now until next Monday. I'll be able to go to Jules' party Sunday night, but I can't get out of work Monday night because some of the other girls are on vacation. I'll just have to suck it up.

This whole having a social life thing is really starting to interfere with my work schedule. I laugh at the thought, start my old car and head toward home.

Yes, having Will, and his huge family, in my life is complicating things, but I wouldn't change it for anything. It's added some fun to my life.

He's reminded me that there's more to life than work.

Leo would be proud.

My stomach twists the way it always does when I think of Leo. I miss him. He was my brother in every sense of the word, and having him gone from my life has left a big hole. Jules is right, his number probably hasn't changed, but what would I say? He's been gone for years now. He's a big time rock star with a band, a tour schedule, fans and responsibilities. He made it clear when he left what his priority was.

I shake the thought of Leo off and stop at a red light in a deserted part of downtown Seattle. Hell, any part of Seattle is pretty much deserted at three am. Just as the light turns green, and I step on the gas, my car dies.

What the fuck?

I turn the key, but there's absolutely no response. Not even a clicking noise.

Goddamn car!

I hit the steering wheel in frustration and then lean my forehead against it. *Fuck.*

Well, I can't sit here in the middle of an intersection all night. I make sure the car is in neutral, open the drivers' door, get out and push it to the side of the street, park it and climb back in, locking the door.

This is downtown Seattle in the middle of the night.

I call Will's number and cringe. He's going to have to get up in a couple hours to go train.

"Hello?" he answers sleepily.

"Hey, babe. I'm sorry to wake you," I murmur.

"What's wrong?" I hear him sit up. "Why aren't you here?"

"Well, I was on my way there, but my car broke down."

"Where are you?" He's moving around, probably looking for clothes, and I sigh.

"I'll call a tow-truck, Will. I just didn't want you to worry when you woke up and I'm not there."

"I'll come get you. Where are you?" he asks again.

"Downtown."

"*What?*"

"I'm downtown. In fact, I should call Jules. Their condo isn't far from here."

"Hell no, I'll be there in ten minutes. Call a tow. I'm on my way."

He hangs up and I rest my forehead on the steering wheel again. He sounded mad. Well, screw him! He didn't have to come get me. I told him I'd call a tow.

Speaking of a tow, I call a local company, give them my location and my insurance information, and wait.

Less than ten minutes later, Will pulls up behind me in the Rover. I get out of the car and slide into the passenger side of his SUV.

"Thanks. You didn't have to come get me."

"Like I'd let you sit out here by yourself, Meg. How long did the tow company say they'd be?"

"About a half hour. They'll be here soon."

He just nods and looks straight ahead, jaw tight.

"Will, seriously, I'm sorry. I know you have to get up early…"

"That's why you think I'm upset?" His head whips around to look at me. "Because I'm going to lose a couple hours' sleep?"

"I know you have a busy schedule today…"

"Stop talking." He runs his hands down his face and my jaw drops. Did he really just tell me to stop talking?

"Megan, I'm not mad at you for waking me up, or for having to come get you. You're mine. This is part of my job. I'll gladly come get you every night after work and bring you home, just so I know that you're safe."

"You don't have to…"

"What pisses me off," he continues, ignoring me. "is that I've told you that your car isn't safe, especially for driving alone in the middle of the night, and I've offered you *this* car to keep."

"Will, I can't just take a car from you."

"Why the hell not?"

"Because it's a goddamn car!" I yell back to him. "It's not a pair of shoes or taking me out to dinner, Will. It's an expensive car."

"A car that I barely use." His voice is calmer now. "Megan, I rarely drive this car. Seriously, just use it. If it makes you feel better, just borrow it indefinitely."

I frown at him.

"You don't have much choice. I have a feeling that thing is past the point of return." He points to my little red car and I sigh.

"I know."

He takes my hand. "I'm sorry I yelled at you, but babe, this is silly. Just use this car, okay?"

"Why do you always get your way?"

"Because I'm charming and handsome and rich."

"And so incredibly modest." I shake my head at him and then climb over the console into his lap. "Thank you for coming to get me and for letting me borrow your car."

"You're welcome."

"How can I ever repay you?" I ask and weave my fingers into his soft dark blonde hair.

"Hmm… I think we can work on payment when we get home." His eyes are happy now, a smile plays on his lips and I tip my head to lay my own on them.

"You smell good," I whisper.

He wraps his arms around me and kisses me softly, nibbling my lips playfully, then across my jawline and over to my ear where he knows I'm ticklish.

"You taste good," he murmurs.

Just then a tow truck pulls in front of my car and backs up to my front end.

"Stay here," Will instructs me as he gets out of the car. "And lock this door behind me."

"Yes, sir," I respond playfully.

"I'm gonna spank you later."

"Oh, good," I grin at him and he shakes his head as he meets the driver by my car, giving him instructions.

Chapter Twenty-One

"Who called them?" Natalie asks and points a drunk finger toward the door. We follow her manicured hand to find Caleb and Matt sauntering to us, trying not to smile.

Gosh, the Mungumrys are pretty.

"We don't want to go home yet." Jules pouts.

"The bar is trying to close, Jules," Matt tells her. "We need to start taking you guys home."

"I'll call Nate and have him pay them to stay open longer," Jules reaches for her phone, but Matt just laughs at her.

"Uh, Jules, it's against the law for them to stay open any later than this."

"Well, shit," Sam mutters.

"Yeah, shit," I mutter in agreement. "Okay, let's go." We all slam our last shot, grab our bags and head toward the door.

Thank goodness my feet are still intact this time.

"I'm gonna go get some orgasms!" Natalie announces to all of us as we stand on the sidewalk and wait for Caleb to bring the car around.

I grin and raise my fist to bump hers. "Hey! I can get some this time too! Wait." I turn my blurry eyes to Matt. "Did Will get home?"

Will had to travel to New York this weekend for an away game. I hate it when he's gone.

"Yes, he's waiting for you at home," Matt replies with a half-smile.

"Good! Orgasms for me!" The girls all laugh and high five each other, half of us missing the others hands in our drunken stupor.

Caleb pulls up to the curb in a mini-van that he must have borrowed from someone to cart us all around in. He hops out of the drivers' seat to help Matt get us all in and settled, then Matt gets in the drivers' seat and Caleb in the passenger seat.

"I need orgasms," Brynna pouts. She is *hilarious* drunk. This dark haired woman is a vixen when given some liquid courage.

"That one guy who was dancing with you would have given you some," I remark with a smirk and Caleb's head whips around to glare at us.

"What man?" he asks, his voice low and hard.

"Just some dude who wanted to get his groove on," Natalie responds. "And by groove, I mean giving Bryn some orgasms."

We all laugh, like that's the funniest thing we've ever heard. 'Cause it is.

"Hey, are you guys good at giving orgasms?" I ask the brothers and then smirk when Matt shakes his head ruefully and Caleb puts his hand over his eyes, trying to hold onto his patience. "I bet you are. I bet it's 'netic, 'cause Will can give some fucking good orgasms."

"I want some rough sex," Sam responds. "I like to be spanked."

"Seriously?" Brynna asks, her eyes wide.

"Haven't you ever been spanked?" Sam asks her, and Brynna shakes her head no.

Hmm… I think I'll have Will spank me tonight.

"It's totally hot," Sam tells her and we all nod in agreement. Matt shakes his head again as we turn a corner.

"What's wrong, Matt?"

"Must you guys talk about sex?" he asks. "I'm related to most of you."

"What's wrong, you don't like it rough?" Brynna asks with a smirk.

Because I'm sitting right behind him, I hear him mumble, "You have no idea how rough I like it."

"Dude," Caleb scolds him. "Shut it."

"What? They're talking about it."

"Yeah! I need to get laid," Brynna mumbles again. "Seriously guys. Like laid for days. Like, we just do it over and over and over…"

"Enough!" Caleb yells, startling all of us.

Matt laughs at him as we all look at each other.

"I think Caleb needs to get laid too," Jules remarks with a smug smile. "Nat, how do you spell orgasm?" she asks, her face practically pressed to the screen of her phone.

"You don't spell it, you feel it."

"No, I'm texting Nate and I'm gunna tell him I need some."

"I think he knows," I tell her. Well, the one on the right. There are three of her. "Nate looks like he gives really good orgasms."

"Oh, he seriously does. I never realized what that apa could do until I met him." She's nodding and texting and I'm stunned.

"He's pierced?" I squeak.

"Yep."

"Holy shit!"

"No way!"

"Why?!"

All the girls are stunned, throwing questions out at once, but I'm speechless. Holy shit. He's pierced.

Lucky Jules.

"I wonder if Will would get pierced?" I ask the van at-large, but both Matt and Caleb respond with a loud, "No!"

Suddenly, Caleb's phone is ringing. "Hey, man."

"Who is that?" Jules asks.

"Yeah, we have them and we're on the way to your place first." Caleb says as he looks back at Nat, who is curled in a little ball with a grin on her pretty face.

"Are you thinking about orgasms?" I ask her.

"Mmm hmm." She confirms. "Luke's good at them too."

Lucky bitch.

We're all lucky bitches.

Well, those of us getting orgasms.

"Luke's waiting for you, Nat." Caleb tells her as he hangs up the phone.

"I know," she smiles.

"There is no one at home to smack my ass," Sam remarks darkly, a scowl on her beautiful face.

"You should have picked someone up at the bar," Jules replies. "Nat, how do you spell pussy?"

Matt chokes on the soda he was drinking. "Seriously, Jules, shut up! You're my sister!"

"Oh, stop. I'm a grown up. I've been having sex for more than a decade." She waves him off. "Meg, how do you spell cock?"

"I don't know," I wrinkle my forehead in thought. All my words are gone. "Shit, I have 'nesia!"

"Shit," Brynna replies. "I think you spell it c-o-c-k. But you're not supposed to spell it, Jules, you're supposed to suck it."

"Sonofabitch," Caleb mutters and answers his ringing phone. "Hi Will. I sound like this because these drunker than fuck women won't stop talking about sex…"

I rip the phone out of his hand. "Hey, sssssexy football player."

"Hi, honey. Are you having fun?"

God, his voice is hot.

"Yeah. I want orgasms. I get to have them this time, right?"

He laughs in my ear and I smile. "As long as you don't throw up, yes."

"I won't throw up," I frown. "I want you to smack my ass. Sam reminded me that I like that. But I have 'nesia 'cause I can't remember how to spell pussy."

"Uh, Meg, my brothers are right there."

"I know your brothers are right here!" I roll my eyes and giggle.

"They're my brothers too!" Jules yells at him.

"Jesus, you guys got really drunk." Will chuckles.

"Well, yeah. It's a bitcherlet party, Will." I squirm in my seat. "Now, as I was saying. You know where I have my clit…" Before I can say another word, Caleb takes the phone back, scowling at me.

"Dude, what is up with all these horny women?" he asks Will.

"Hey! I wasn't done!"

"Meg," Jules peers over at me. "My brothers don't want to know that you have your clit pierced."

I hear Will yelling on the phone, even over the girls gasps, and then Caleb pinches the bridge of his nose and sighs. "Yes, she told."

Matt glances at me in the rearview and I shrug. "What?"

He laughs and shakes his head. "Nothing."

"Hey, it makes things interesting."

We pull up to Nat's house, and Luke comes out to gather his girl. He smiles sweetly at her as he lifts her out of the van.

"Welcome home, baby."

"Hi, handsome." She cups his face in her hands and kisses him deeply as he carries her inside and waves back at us.

"Orgasms," Brynna sighs and sits back in her seat.

Next stop is Nat and Jules' old house where Brynna and her girls have been living for the past few months. Brynna steps out of the van, but stumbles, and Caleb easily lifts her in his arms and smiles down at her as she wraps her arms around his neck.

"You don't have to carry me," she murmurs to him as he walks to her front door.

"It's okay, sweetheart," he mumbles back and I sigh. Gosh, he's sweet. All the guys are so sweet.

"I like sweet guys," I announce.

"Why?" Jules asks.

"I dunno." I frown and think about it. "They taste good."

Sam nods in agreement. "They do. But they taste good when they're naughty too."

"Oh, yeah." I remember. "Okay. I like sweet, naughty guys."

Caleb climbs back in and we take Sam home. "You okay?" Matt asks her as she climbs out of the van.

"Yeah, I'm fine. I have to go call Brandon."

"Who's Brandon?" Jules asks.

"Fuck buddy. I need to be spanked. 'Night all!" And with that she disappears into her downtown apartment building.

"Atta girl!" I yell at her. "You go get some."

Jules smirks and looks over at me. "I'm so glad we did this."

"So fun," I agree.

"We'll do it again when you get married."

I frown at her and shake my head. "Not getting married."

"Why?"

"Will will leave me before that." I shrug and sigh. "But I'll enjoy him for now."

I look up to find Caleb and Jules both scowling at me, and Matt eyeing me again in the mirror.

"What?"

"Why would he leave you?" Caleb asks quietly.

"They always leave."

"Who?" Matt asks.

"People I love." I sigh again and look at Jules who is watching me with understanding eyes. She and Nat are the only ones who really know. "I can't tell him, Jules. If I tell him I love him, he'll go."

"No he won't, sweetie." She squeezes my hand and then grins. "He'll fuck the shit out of you."

"No he won't." I shake my head. "He says he never fucks me. Even when he fucks me."

"What does that mean?" she asks with a frown as the guys up front share a glance.

"I dunno." We pull up to Jules' building. "Go get your apagasms."

"Okay." She smiles widely at the tall, devastatingly handsome man walking out to the curb to claim her. "See you Saturday."

Nate lifts her in his arms and waves at us before carrying her back inside out of the cold. They're so pretty together. Their babies will be knock outs.

I snort.

Knock outs. Nate used to fight. Why this is so funny to me, I'm not sure, other than it's still the alcohol talking.

I must fall asleep because suddenly the van door opens again and Will leans in, smiling gently at me. "Hey, lazy girl. Let's get you inside."

He lifts me easily out of the van and I wrap myself around him, so happy to be cradled in his strong arms.

"Thanks guys. Have a good night."

"No problem, man. Good luck with her."

My eyes are closed, but I can hear Caleb's grin.

"Good night, boys. Go find some orgasms," I instruct them and can't help but smile at their laughter.

I love these guys.

Will carries me inside and sets me on the kitchen counter. I brace my hands on the edges of the dark granite and dangle my feet, watching him move about, pouring a glass of water and grabbing pills out of a drawer.

"Here, take these and drink the whole glass and you won't be hung over tomorrow."

"Did you win tonight?" I ask and do as I'm told.

"Yes." His eyes are happy as he watches me follow his directions. When the glass is empty, I wipe my mouth with my arm and lick my lips.

"Thanks."

"You're welcome." He puts the glass in the sink and then stands between my legs, his arms wrapped around my ass, and nose even with mine.

"Did you get tackled a lot?" I ask with a frown.

"No, not much," he responds with a soft smile.

"I don't like it when you get bagged."

"That's sacked, sweetheart," he chuckles. "I'm fine."

"You're so tall."

He just smiles at me. "You're so beautiful."

"Nah, I'm just a normal girl. Your groupies are beautiful."

"They're not my groupies. And they're not beautiful. You are. I love your hazel eyes and soft auburn hair. I love your soft skin." He wraps his arms tightly around me and nuzzles my nose with his. "I love you, Megan."

I sigh and wrap myself around him, legs around his hips, arms around his neck, and bury my face in his neck. He lifts me and carries me upstairs like this, and helps me out of my clothes, then tucks me into the bed.

He's standing at the side of the bed, looking down at me with humor and love. I hold my arms out. "Come to bed."

He strips down, and I'm reminded of that first night in my townhouse when he took me home from the engagement party, and how far we've come since then. He slips in behind me and pulls me to him, wrapping his arms around my middle. My eyes are heavy from the alcohol and the dancing.

"Sleep," Will whispers to me.

"But I wanted orgasms," I whisper back. Will chuckles softly and brushes my hair back off my face.

"I'll give you lots of orgasms tomorrow."

"Okay." I sigh and link my fingers with his. "Love you, too," I whisper so softly, just before I drift to sleep, and don't hear Will's gasp of surprise, or feel the wide smile spread across his face.

* * *

I wake to sunshine and the smell of bacon.

Oh, sweet God, bacon. I lay in the bed, flat on my back, and take stock. Stomach isn't rolling. Room isn't spinning. Head doesn't hurt.

I sit up and run through the same list. All systems are a go. And the bacon is making my mouth water.

I love Monday mornings. Will usually has the day off, which means I get to spend the morning with him.

I hurry to the shower and scrub last night off my body. Face, hair and body are all buffed and washed and scrubbed until I'm squeaky clean and feeling ten times better. I brush the hell out of my teeth, comb my wet hair, pull on one of Will's old jerseys and his boxer-briefs and go hunt him down.

He's in the kitchen, adding fruit to two small bowls. He's made pancakes and bacon and he looks delicious himself in faded, torn blue jeans and an old black t-shirt. The arms of the shirt hug the muscles in his biceps and I can't stop myself from walking over and kissing him there, just below the hemline.

"Good morning," I murmur.

"Good morning." He smiles down at me and kisses me chastely. "How do you feel?"

"Better than I expected to."

"No hangover?"

"No. I feel good. The shower helped too."

"Good." He hands me the fruit bowls, grabs the plates and leads me to the dining table where he's set up coffee and juice.

"This is fantastic. Thank you."

"You're welcome, sweetheart." We dig in and oh my God, it tastes like heaven.

"I had no idea you could cook."

He laughs and shrugs. "I really can't. Breakfast is all you'll really get out of me."

"Mmm." I take another bite of pancakes. "Really good."

"You were hungry," he remarks with a smile.

"Yeah. We didn't eat much last night."

"I figured as much. Do you remember much of it?"

I wrinkle my forehead and think back. "I remember dancing and laughing and drinking a whole lot."

"Do you remember the ride home?" His eyes are dancing with humor.

"I think I talked to you on the phone."

"You did."

"And we were all talking about orgasms. I didn't get any, did I?"

He shakes his head and laughs. "Uh, no. You passed out on me."

"Typical." I shrug. "It was a lot of fun."

"Good. You deserved it."

"I guess work won't suck too badly today."

"You have to work today?" He asks with raised brows. I finish my meal and sit back, juice in hand.

"Yeah. Some of the others are on vacation and I couldn't rearrange the schedule." I shrug again. "It's okay. I work tonight through Thursday and then I'm off until next Tuesday."

"Four nights this week?" Will asks as he clears the table. I stand to help him, but he waves me off. "I've got this. Just relax."

"Yeah, I picked up an extra shift." I don't tell him it's because I could use the extra money to replace my car. "So, before our drunken stupor last night, Jules offered to help me get ready for the ball on Saturday. She has a dress for me to borrow and everything, so that'll be fun. I think Nat and Sam are going to come too."

"That'll be fun. I'm sure you'll look beautiful." He smiles at me, but I feel like something's wrong.

"What is it?"

"What?"

"Something's wrong." I stand and cross to him. He leans his ass against the countertop and I lean against him, wrapping my arms around his waist, looking up into his handsome face. He frowns and tightens his lips.

"I was hoping to spend the day with you today. I was gone for three days, and I missed you."

I raise myself on tip-toe and kiss his lips softly, pulling on his lower lip with my teeth. "I missed you too, football star."

His hands slide from my thighs over my ass, under his jersey and up my back. "You feel so good."

I raise my arms and he pulls the jersey over my head and throws it on the floor. I pull the hem of his shirt up and he helps me pull it over his head, and I can't help but step back and take in the muscled perfection before me. God, all that hard work pays off.

"You are so fucking hot," I whisper, my eyes roaming over his torso. I pull at the buttons on his jeans and strip him out of those too, and run my fingernails up his legs to his hips, and trace the V there.

"You make me crazy," he murmurs as I take his erection in my hand and smile sweetly up at him.

"I do?"

"You know you do."

"I know you make *me* crazy." I kneel and trace the rim of the tip of his cock with my tongue and smile when he sucks air in through his teeth. "I know I love your hard body."

I sink down onto him and grip his cock tightly with my lips and pull up, all the way over the tip and watch a little bead of moisture form there. I lick it off and then sink over him again. He weaves his fingers in my hair, but doesn't try to control my movements. He just needs to touch me.

"I love watching your little pink mouth on my dick, babe."

I moan and pull up, jacking him as I do, and cup his balls with my other hand. Before I can do anything more, he grips my shoulders and pulls me to my feet, and kisses me, deeply. His tongue dancing with mine, he pulls his shorts off me and lifts me onto the countertop.

"I remember being up here last night."

He grins at me and kisses my neck and down to my breasts, holding onto my ass. He pays extra attention to each nipple, licking and pulling at them with his teeth, and one hand finds its way between my thighs.

"God, Will." I moan. He smiles against my breast and finds my center.

"Fuck, you're wet."

"You're sexy as hell, Will." I lean back on my elbows and watch him kiss his way down my flat stomach, his fingers are massaging my folds.

"Watch, Meg." He looks up and pins me with his hot, blue stare, and then down at his fingers, playing me like a musical instrument.

I sigh deeply and moan. "God, that feels good."

He sinks two fingers inside me and moves them, oh so slowly, in and out, stretching me just a little at a time.

"Will."

"Yes, sweetheart." He leans down and sucks on a nipple, pulling it in his lips and I gasp.

"Need you, babe."

"Where?"

"Inside me."

He grins up at me, then watches his fingers again, and pushes his thumb against my metal, pushing me over the edge.

"Ah, shit!"

"Let go, honey."

And I do. Holy shit, the orgasm works through me and I pulse and shudder against Will's hand.

Suddenly, he pulls me off the counter top, spins me around so I'm leaning against the granite, warmed from my body heat, pulls my hips back and pushes himself inside me.

"Oh God," he growls. "You're so fucking tight."

He eases all the way in and then starts to really move, pumping in and out of me, gripping my hips and ass in his huge hands until I think he'll bruise me.

It feels fan-fucking-tastic.

"Spank me," I tell him, looking over my shoulder to see his reaction. His eyes widen and then narrow.

"You want it rough?"

"Why not?" I ask him.

He gives me a naughty grin and smacks my ass, softly at first, and grips my hair in his fist, pushing my face down to the smooth countertop.

"Is this okay?" he asks softly.

"Fuck, yes."

He smacks me again, harder this time, and I groan, loud.

"Again."

He complies, just a little harder, and I feel the blood rush to my ass. His grip on my hair tightens and he pulls back, bringing me up so he can kiss my neck, biting and sucking it hard as he slams into me, over and over, harder and harder.

I grip the edge of the counter and push back against him, feeling the rush building in me once more.

"I'm gonna come."

"Not until I tell you to," He growls, and my brows climb into my hairline. Holy shit.

That's fucking hot.

"Please?" I ask.

"Not yet." He spanks me once more, then pulls out, spins me around, and lifts me, sliding easily back inside me and pins me against the fridge. There's sweat on his forehead, his eyes are glacial and narrowed, and he's panting as though he just ran seventy-five yards for a touchdown.

"I love this," he growls and kisses me deeply, pushing harder and harder inside me.

"Will, I have to come."

"Almost."

"Will."

"Almost, damn it." His hands on my ass tighten and I squeeze around him like a vice, my hands pulling on his hair. "Now!"

We both explode, our bodies shuddering and shaking with the force of our climax. Will leans his forehead against my shoulder, his whole body shaking.

"Hey," I murmur, caressing his back gently. "Will."

He pulls back, his eyes wide. "Are you okay?"

"Oh honey," I grin. "I'm more than okay."

His whole body sags in relief. "Thank God."

He pulls out of me and sets me on my feet. "I want to carry you upstairs, but I don't have any strength. You just decimated me."

"Really?" Why this makes me so proud, I don't know, but I'm preening.

"Oh yeah. Come on, let's clean up."

Before leading me out of the room and up the stairs, he leans down and kisses me softly, longingly. Beautifully. "You are mine, Megan McBride. Don't ever forget that."

Chapter Twenty-Two

"Seriously, guys, this is just way too much." I gaze down at the red Louboutin stilettos with lust-filled eyes.

"Honestly, we wanted to do this for you today." I look up at my three friends and giggle. I don't remember the last time I giggled over shoes.

Maybe that's a problem.

Because, holy crap, these are just to-die for, and are perfect for the dress Jules is lending me.

The dress that I'm going to beg her to will to me when she dies because it fits me like a glove and I want to wear it every single day.

And now I want to wear these shoes every single day too.

"But you already got me the gorgeous underwear and took me to the spa, and really, guys this is just crazy. Who lives like this?"

Samantha smirks and smooths lip gloss on her plump lips, her blue eyes smiling. "We do."

"Meg, you were born for these shoes," Nat sighs. "They're perfect for the dress."

We are in my bedroom, and they're helping me get dressed. Jules has spent over an hour teasing and curling and fussing with my hair to make it look, well, hot. It's all up, but it doesn't look stuffy or serious.

It's fun.

"I don't know how I can ever repay you guys for all of this."

"Oh please," Nat waves me off and chuckles. "There is no need to repay us. We love you."

"Well, there is one thing you could do," Jules murmurs and bites her lip, her blue eyes wide.

"What?" I ask.

"Sing at my reception."

"Jules…" I shake my head and prop my hands on my hips.

"Just listen," she pleads and grabs my hand, holding on tightly. "Meg, I love your voice. I always have, and you know that. I was always your biggest fan."

"Hey!" Nat protests, and I grin at her.

"Jules, I haven't sang in front of an audience in years."

"It's not like you've forgotten how, sweetie. You don't have stage fright. You will kick ass. Just one song, please?"

I bite my lip and look over to Natalie and Samantha who are both smiling at me.

"Who did you hire to play at the reception?" I ask.

"I don't know, Luke took care of it."

"Luke?" I ask, my eyebrow raised.

"Luke knows everybody," Nat rolls her eyes. "I'm not sure who he got, but he wanted it to be our gift to Jules and Nate."

"So it'll probably be someone famous. Not a local band."

Jules shrugs. "Probably just some up and comer band. But Luke knows the kind of music we like, so I'm sure they'll be great. But you don't have to sing with them. You can borrow a guitar and do just one song. I'd love for you to play the song for our first dance. Please, it can be your gift to me."

Her eyes are pleading me. How can I possibly say no?

"What song?" I ask with a sigh and she smiles widely, her beautiful face beaming, and I can't help but smile back as she hugs me tight.

I Won't Give Up by Jason Mraz."

"I actually know that one," I grin at her and then Sam and Nat. "I guess I'd better start practicing."

"This is so awesome," Nat hugs Jules. "I can't wait to hear you."

"And I can't wait to hear you for the first time," Sam says with a grin. "Sounds like it'll be a helluva show."

"I'll do my best."

I turn and take one last look in the mirror. "Are we sure about the dark lipstick?" It's a dark raisin color, giving my lips definition and is a stark contrast to my white skin.

"Definitely. It's hot. And it's color-stay, so Will can kiss you all night and it won't smudge or come off." Sam winks at me.

"Okay. Wow, I clean up well, if I do say so." The doorbell rings and I suddenly feel my stomach roll with anticipation.

"That's Will." The girls jump up and head out of my room. "Stay up here for a few minutes." Nat kisses my cheek. "Take a deep breath. Let him wait for you. You're stunning. Have fun." And with a smile and a wave, she follows the other two downstairs to let Will in.

I hear his voice and smile. That deep baritone does things to me.

I bet he can sing well.

"Where is she?" he asks.

"She's just finishing upstairs. She'll be down in a second." Sam tells him.

"I'm going up." I hear him head for the stairs.

"No, you won't," Jules laughs. "Be patient. She'll be right down. Have fun tonight."

"Be good," Nat says and then I hear the front door open and close and Will sets the alarm.

What is it with him and that alarm?

Suddenly, I hear him take the stairs two at a time and he's standing in my doorway, staring at me. And I just stare back. He's in a tux, looking all 007, and hot and… *mine.*

"What happened to you waiting downstairs?" I ask with a raised brow.

"Fuck that, I want to see you." He swallows hard. "Wow."

"Yeah?" I look down at the dress and turn a circle so he can see the whole thing. "You like?"

"Hmm," he murmurs. "You are absolutely gorgeous, but you're missing something."

"I am?" I look down again, then turn to the mirror, making sure my hair is still in place. "I think Jules covered everything."

He moves up behind me and catches my gaze through the mirror. As he leans down and kisses my neck, right below my ear, he wraps an arm around me, palm up, with a blue Tiffany box, wrapped in a white bow, sitting on his hand.

"I think this might complete your outfit," he murmurs into my ear.

"You've already given me so much," I whisper, eyes glued to the tiny blue box.

"I would give you the world if I could, sweetheart." My eyes fly back to his in the mirror and he's smiling softly.

"You are my world," I whisper. His eyes widen, and just when I think he's going to go all mushy on me, he smirks.

"Who's cheeky now?" he asks, reminding me of the café in New Orleans.

"Cheeky?" I ask with a chuckle.

"Cheeky," he mouths to me, his face happy. "Open it."

I pluck the box from his hand and he rests his hands on my shoulders as I open it. Nestled inside are the most over the top chandelier diamond earrings I've ever seen. I pull one out and hold it up to the light, watching the light reflect off the diamonds. They're swirly, with a huge princess cut diamond in the middle, set on its side. They are totally my style.

And totally the most expensive things I've ever had my hands on.

"Will…" I try to protest, but he takes the earrings from me and turns me around gently.

"When I saw these," he begins and fastens one to my right ear. "I knew they belonged on your perfect little ears." He fastens the left one and then turns me back to face the mirror so I can see them. "See? Now your outfit is complete."

I push one of the earrings with my index finger, watching it dangle along my jaw line, then turn in Will's arms, loop my arms around his neck and kiss him, softly, thoroughly. He rests his hands on my hips and patiently lets me explore his lips with my own until I back away and grin shyly up at him.

"Thank you."

* * *

The ball is exactly what I expected. We are at a posh hotel in downtown Seattle, surrounded by gorgeous people, tall flutes of champagne, tiny bits of food being passed around on silver platters and lots and lots of money.

It looks exactly the way it does in the movies.

Surprisingly, I'm not nervous. Jules was right, I rarely have stage fright, and I'm completely comfortable with Will at my side, his hand resting on the small of my back. He's charming, talks easily with everyone who stops him, but makes sure that he always knows where I am, who I'm with, or draws me into the conversation.

Will and I wander through the silent auction room, looking through all of the items up for bid. There is everything from spa days to art work to a week in Italy. When Will sees the week in Italy, he looks down at me with a wide grin.

"Ever been to Italy?"

"Uh, no."

"Wanna go?" He offers me that cocky side grin, the one that used to make me roll my eyes, and I laugh.

"Yes, Will, I want to go to Italy." I shake my head and take a sip of champagne.

"Okay," he shrugs and grabs the pen, writes down his name and a very, very large sum of money to place his bid.

"Holy shit!" I whisper to him.

"What?" His eyes are wide, brows raised. "You said you want to go."

"Well, of course I *want* to, Will, but I didn't think you'd actually bid on it."

"You confuse me," he frowns down at me. "If you want to go to Italy, I'll take you."

"Just like that?" I ask.

"Just like that." He places a chaste kiss on my lips and guides me down to the next item up for auction. We come to a signed jersey of Will's and I gasp.

"When did you donate this?"

He shrugs and looks down at the bids, then smirks. "I don't know, not long after they sent the invitation. Some idiot has bid ten grand on this thing already."

"I wonder how much I could get for the ones I sleep in on eBay?" I ponder, taking a sip of my champagne, making Will laugh.

"Gonna start selling all my shit now?" he asks and leads me out of the room. He's bid on the trip to Italy, a weekend in Mexico, and another week in Hawaii. Apparently he plans to travel a lot this year.

"Maybe," I shrug. "Could be a good side business."

"Now I'm just a side business. You wound me, babe."

He leads me laughing out into the main ballroom where there is a band playing classic hits, like *It Had To Be You* and *Fly Away* and Will sweeps me into his arms and across the dance floor, holding me close, looking down into my eyes.

Wow, he's a good dancer.

"You move very well," I remark. He just shrugs and smiles and pulls me closer.

"You fit well, right here."

"Hmm," I agree and smile up at him, lost in his blue eyes. It's as though we're the only two in the room. "This is fun."

"Do you know any of the people here from the hospital?" he asks.

"No," I shake my head and look around. "I know some of the faces, but these people are way above my pay grade."

"You do look beautiful tonight," Will murmurs.

"Thank you. So do you."

"I hate dressing up," he grins and shrugs. "But if I get to have you with me looking like this, it's worth it."

"Cheeky bastard," I mutter and kiss his chest through his white shirt.

"Ladies and gentleman," An older man takes the stage, looking distinguished in his formal tux, gray hair slicked back. "Before we wrap things up for the night, I want to announce the winners of the silent auction."

We stop where we are on the dance floor, arms wrapped around each other, and listen to Mr. Richards, the CEO of Children's read the highest bidders. The winners whoop and applaud excitedly. When he gets to the trip to Italy, he announces Will's name.

"Holy crap!" I look up at him with wide eyes, and he winks down at me.

"Looks like we're going to Italy in the spring," he says with a grin.

We're going to Italy in the spring!

Will also wins the weekend in Mexico, but the week in Hawaii goes to another of his teammates.

"Thank you, everyone for bidding," Mr. Richards continues. "And, it's my honor to announce that you have raised more than three million dollars tonight for our hospital."

The room erupts in applause and I can't help the wide grin on my face. This is fantastic! Oh, the things we can do with that money.

Will is smiling down at me, enjoying my reaction. "I think this just became an annual event for us," he murmurs.

I look up in surprise. *He's plans on being with me in a year!*

"Are you ready to get out of here?" He asks.

"Yes." His eyes heat. He takes my hand in his, laces our fingers and leads me to the doors. "Don't you have to say goodbye to some people?"

"No."

"Why are you suddenly in such a hurry?" I ask with a breathless laugh.

He stops and turns to me, pulling me against his hard body, and leans down so he can whisper in my ear, "I'm in a hurry to get you home, out of this sexy as fuck dress, and bury myself in you for the better part of the night. Is that okay with you?"

"Um, yeah. That works."

He leads me out to the valet, hands the man his ticket and we're quiet while we wait for the car.

"What are you humming?" Will asks.

"I was humming?"

"Yeah, what was it?"

"I didn't realize I was." I shake my head and smile up at him. "It was probably the song Jules asked me to sing at the reception."

"You're singing at the reception?" His eyebrows climb into his hairline in surprise.

214

"Yeah, she begged. It was embarrassing. I put her out of her misery." I wave him off and laugh. "It's hard to tell her no when she gives me shoes like these." I pull my skirt up so he can see my amazing Louboutins.

"Dear God, those have been under there all night?"

"Yep," I smile smugly.

"What else do you have under there?"

I purse my lips and tilt my head like I'm thinking really, really hard. "It's hard to remember. I'm prone to amnesia these days."

The valet pulls up with the car, and Will holds the passenger door open for me, then hops in and takes off toward home.

God, I effing love this car.

I reach over and untie his bowtie, letting it hang onto his chest, and unbutton the top two buttons of his shirt.

"Thank you," he sighs. "Damn monkey suit."

"You look hot in that monkey suit," I remind him.

He grins over at me, then lets his eyes wander down my dress. "That dress is perfect on you."

"I'm surprised Jules had something that fits me so well. She and I are built differently."

"She just probably hadn't had time to have it tailored yet," he shrugs. He's probably right.

And I decide to play with him.

"Gosh, it's hot in here," I say innocently, my eyes wide, and start hiking my skirt up with my fingers, pulling it until it's gathered around my thighs, just above where my blush-colored thigh-highs attach to the matching garter.

"Holy fuck," he whispers.

"Keep your eyes on the road," I suggest and bite my lip.

"Pull your dress down, sweetheart."

"Why?"

"Because I can't drive with you sitting there like that," he growls, making me laugh.

I leave the skirt where it is, lean back in the seat, spread my thighs, and run my fingertips up the insides of my legs. "Hmmm."

"Are you trying to kill us?"

"No, this just feels good. These stockings are silk." I look over at him and grin. "Can you imagine how they'll feel wrapped around your waist?"

"Sonofabitch," he whispers as if he's in pain and steps on the gas harder, propelling us down the freeway.

I move my fingers up higher on my thighs until I'm touching my pussy, and I squirm. Suddenly, Will reaches over, grabs my hand and pulls it up to his lips, kisses it and keeps it in his lap, not taking his eyes off the road.

"If you don't stop," he says softly, "I will wreck this car. I'm not kidding."

I slide my hand away from him and grin sassily. "Then don't watch."

I resume playing with myself, circling my clit with one hand and pushing two fingers into my wetness with the other. I bite my lip and groan.

"Fuck, that's hot." Will's voice is steel. I look up at him and his jaw is clenched, hands fisted on the wheel. He glances down to watch me pleasure myself, and then looks me in the eye.

"Lick your fingers."

I do as I'm told and lick my own sweet essence from my fingers, then stick them back inside me, watching him watch me.

"Fuck, babe, I'm gonna come."

"Do not make yourself come."

"What?"

"I want to do that."

"Then here," I grab his hand and pull it between my legs, and he gladly rubs my clit, over my metal, pushing it against my clit.

"Oh, Fuck." I come apart, pushing against our hands, and cry out his name as the orgasm pushes through me.

He grins down at me wolfishly as he pulls through the gate and into his garage. Not waiting for him to open the door, I climb out and he's suddenly beside me, pulling me into the house, through the kitchen and into the living room that looks out onto the sound.

It's dark in the house, the only light coming in through the floor to ceiling windows facing the water. Lights twinkle at us from the islands across the way.

We stand here, for a moment, in the moonlight, looking at each other. His blue eyes reflect the light and shine with love and carnal lust, and I know they reflect my own.

"So beautiful." He slides a finger into the neckline of my dress and drags it against my skin, following the hemline. "You were wonderful tonight."

His voice is soft, seductive. I don't know what to say, so I just watch him seduce me. He steps closer to me, so he's only a few inches away and wraps his arms around me to pull the zipper of my dress down, then pulls it down my arms, over my breasts, and lets it pool at my feet.

"Dear God," he whispers, his eyes wide, as he takes in my blush-colored corset, garter and stockings.

I'm not wearing panties, as usual.

He swallows hard. "It's a good thing I didn't know that this was under that dress."

"Why," I whisper.

"Because I would have locked us in a bathroom and stripped you naked and kept you to myself all night. My God, Megan, you're stunning."

I smile shyly and push his jacket off his shoulders and down his arms and lay it nicely on the end of the couch. He's started to pant, his hands are in fists at his sides, and it's killing him not to just pull me to him and ravage me.

But tonight isn't the night for that. We both feel it.

I carefully unbutton his shirt, unfasten his cuff-links, and let the shirt fall to the floor, then make quick work of his pants as well until he's standing before me completely naked, hard and ready.

"I love your body," I murmur.

"Megan," not able to hold back any longer, he pulls me to him, sinks his hands in my hair and kisses me with all he's got, tangling our tongues, biting my lips, devouring me.

When we're completely gasping for breath, he nibbles his way along my jaw line to my ear and nuzzles one of my diamond earrings with his nose.

"You need to keep the earrings and the stockings on, babe."

"Okay."

He spins me around and unlaces the corset, slowly, pulling the laces through the loops until it falls forward into my arms. He reaches around and cups my breasts in his hands, massaging and soothing them from being bound so tightly, and I moan in appreciation.

"Feel good?" he asks.

"Mmm."

"Oh, baby, the things I want to make you feel tonight."

My breath catches at his words, my thighs tighten and I turn so I can kiss him again, bury my fingers in his hair and just hold on to him.

He lifts me and sits in a loveseat, right in the middle, and cradles me in his lap, kissing me deeply, his hands roaming all over my body, leaving a trail of fire behind them. I grip his face in my hands and hold his mouth to mine, and show him how much I love him.

Finally, I crawl off his lap, headed to kneel on the floor and suck him, but he stops me. "Wait."

"What?"

"I don't want you to do that tonight."

"Why not?" I frown. I thought he liked it when I did that?

"Because tonight is all about you, my love."

"Huh?" I tilt my head and look down at him, straddling him, in the moonlight. He places his palm flat on my chest between my breasts, and then glides it down my stomach.

"Let me just make love to you."

"You always make love to me," I whisper and kiss his cheek. "Remember?"

"I know, but," he stops himself, a war raging on his face.

"What, babe?"

"You deserve so much. You should never, ever be on your knees." He lifts me and lays me gently on my back along the couch, kneeling between my thighs, and covers me with his large body. I wrap my silk-covered legs around his hips, and he settles against me, his long, hard cock nestled in my wet folds. He teases my metal with the tip and I gasp.

"I fucking love that piercing," he grins down at me and pushes his fingers into my hair, brushing the loosened tendrils back from my face.

"I'm glad." I sigh as he runs the backs of his fingers down my face. "Will?"

"Yes, my love." He runs his nose down along my own, nuzzling it.

"When I can say the words, when I can finally tell you how I feel, please don't leave me." The words are barely a whisper, spoken so softly at first I don't know if he hears me. I run my hands down his back to his ass and up again, watching his face. Watching his eyes. They haven't changed, but I can see the wheels turning in his handsome head.

"Megan, the thought of being without you destroys me," he whispers, just as softly, and sinks into me, slowly, until he's completely buried in me. He's holding my head in his palms, his elbows braced on the couch under my shoulders, his face less than an inch from my own. "Just the thought of you not being in my life is my undoing. When you feel safe enough to say what I know you feel, it will be the best moment of my life."

I cup his face in my hands as he starts to move inside me, gently, in long smooth strokes. Holding my head firmly, he lowers his lips to mine, and makes love to me, completely connecting his body to me, until in a slow-building crescendo, we both let go and come apart in each other's arms.

Chapter Twenty-Three

"I just won a hundred bucks!" I exclaim and grin over at Samantha, who is sitting two machines down from me.

"I just lost two hundred. Jesus, why are we here again?" She scowls as she takes a long sip of her diet soda. "And why can't I drink?"

"Because we're the drivers tonight. They were our drivers last week, this week it's our turn."

"This sucks." She mutters and feeds another hundred dollar bill into her machine.

"It probably sucked for them, too," I laugh. We are at the casino north of Seattle on Monday night, waiting for the guys to need a ride home. Will has tomorrow off of training, so they decided tonight was the best night for a bachelor party. They've been up in the high roller room for a few hours now, most likely smoking cigars and drinking whiskey and playing poker. It's all very Hollywood in my head as I imagine it.

But there's no way in hell that I'm going up there. I just pray to God no one needs to be carried out to the van because these guys are big, and there's no way that Sam and I can carry them.

They'll have to sleep on the casino floor.

"You're a bad fucking loser!" I twirl at the sound of our group, and sure enough, here they all come, tripping over each other, laughing, drunk as shit.

"I am not a bad loser," Nate slurs. "But you took ten thousand fucking dollars. Do you know what I can do for your sister with that kind of money?"

"Yeah, probably buy her another pair of shoes she doesn't need," Matt responds happily, completely sober.

"Why are you sober?" I ask him.

"Because he's a pussy," Will explains, earning him a punch to the arm. "Watch it! That's my throwing arm, asshat."

"Charming," I murmur and look over at Sam. "Did we act like this?"

"Yes," Matt responds with a grin. "Except these guys aren't talking about sex."

"Yet," Isaac adds with a happy grin, then frowns deeply. "Except I don't get to have sex for another month. Damn babies."

"Dude, that's your kid."

"Yeah, he's great." Isaac grins goofily and I start to herd them toward the door like I'm herding cattle.

"Come on, guys, let's go home to the ladies."

"What lady," Caleb asks. "Ain't got no lady."

"I'll be your lady, handsome," Sam grins at him sassily and Caleb smiles wide and puts his arm around her waist, leaning on her.

"Now, that's a nice offer," he murmurs.

"Get your ugly hands off my sister, dude," Luke's voice is hard and not quite as slurred as the others.

"Oh yeah. You're family," Caleb pouts and hugs Sam before setting her aside. "Why do all the hot women in the world have to be taken?"

Will saunters over to me with a loose, happy grin on his handsome face. "Hi."

"Hi."

"Let's go home and get naked."

"Holy shit, you're Will Montgomery!" We all turn at the woman's voice to find a tall, slender, long-haired blonde smiling widely. She's all tan, with too much makeup and not enough clothes.

"That I am," Will slurs as he walks to her and very deliberately looks her up and down, then smiles back at her. "What's your name, sweetheart?"

He fucking called her sweetheart!

"Amanda," Barbie responds and holds her hand out for a shake. I look over at the brothers, all of whom are shifting uncomfortably. "Can I give you a hug?"

"Hey, I always welcome hugs." He opens his arms wide and she steps up to him, presses her perky little body against him and

221

hugs him around the neck.

"Seriously?" I ask the room at large.

"Can I give you my number?" Amanda asks as she pulls out of his arms.

"Fuck, no, you can't." I stomp over to my way-too-drunk boyfriend and slip my arm around his waist. He smiles down at me happily.

"Hey, babe. This is Amanda."

"Fantastic," I sneer.

"Amanda, this is Megan, my beautiful girlfriend."

Amanda blinks at me, then up at Will. "Uh, sorry."

"Always happy to meet the fans," Will slurs and waves goodbye to her as I turn him toward the door.

"Fucking moron," Caleb mutters.

When we get outside, Sam has pulled the van up, and all the guys climb in, Will last.

"I'm an idiot when I'm drunk," Will slurs, serious now. "You know I wouldn't have taken her number, right?"

"Right," I sigh and motion for him to get in the car.

"'Cause I love you, babe."

"I know. Get in the car so we can take everyone home."

This ride home is amazingly more calm that the one last week. Most of the guys pass out cold, snoring away. Matt sits quietly behind me and to my left, typing on his phone. At each stop, the girls come out to gather their men, and when we get to Caleb's, Matt helps him inside, then takes his own car from Caleb's home.

Sam drops us off last.

"See you at the wedding on Saturday." I smile at her and help Will inside, get him up the stairs, stripped down, and in bed.

"I need to get you something for that headache you're sure to have tomorrow."

He pulls me down with him into the bed and loops a heavy arm around my waist. "You're so pretty."

I smile and cup his face in my palm. "So are you."

"I wasn't really flirting with that girl, Meg." His eyes are droopy, falling shut, but then he fights then open again.

"Are you worried that I'm mad about that?"

"Yeah," he sighs, his breath smelling of horrible cigars and beer.

"I'm not." I sigh back. Amazingly, I'm not. Even if I hadn't been there I trust that he would have told her no.

"M'kay." And he's asleep.

I slide out from under him and take a shower, dry my hair, and pull on one of the jerseys that I've come to claim as mine when I'm here. I pull on his underwear and wander downstairs, leaving the lights off.

I sit in one of the plush armchairs that faces the water and pull my knees up to my chest, wrapping my arms around them, and take a deep breath.

I didn't lie when I said I wasn't mad about Will flirting with that woman tonight. I'm not mad. But it did reiterate to me that Will can literally have any woman he wants. All he'd have to do is crook his finger, and they'd come running.

I know he loves me, but what happens when he gets tired of me, and that tall, beautiful blonde starts to look more appealing?

I want to trust him when he says that he loves me. I believe he means it. And I love him so much it hurts.

I should go up and go to bed, but I'm not sleepy, so I reach over for my guitar. I left it here last night with the intention of practicing for Jules' wedding, and there's no time like now.

I don't think anything could wake Will up right now.

So I strum and sing, playing the song over and over, tweaking the arrangement here and there to fit my voice. It's a beautiful song. I wonder how it came to be Jules and Nate's special song?

And it occurs to me, that Will and I don't have a special song yet. Well, there was the song that the kid played on the sax while we danced in New Orleans, when Will first told me he loves me, but I don't know what the song was.

I smile and start playing a song I learned recently that I just can't ever get out of my head. It's by Christina Perri, called *A Thousand Years*, and it fits my voice perfectly.

The intro is supposed to be on the piano, but I've changed it for my guitar, and start to sing about a love that I've waited for for a thousand years, about being brave to love. The lyrics are sweet, and the song itself is soft and romantic.

When I finish, I set my guitar aside, finally sleepy and stand to go upstairs, but when I turn around, Will is sitting on the couch and startles me.

"Holy crap!"

"Sorry, I didn't want to interrupt you. That was beautiful."

"Thank you. How long have you been down here?"

"Just a little while. I woke up and you weren't there, so I drank some water and took something and sat down to listen. I hope that's okay."

He looks unsure of himself, and I hate that.

"Of course it's okay." I cross to him and climb in his lap. "Did you have fun tonight?"

"Yeah, it was fun. Lost some money, razzed the guys." He shrugs and I smile against his chest.

"Let's go up to bed." I climb off him and hold a hand out, helping him to his feet. "How do you feel?"

"Still a little drunk," he answers with a half-smile.

* * *

A hung-over Will is not a fun Will. He's been surly and grouchy all day, so I left him when he finally lay down to take a nap and decided to return Jules' dress to her.

I hate to give it back. It's so damn pretty.

I walk into Jules and Nate's downtown office and whistle softly. Wow. Nice digs. Very high class.

There's a kind-looking older woman manning the reception desk. Her name plaque reads Jenny Glover.

"Hi, I'm Meg. I'd like to see Jules if she's free."

"Do you have an appointment?" she asks.

"Uh, no. I'm sorry, I'm a friend. I didn't realize I should make an appointment."

"Please have a seat and I'll see if she's free."

Jenny calls Jules' office, and less than fifteen seconds later, Jules opens her office door with a wide smile on her pretty face.

"Hi! Come in."

I follow her into her office and am stunned by the view of the Space Needle and the Sound.

"Wow, that's some view."

"I know. We lucked out on this space." She grins and leads me to a couch. "What's up?"

"I just wanted to return your dress, and honestly get the hell out of Will's house for a while. That man is grumpy as hell when he's hung over."

Jules laughs and nods. "Yeah, he's not a good patient. If he's ever sick, just steer clear."

"I could have used that warning yesterday." I try to hand Jules her freshly dry-cleaned dress, but she frowns at me.

"Why are you returning the dress?"

"Because it's yours." *What the hell?*

"No, it's not."

"What are you talking about?"

Jules sighs and pinches the bridge of her nose. "Will didn't tell you?"

"Tell me what?"

"Meg, Will bought the dress for you. He just had Natalie and I call the designer and make the arrangements. This was never my dress." She smiles softly.

I'm stunned. My mouth drops, and I look at the beautiful dress in my hands.

"How much was this dress?" I ask her.

"It doesn't matter; it was a gift, Meg."

God, she sounds just like her brother.

"What about the spa? The shoes? The underwear?"

"Those were all Nat and me. Will just bought you the dress."

"And the diamond earrings," I murmur.

"He got you diamond earrings?" she asks with a wide smile.

"Yeah, they're gorgeous." I sigh happily. "I should be mad, but honestly, I love this fucking dress. I want to wear it every day."

Jules laughs. "It's so perfect for you. Will picked it out himself, you know."

"He did?"

"He did," she confirms. "I heard about what he did last night when you guys were leaving. Wanna talk about it?"

I squirm uncomfortably in my seat. "I'm not mad about it."

"But you're not happy."

I shrug. "He was drunk."

"Spill it, McBride." Her voice is firm, and I know I'm not leaving here without talking to her, and frankly, I need to talk to her.

I need to talk to someone.

"Jules, what the hell does he see in me?" I frown and look down at my hands. "I guess that's what it comes down to. He can have anyone he wants."

"Why is it so hard for you to believe that he wants you? Meg, you're fantastic."

"But…" I shake my head, but she interrupts me.

"No buts. Will adores you, Megan. I've never seen him like this."

"He'll get tired of me."

"Stop it. Now you're just being a pussy, and I don't have time for this shit." My eyes go wide and I raise my eyebrows.

"How do you really feel?" I ask dryly.

"Will is famous, Meg. None of us can change that, and I don't think he wants to change that. He's good at what he does."

"Yes, he is," I agree.

"There will always be groupies. He will always get recognized, especially around this town. Will's never really cared about all that bullshit." She shrugs. "It just goes with the job. But Meg, if every time a woman tries to get his attention it makes you start to question his feelings for you, or whether you deserve him, you will never be able to make this relationship work."

"What are you saying?" I ask her.

"If you aren't in it for the long haul, willing to pull your big-girl panties up and deal with the bullshit that comes along with being famous, then cut your losses now rather than later."

I don't have any words. I just sit and stare at her, then look over at the dress, and back to her.

"The thought of being without him kills me," I whisper.

"Then trust him when he says he loves you. He means it. Enjoy him. Love him back."

She looks so damn proud of herself.

And she's right. He's never given me a reason not to trust him.

"Okay. Thank you. For everything."

"You're welcome." She pulls me into a tight hug and then walks me to her door. "I'll see you Saturday."

* * *

Just when I walk through my front door, my phone rings. *Football Star* reads on the display.

"Hey there," I answer.

"Where are you?" God, he's so grouchy.

"I'm at home. Just got here."

"Why?"

"Because I just left your sister's office and I needed to come home for a while. I see you're still as charming as you were this morning."

He sighs. "Sorry. I slept too long."

"Jules told me about the dress, Will."

He swears under his breath. "Great, so now I guess you'll bitch at me about spending too much money on that too?"

"Actually, I was going…"

"Because I'm sick of trying to give you nice things and you keep telling me I shouldn't," he interrupts. "Do you have any idea how much money I make?"

"No, I don't care…"

"I just signed a one hundred million dollar contract, Megan."

Holy fuck.

"I can afford to buy you dresses and earrings and take you on trips."

"Okay."

"Okay?"

"Yes. I was going to thank you for the dress because I really love it and I love that you picked it out. But clearly you're still in jack-ass mode, so I'm going to let you go get over this fucking

227

hangover that has you growling at me like a wounded bear and get some things done around my own house. I'll see you later."

I hang up before he can respond and toss my phone on the counter top in the kitchen.

I throw in a load of laundry, tidy my bathroom and clean out the fridge, swearing at grumpy football players who don't know how to hold their liquor.

Jackass.

And then it occurs to me: I don't think he's eaten today. Unless he ate while I was out, but Will requires a hell of a lot of food, and with that hangover, which he's not used to, I'm quite sure he hasn't eaten.

So I take a quick stock of my freezer and pantry and send him a text.

Be at my place in an hour.

* * *

The lasagna is resting on the tabletop and I'm just pulling the garlic bread out of the oven when Will rings the doorbell.

I open the door to find him standing there, freshly showered, with a dozen pink roses, and I melt just a little.

"I'm sorry I'm a jackass."

"Come inside, jackass." I let him in and push the buttons on the alarm like I'm supposed to when I open the door, earning a wide smile from Mr. Overprotective.

"You set the alarm."

"I did." I shrug like it's no big deal. "You seem to like it when I do that."

"I do." He holds the flowers out to me. "These are for you."

"Thank you." I bury my nose in them and take a deep breath. "They smell wonderful."

"Like you," he whispers.

"Don't think being cheeky will redeem you from your jackassery."

"Jackassery?" He asks with a laugh. "Where do you come up with these words?" He follows me into the kitchen where I put the flowers in the water.

"Where did you get that lasagna?" he asks, his eyes wide and pinned to the pan of bubbly goodness on the table.

"I made it."

"What?" His eyes dart to mine and he pins me with a glare. "You *made* that?"

"Yeah." I toss the bread in a basket and set it on the table, along with plates and silverware.

"You can cook?"

"Of course."

"You've been holding out on me?" He crosses his arms over his chest and looks down-right pissed off, which makes me laugh.

"Will, you never asked me if I could cook. You just assumed I couldn't." I smile softly at him. "Are you hungry, babe?"

"God, I'm fucking starving." He sits at the table, but instead of letting me sit in my chair, he pulls me into his lap and kisses me hard. "I'm so damn sorry for today and for last night. Did I really flirt with another woman with you standing right there, or was that a nightmare?"

"You did." I cup his cheek in my hand. "I'm okay."

"I'm never drinking again. I swear."

"I'm okay, Will. I trust you." I smile up at him as I pull my fingers down his sexy face. "I thought you were hungry."

"God, yes." He pushes me out of his lap and digs into the lasagna. "And after I eat this, I'm hungry for you." His blue eyes follow me as I sit in my chair and take a bite of garlic bread.

"Sounds like a plan."

Chapter Twenty-Four

It was, perhaps, the most beautiful wedding I'd ever been to in my life. We've just left Jules and Nate's wedding and are riding in limos to the reception site, a beautiful country club in Bellevue. Jules chose to play it safe, with it being fall, and is keeping the whole event indoors.

I lean on Will's arm, link our fingers, and sigh happily.

"That was beautiful."

"Jules looked really happy," Stacy agrees. We are riding with Stacy and Isaac and their kids and Caleb and Matt.

"The twins were adorable flower girls," I remark. Josie and Maddie had fluffy, soft pink dresses on and their hair twisted up in sweet little up-do's.

"I think it was sweet of Jules to have Livie and Soph wear similar dresses too," Stacy says with a soft smile.

"Are we going to talk about dresses all day?" Caleb asks with a frown.

"Uh, Caleb, it's a wedding," I reply dryly. "We're going to talk dresses and shoes and flowers all day."

"Shit," he mutters and pulls on the collar of his white suit shirt.

"You look very nice," I tell him with a sweet smile. And it's true. He looks damn hot in a suit, all broad shoulders and tan skin. He grimaces.

"Thanks."

"Are you flirting with my brothers again?" Will asks me with a grin.

"Yep. Get used to it." I kiss his cheek. "But you're my favorite."

"Gee, glad to hear it, babe."

"Here we are." Isaac props little Liam on his shoulder and we all follow him out of the limo. The other cars have pulled up around us, so all the family is arriving at the same time. The rest of the guests should already be inside.

I can hear the band playing inside. They sound good. I wonder who Luke got to play?

"Ready?" Will asks and holds his arm out for me.

"Yes, let's party!" I take his arm and he escorts me inside along with everyone else, Jules and Nate bringing up the rear.

Once we're all in, Jules' dad takes a mic and announces the newly married couple.

"It is my great honor to introduce you all to Mr. and Mrs. McKenna!"

Applause erupts and the happy couple enters the hall, smiling broadly, absolutely glowing.

If it wasn't so fantastic, it would be disgusting.

Jules' dress is just flat-out amazing, which doesn't surprise me. It's white, and almost Grecian in style, flowing up one shoulder and gathered with rhinestones. Rhinestones cascade down the mostly-open back, holding the dress together. It's floor-length, and as she walks, Tiffany-blue shoes peek out. Her something blue.

I scan the elegant room, taking it all in. The guests are beautifully dressed, wandering around, chatting or finding their assigned seats at one of the many round tables, set with soft pink linens and large pink bouquets of flowers and tea-light candles.

The whole room glows. The band is playing out of my sight, in an adjoining room, where I'm assuming the stage and dance floor are. I can see French doors that open between the two rooms, so those seated at the tables can watch the band and the dancers. People are already wandering in to listen, and they seem to recognize the band.

"Come on, let's mingle," Will smiles down at me. "I want to show you off."

"Right," I smirk.

"You are gorgeous today. Well, every day, but I love this dress." He brushes his hand down my naked back and settles it right above my ass. "I can see your dimples."

I grin up at him, enjoying that lustful look in his eyes. "I did that on purpose." My dress is simple, but pretty. Its eggplant, and floor-length. The bodice is v-shaped, ending right between my breasts with a tiny rhinestone broach. It's sleeveless, the straps only about an inch wide, and there is no back to speak of.

"Yeah, I thought so," he laughs. He looks amazing in his dark suit. Like his brothers, he's broad-shouldered and tall and just delicious.

I want to eat him up.

He grabs us each a glass of champagne and we start to wander about the room, chatting and laughing with the other guests. I'm introduced to friends of Nate's from his fighting days, all of whom are funny and nice, and clearly uncomfortable in their suits. Finally, we make our way back to Nat and Luke.

"Who's the guy with Luke?" I ask Will.

"Oh, you haven't met Mark yet. That's his brother. He's usually in Alaska working." He leads me to the threesome and introduces me to Luke's handsome brother.

Holy shit, I didn't think it was possible to be hotter than Luke Williams.

I was wrong.

What is up with the water these women drank when they were pregnant? Seriously, it's crazy.

"Hi, Meg, nice to meet you." Mark offers me a cocky grin as he shakes my hand. "Too bad Will's already snatched you up."

"Watch it, dude. You've been back all of two days. Don't make me kill you." Will growls good-naturedly.

Mark just grins at him. "You'd miss me."

Suddenly, Jules is walking briskly to me, her eyes wide and worried. "Um, Meg, we need to talk."

"Why?"

But before she can say anything, I hear it. *Lonely Soul* starts to play, the song I wrote with Leo.

And it's Leo singing it.

"Luke, who did you hire for this?" I ask, my eyes pinned to Jules'. I already know.

"Nash," he replies, his voice confused. "Why, you don't like them?"

I close my eyes and take a deep breath. *Holy fucking shit.*

Natalie gasps, and Will wraps his fingers around my arm, pulling me around to face him. "What is it?"

"Meg, I'm sorry. I didn't know." Jules runs her hand down my back. "I really didn't."

This is Jules' wedding. She's one of my oldest and dearest friends. I will be fine. I will do what I need to do to get through tonight, and it will be fine.

I paste a smile on my face and hug her tightly. "It's fine, sweetie."

"What did I do wrong?" Luke asks.

"Nothing." I shake my head and smile over at him. "Nash is a fantastic band."

"What am I missing?" Will murmurs down to me. I sigh.

"Leo Nash is *my* Leo, Will."

"What?" he asks, frowning. Natalie curses under her breath. Jules is still worried, biting her lip.

"I'm fine." I look around at the group of people who have come to mean so much to me. They have become like family to me. "Honestly, this is great. The guests will love them."

Will is watching me closely, questions in his eyes, and I feel like shit for not telling him the whole story before. But it was too painful to admit to him that Leo left me here while he went and became a big rock star.

That he just forgot about me.

"Luke, how did you manage to get Nash?" Jules asks him.

Luke shrugs. "They're doing the soundtrack for the new movie I'm producing. They just wrapped up a tour, and are taking some time off, so I asked if they would do this event before their vacation, and they agreed."

"You're so sweet," Nat murmurs and kisses him.

"Maybe I should have checked with you guys, though. I didn't think you knew any rock stars."

I shrug. "We used to."

Everyone is watching me. "Stop. I'm fine. What's next? Dinner? When do we get cake?"

"Yeah, when do we get cake?" Will asks, making us all laugh, but his eyes are still serious and pinned on me.

"After dinner," Jules replies dryly. "Which I think they're about to serve."

The band stops playing, and a DJ takes over while we have dinner and go through the motions of the cake cutting and the toasts.

Natalie stands and takes the mic offered to her and smiles shyly to the room at-large.

"My husband is usually the one to speak to large audiences, but I'm happy to talk to you all about my best friend." She looks over at Jules and smiles widely.

"Are you going to embarrass me?" Jules asks.

"Maybe," Nat winks. "See, she can never break up with me because I know too much." We all laugh and Nat sobers.

"I don't remember a time in my life that Jules and her family weren't in it. You have shared everything that has ever mattered with me, even the birth of my baby. When Jules and Nate got together," Natalie turns to the audience and smiles. Will takes my hand in his and kisses my knuckles. "I was astonished to watch the change in her. Jules is a kick-ass girl. She's not big on public displays of affection, which she reminds me of almost daily."

"Seriously, you guys are gross," Jules rolls her eyes, but I can see the tears threatening to spill over.

"But Nate brought out that soft side of her. He makes her better. And I think she does the same for him. I just couldn't have found anyone more suited to you, my friend, if I tried." Nat raises her glass and we all follow suit.

"So, to my new brother-in-law Nate, and my sister of the heart, his Julianne. May your love continue to grow every day."

"To Jules and Nate!"

Even I wipe a little tear away from the corner of my eye and laugh when Will smirks at me. Gosh, I love those girls. I understand what it is to have a sibling of the heart. Mine is in the next room.

Holy shit.

"Are you nervous?" He asks me, sensing my tension.

"To sing?"

"Yeah, are you okay?" He wraps his arm around me, resting it on the back of my chair. I grin up at his handsome face.

"I'm fine. I don't usually get stage fright. And I've been practicing a lot."

"I love the arrangement you've done with the song," he murmurs and kisses my cheek. "You're going to knock them dead."

I smile and lean into him. "Thank you. I hope so."

"Are you okay with Leo being here?" he whispers down at me.

The mention of Leo makes my heart stop. God, I'm going to have to talk to him. I don't think he even knows I'm here.

What will he say? How will he react?

"I don't know," I whisper back.

"Hey," he pulls my face up with his fingers so he can look into my eyes. "It's going to be okay. I'll kick his ass if you want me to."

I laugh and cup his cheek in my hand. "That's okay. The time for that was about three years ago." God, I love this man. He's always so ready to protect me.

"I love you, sweetheart."

I smile softly and kiss his lips, tenderly. "I know."

"And now, ladies and gentlemen," Jules' dad, Steven, announces, "I am proud and pleased to introduce you to a very good friend of Jules, and the woman who seems to have snagged my son, Will's, heart. Megan McBride is going to sing the song for the first dance. Meg? Where are you, honey?"

"Here goes nothing," I murmur at Will and he smiles widely and follows me, along with everyone else, into the ballroom.

And there by the stage is Leo, his mouth gaping open, watching me cross the dance floor to him.

"Can I please borrow your guitar?" I ask, cutting to the chase.

"Meg-pie," he murmurs, shocked to see me. The old knickname almost brings me to my knees.

I lock them.

"Leo, I just need your guitar, please."

He can't move. He's just staring at me. God, he looks good. He's tall, about six feet. His light brown hair is cut short on the sides, and a bit longer on top, styled into a faux-hawk. He has a small guage in one ear with a hoop through it. His lip and eyebrow are pierced. He's covered in tattoos.

And his sweet, soft dark-gray eyes are pinned to mine.

"Leo," I say again, a bit stronger, and he blinks.

"Meg," he clears his throat. "I didn't know you'd be here."

"Same here," I reply with a grin. "I need to borrow your guitar, please."

"Oh, sure." He holds it out to me, and offers me a half-smile. "You've played it often over the years."

I learned to play on this guitar.

I bite my lip as I loop the strap around my shoulder and back, and look up at him. "Thank you."

I climb the stage and move the stool that's been set in front of the mic for me. "I don't think I can gracefully sit on that thing in this dress," I say to the audience with a smile, earning laughter and applause.

"So," I begin, "Jules and Natalie and I have been friends since college, so they knew me back when I used to play with a local band here in Seattle." I smile out at them. All the guests have gathered in a semi-circle around the stage, Jules and Nate and the rest of the family and bridal party up front. Will is gazing at me with warm blue eyes.

I look to my left to see Leo standing by the stage with his arms crossed over his chest, watching me intently. I swallow hard and focus on the task at hand.

Just get through this one song, Meg.

"I was a bit surprised when she asked me to sing tonight because I haven't sung in front of an audience in quite some time, but I'm honored to sing for Jules and Nate's first dance together as a married couple." I smile again and strum the guitar, making sure it's in tune.

It is, of course.

"The song they've chosen is *I Won't Give Up*."

I begin to play the intro as Jules and Nate take the dance floor. Nate pulls Jules into a firm embrace and moves her effortlessly across the floor.

I'm taken away by the song and watching my beautiful friends dance so gracefully, gazing into each other's eyes. Nate is singing along with me, to his girl, and the romantic in me melts at the sight. He leans down to murmur something in her ear, then kisses her naked neck, below her ear, and sweeps her around the floor again, much to the crowd's delight.

I find Will's eyes across the dance floor. He's smiling at me, watching me intently. God, I love him.

I've got to tell him.

The song ends, and the room erupts into applause and whistles. I smile and back away from the mic to offer a little curtsy, and then walk to the end of the stage, ready to hand Leo back his guitar.

"We have to do a song together," he says, his face serious.

"No, thank you."

He takes his guitar and hands it to someone else, then grabs my arm and pulls me back to him and whispers in my ear.

"Megan, please. I've missed you. Let's do the song we used to do at weddings back in the day."

I sigh and tears threaten.

"Leo…"

"Please. You sound great. We'll blow them away."

"You don't need me to do that, remember?" I ask, my voice cold. He scowls.

"I never said that." He sighs. "Come on, people are watching."

I don't have a choice. I do not want to make a scene at Jules' wedding. So, I follow Leo up the stairs and stand at his side as he speaks to the audience.

"Hey, everyone, are you having a good night?" He asks, and the audience applauds and whistles. "Good! I'm honored to be here tonight with my band to entertain you all and celebrate with Jules and Nate. I knew Jules, back in her college days, and I'm happy to see she found a dude worthy of her." He winks down at

He offers the audience that killer smile of his, and I swear half the women in the audience, including Samantha, look about ready to throw their panties at him.

I can't help but roll my eyes.

"I kept Meg up here because Nash is that little local band she told you about earlier. She and I go way back." He smiles over at me. "And she's agreed to sing one more song with me before she joins you guys to get drunk and be stupid while I work my ass off up here."

The audience laughs and I join them. I find Will in the audience, and he's watching, standing still. I can't read his face.

Someone hands me a mic, and Leo takes his mic off the stand and sets the stand aside.

"Don't we need a guitar?" I ask into the mic.

"Nope, we have backup." He winks and nods at one of the guys to join us on stage with a guitar. He leans in and whispers the song in the guy's ear. I don't know him; he must have joined the band after they got to L.A.

"This song," Leo says into the mic and looks up at me, his dark gray eyes happy. "is called *Marry Me* and was originally done by a band who is also from Seattle, Train."

The audience applauds again, and I can't look away from Leo. We always nailed this song. It wasn't originally written as a duet, but we alternate the verses and join together for the chorus.

I start, while Leo watches, lip singing along with me, his eyes bright and happy and encouraging, and I offer him a sassy smile as I start the song.

He joins me for the chorus. This tall, tattooed rock star, singing a sweet love song. It looks all wrong, but God, his voice is amazing. As his voice joins mine in perfect harmony, goose bumps break out on my skin and I smile widely at him.

I lower my mic to my side and watch Leo take over the next verse. I've always loved to watch him sing, even when I was very young, in the first foster home with him. He would sing to me all the time, and then let me play his guitar, showing me so patiently where to put my fingers and make the sounds perfect. He taught me how to control my voice.

He taught me everything I know about music.

As he sings these lyrics, I can't help but wonder if he has a special woman in his life now. I hope so. He deserves one, although I know his trust issues go deeper than mine.

For the last half of the song, we sing it all in harmony. I hear Jack, our original pianist, join the guitar and I'm just completely swept up in the moment. We step closer together, passionately singing about this sweet love, just inches apart.

We smile at each other after that last line, and then finish the song.

The music fades and Leo smiles at me, offering me that secret smile he used to give me when we were kids and we knew we might get into trouble for something we planned to do.

But he never got me into trouble. He always protected me.

He pulls me into a tender hug, then pulls back and gazes down at me. I don't hear the applause around us, or the audience asking for more.

Leo leans in and whispers in my ear, "I've really missed you, Meg-pie. I love you."

He kisses my cheek, right next to my lips, and backs away, and I grin at him. "I love you too."

Chapter Twenty-Five

~Will~

I stand transfixed and watch the woman I adore sing my favorite love song with another man. And even though I know she loves Leo as a brother, I want to punch him.

Hard.

Her sweet voice fills the air, and I am even more in love with her in this moment than I was before she walked up on that stage, and I didn't know that was possible.

She's so fucking talented.

And sexy as hell in that dress, with her hair up, showing off her slender back and soft neck, and the diamond earrings I bought her a few weeks ago. I can't wait to get her out of it and make love to her. I just never get enough of her.

Forever can never be long enough for me.

Damn if that isn't the truth.

The song comes to an end, and Leo pulls Meg in for a hug, whispers something to her, and because I'm standing straight ahead, I can't tell if he kisses her on the cheek or the edge of her lips.

My hands tighten into fists.

Then he pulls away from her and she mouths the words, "I love you too."

Fuck me.

Chapter Twenty-Six

~Meg~

I wave at the crowd and carefully walk down the stairs in my heels. That felt fantastic. I didn't realize how much I missed playing in front of an audience, especially with Leo. I hope I get to see him again while he's in town.

I cross the dance floor, and Jules and Nate meet me in the middle to hug me.

"Thank you so much. That was so beautiful," Jules murmurs in my ear as she hugs me.

"You're welcome."

"Thank you, beautiful girl," Nate hugs me close too. Wow, holy muscles on this one. I smile up at him shyly.

"My pleasure. Congratulations, you guys."

The family all hugs me and tells me that they loved the songs, but my eyes are searching for Will.

"You didn't tell me you knew Leo Nash, girl," Samantha mutters with a grin. "I'm going to want to hear this story."

I laugh. "We'll get together soon and I'll tell you all about it."

Finally, I find Will, standing back from the crowd. His face is sober, hands in his pockets, and the light has gone out of his eyes, and my stomach falls into my feet.

Something is very wrong.

"Hey," I say as I approach him.

"Hey," he responds.

"What's wrong?" I ask, but he just shakes his head.

"Meg, that was amazing," Natalie and Luke are suddenly at our side.

"Seriously, Meg, I know people," Luke's smiling, but his voice is all business mode. "I could make some calls on Monday. You should be singing for a living, my friend."

I'm shaking my head and holding my hands up for them to stop. "No, thank you."

Will's eyes narrow on me, but he stays silent.

"But, why? Meg, music has been your life for as long as I've known you," Natalie responds.

"It's not my life now." I shake my head again and sigh. "I love music. I always will, but I love my kids at the hospital." I shrug. "I'm happy here. I don't need to be the center of attention."

"If you change your mind, just say the word." Luke leans in and kisses my cheek. "I could help make you a very rich woman."

"I'm already rich," I respond with a smile. "I don't need the money."

Luke tilts his head and a slow smile spreads across his incredibly gorgeous face. "Fair enough."

Nat winks at me and they walk away, off to mingle with other guests.

"Talk to me," I whisper up to Will when he still says nothing, just gazes down at me with sober eyes.

He shakes his head. "Not here. We'll enjoy the reception. But we will talk later."

My mouth gapes open and I just stare up at him. *What the hell did I do?*

"Okay," I murmur. He nods once, sharply, and leads me back into the crowd to mingle and chat. He smiles and plays the perfect brother for the rest of the evening, but never puts a hand on me. Never looks at me. If I rest my hand on him, he steps away from my touch.

It's fucking killing me.

"Will..." I begin when we have a moment alone, but I see Leo approach from the corner of my eye and I sigh as Will stiffens next to me.

This is the issue.

"Hey, Meg, we're taking a break. Is this Will?" he asks and I raise a brow in question. "Jules' dad mentioned you'd snagged Will's heart," Leo answers my unspoken questions and I grin.

"Yes, this is Will. Will, this is Leo."

Will offers his hand to shake, but his face is anything but friendly. "Hello."

"Hey, I'm a big Seattle football fan," Leo tells him with a smile.

"Cool," is all Will says, and Leo steps back, narrows his eyes and looks between Will and I skeptically. Finally, his dark gaze finds mine.

"Problem?"

I shake my head and force a smile. "No problem."

I search the room with my eyes, trying to find someone to come save me. As much as I want to catch up with Leo, I need to talk to Will. His silence is killing me.

Samantha catches my gaze from a few feet away, and immediately steps into action, God love her.

"Leo, have you met Samantha?" I ask him as Sam joins us.

"Uh, no." He doesn't look down at her, not really caring who she is.

"She's Luke's sister," I explain further, and he smiles in recognition. Sam is drop-dead beautiful, and Leo grins down at her, nods, but then looks back at me, in full protective brother mode, sensing the tension between Will and I. I don't need him to start something.

"Sam," I grin at her, "Leo hasn't seen Jules in a long time. Would you take him over to see her and meet Nate?"

Leo continues to scowl at me, but then sighs and smiles down at Sam. "Hi, Samantha."

"It's just Sam," she responds and tucks her arm in his. "Let's do the obligatory walk away thing where we don't sense the tension over there and find somewhere else to be."

Leave it to Sam to not beat around the bush.

"Will, this is crazy. Talk to me. What did I do?"

But he frowns stubbornly and shakes his head again. "Not here."

"You're scaring me." I whisper.

"This is not the time or the place," he mutters, still not meeting my gaze.

"Time to toss the bouquet!" Jules announces. "Meg, get your sexy ass in here!"

I keep my eyes on Will's face, begging him to talk to me.

"Go, Jules is calling for you," he mutters and turns his back on me and walks away.

Fuck.

All the single girls are gathered in a semi-circle before the stage. In this crowd, there aren't many single girls, maybe fifteen. Sam is nowhere to be found, probably still chatting with Leo.

Traitor.

I paste a smile on for Jules and wait patiently for her to make a big show of tossing the bouquet. I try to step aside so Brynna can catch it, but wouldn't you know it falls right in my hands.

Sonofabitch.

I just laugh and hold it above my head. Jules hugs me and we pose for photos. The photographer asks for a few more posed family photos, and when the last photo is taken, Will returns to my side.

"Is all the wedding crap over?" he asks.

"Yeah, all that's left is dancing and getting drunk," I respond.

"Good, let's get out of here."

We spend the next hour making our way through the ballroom, saying our goodbyes, posing for a few more photos, and hugging Jules and Nate.

"I'm so proud of you, kiddo," I hear Will murmur to Jules.

"Thanks," she smiles up at him. "And don't call me that."

He laughs, a real Will laugh, and my stomach clenches. God, I love his laugh.

I love him so much, and he's about to break up with me, I just know it.

He escorts me out to the curb and asks the limo driver to take us back to the church where his car is parked. Once inside, Will sits at one side of the limo, and I slide over to the other side, knowing I'm not welcome to sit next to him.

And not being able to touch him is killing me.

So, I'll let him decide when he wants to talk about what's eating at him. We sit in silence all the way to the church. He gets me settled into his sexy car, and is silent all the way to my house.

I notice he doesn't take me back to his place.

When he parks in my driveway, he cuts the engine and we sit in silence, not looking at each other, just looking straight ahead.

Finally, after what feels like forever, I break the silence.

"Will," I whisper, "please talk to me. I can't apologize to you if I don't know what I did wrong."

He scrubs his hand over his mouth roughly, then abruptly gets out of the car, stalks around to my side, and opens the passenger door wide, indicating I should get out.

So I do.

He follows me to my door, watches me disarm the alarm, and then turns to go.

"Please, don't go. Will, come inside and talk to me."

"I can't talk to you," he murmurs, not meeting my eyes. "It hurts too damn much to talk to you, Megan. It's killing me to look at you."

"What the fuck is going on?" I demand, my hands on my hips. "Don't be a pussy, Will, just say what the fuck is wrong!"

"You are!" His head snaps up, his eyes pissed off. "I tell you every fucking day how much I love you, Megan." He moves closer to me, his face inches from mine. "Every single day, I say it. I show you. I make sure you know that I am completely in love with you."

I swallow hard, my eyes wide, and just watch him as he unloads, while my heart is breaking. I feel tears gather in my eyes.

"But you can't say it back," he continues. He throws his arms up and stalks away, but then turns back to me, his mouth set in a grim line. "You can't tell me that you love me, yet you just stood on a stage before two hundred of my nearest and dearest and told another man that you love him."

My mouth drops and a tear falls down my cheek.

"I saw you," he spits out. "I saw you tell him you love him after he whispered in your ear and kissed you, which almost earned him a punch in the jaw." He rubs his mouth again and then plants his hands on his hips and another tear falls down my cheek.

"I'm so in love with you, Megan, I can't see straight. You mean more to me than anything. More than my family, more than football. More than anything." He shrugs and holds his hands out to his sides, as though he's showing me everything he has.

"But you can't say the same to me, even though I know you love me. I just don't think you love me the way I love you."

He closes his eyes and sighs, and then looks down at his feet. He's standing before me, in his suit, and I want so desperately to take him in my arms and tell him how much I need him.

How much I love him.

He slowly raises his head and pins me with his sad blue eyes.

"If you can't love me the way I love you, maybe we're just wasting our time." His shoulders sag and he runs his knuckles down my cheek. "Good luck to you, Megan."

He turns on his heel and walks down my stairs and to his car, and I'm stuck.

What the fuck just happened?

He reaches his car, opens the door, and I spring into action. "Wait!"

Chapter Twenty-Seven

~Will~

I open my car door, my heart in my throat, and have to physically stop myself from running back to her and begging her to forget everything I just said.

I'll take whatever she's willing to give me, for the rest of my life, if I can just have *her*.

But not ever hearing the words come out of that sweet mouth will make me resent her eventually, and that's something I never want to happen.

Ever.

I love her too much for that shit, so it's best to cut our losses now.

"Wait!"

She sounds panicked. I clench my eyes shut and grip the car door tightly. *Just go back to the house, babe.*

"Will, wait." She's at my side now. I look down into her tear-filled hazel eyes and it takes everything in me to not gather her to me and tell her everything will work out.

Because I don't think it will.

"Meg, look…"

"No, you look," she cuts me off, her hands in fists on her lush little hips, fire coming out of her eyes.

I've pissed her off.

"You don't get to drop that bomb on me and then just ride off into the sunset, never to be heard from again, Will Montgomery. And if you think you're breaking up with me, you have another thing coming."

I love it when she's pissed. But the knot in my stomach hasn't eased yet.

"Will," she starts and takes a deep breath, "I love you more than you will ever understand."

The breath leaves me, and I can just stare down at her, my jaw dropped to my knees.

"What?"

"Of course I'm in love with you, Will." She swallows and closes her eyes. Before she can say another word, I take her face in my hands, the touch of her skin a balm to my frayed nerves, and make her look at me.

"I don't want you to say those words just because you're afraid I'll break up with you without them."

Her eyes smile up at me and for the first time in the past few hours, a calm settles over me.

"You're smarter than that," she murmurs in her sweet voice. "And you know me better than that."

I pull her up into my arms, nudge the car door shut with my foot and carry her inside her tiny house.

I plan to sell this townhouse and move her in with me as soon as possible.

Which means next year, because she's so damn independent. God, I love her.

I carry her into her living room and sit on her couch, cradling her on my lap. Her eyebrows climb into her hairline.

"I thought you'd be taking me upstairs."

"Later," I respond and trace her lips with my fingertip. "First, talk to me."

She sighs and bites that lower lip.

"I couldn't tell you I love you because in my life, that's always meant that people would leave." She shrugs and blinks, trying to hold back tears, and it's like a fist clenching my heart.

I hate it when she cries, because she rarely ever does.

"Go on," I whisper and smile down at her. I love the way her small body feels in my arms, all soft and small and like she's meant for me.

"I think I loved my mom when I was small. I don't really remember," her brow creases as she thinks. "But I was taken from her, and honestly, I'm thankful because that was for the best. But then I was tossed from foster home to foster home. I met Leo in the first one, and I latched onto him like he was a lifeline, because for me, he was." She looks up at me with pleading hazel eyes, begging for me to understand, and I think I'm finally beginning to.

"He was the first person I've ever had in my life that was truly family to me. He took care of me, and was kind to me, and didn't want anything from me." She swallows, and brushes the tears on her cheeks. "But then I was taken out of that first home, and Leo was taken away from me. Thank God I didn't lose touch with him."

I cradle her to me and let her talk it out.

"It was always made very clear to me in each of those homes what my place was, and it wasn't as a part of the family I was staying with. I was relieved when the state emancipated me at sixteen and I could go live with Leo."

She pulls back and looks up at me. "But then, after I'd been with him for years, and we'd had the band and done well, he decided to take the band and go to L.A. to try to make it in the business."

"Why didn't he take you with him?" I ask.

"He insisted I stay here and pursue my nursing career. He knew I was good at it, and I'd worked so hard for it. And I think he could see the toll the long hours of working and then playing gigs on the weekend was taking on me. He didn't want me to quit."

I frown down at her. "I hate to say it, but that makes sense, sweetheart."

"Yeah, now it does," she agrees and nods. "But then it just felt like another person I loved, the *most important* person I loved was leaving again."

"I'm not going to leave you, baby," I don't care if she can't stand that nick-name. "I love you so much, Megan."

She cups my face in her hands, the way she always does, and pulls her fingertips down my cheeks, her eyes happy. "I love you too."

Sucker punch to the gut.

"Say it again," I whisper.

"I love you too, Will," she whispers.

I stand with her still in my arms and carry her up the stairs to her bedroom and set her on her feet. With my fingertips, I push the straps of her dress off her shoulders and watch it fall off her delectable body and pool on the floor at her feet.

"Fucking hell, you're naked under there."

She's standing before me in just her black stilettos and diamond earrings, and it's all I can do not to come in my pants like a fucking teenager.

She smiles shyly. "You're entirely over-dressed."

"Undress me," I demand, holding my arms out to my side, but she shakes her head and sits on the bed, then scoots on her ass to the middle of the mattress, leaving her heels on.

"I wanna watch," she responds with a sassy grin, showing off that dimple.

"So damn lazy," I smile down at her and can't get out of this goddamn suit fast enough. Her eyes darken as they roam over my nakedness and I smirk at her.

I will train every day for the rest of my life to keep that look in her eyes when she looks at me.

Finally naked, I climb onto the bed and cover her small body with mine, her hips cradling me, my elbows on either side of her head, brushing little wisps of hair off her forehead with my thumbs.

"I love you," she murmurs with a happy smile.

"God, I'll never get tired of hearing those words come out of your sexy mouth, babe."

She chuckles and grips my ass in her hands. I tip my head down and kiss her, gently at first, and then harder and roll us so she's straddling my hips.

She sits up straight and rocks her hips, rubbing her already wet pussy against my cock. I suck a deep breath in through my teeth. "Easy, baby, or I'll come before we even get started."

"Really?" she looks happy with herself as she continues to torture me, the little vixen.

"Megan," I warn her, and suddenly she's scooting down and sucking on my cock, jacking me off at the same time and I jackknife up on the bed. "Holy fuck!"

She laughs and laps at the head like it's an ice cream cone, and then sinks over it again, sucking as she pulls up. I thread my fingers through her soft hair and moan.

"Meg, come back up here." She shakes her head stubbornly and continues to wreak havoc on my cock.

"I swear to Jesus, Megan, if you don't come up here…"

"What?" she asks after she makes a loud *pop* noise. "You'll what?"

I grip her shoulders and pull her back up to me, kissing her deeply, and reach between us to play with the piercing that I've grown to really fucking love.

It makes her crazy.

"Ah, God, Will," she moans against my mouth and I smile.

"That's right, sweetheart, come for me." Her hips are moving quickly against my fingers, and I know she's so close, and when I feel the shudders start, I guide myself inside her, and feel her sweet muscles milk my cock as I sink farther and farther in.

I grit my teeth and hold onto her hips tightly to keep from coming with her.

As her inner muscles relax, I begin to move her, and she takes over, riding me hard and in the sweetest rhythm. She sits up and pulls her arms up, resting her forearms on the top of her head as she rides me, and I reach up and cup her breasts in my palms, tweaking the hard nipples with my thumb and forefingers, making her even more crazy.

She throws her head back and leans her hands on my chest, and I reach between us again, looking down at where I'm buried deep inside her, and run the pad of my thumb over her clit and piercing, and I feel her orgasm build again.

"Look, babe," I instruct her, and she complies, looking down at us, at me rubbing her clit, and she falls apart, crying out.

She bears down on me, clenching and shuddering, and I have no choice but to come with her. I reach up and grip her hair in my fist and pull her down to me kissing her hard as I come inside her violently, pushing my hips up, burying myself as deep inside her as I possibly can.

She collapses on me, and I roll us onto our side, still inside her, gazing at her flushed face, eyes closed, lips parted as she pants.

This, right here, is my whole world.

"I love you, Will," she whispers, and I can't help the wide grin on my face, or the way my cock twitches inside her at the sweet words.

"I love you too, sweetheart."

* * *

Meg fell asleep about an hour ago, but I'm not tired. I can't stop looking at her sweet face, can't stop running my fingers through her soft hair.

She loves me.

I smile, remembering how the words sound coming from those sinful lips, and can't wait to hear them again.

It kills me that she thinks that loving means leaving, that if she admits to me that she loves me I'll bail on her.

I'm never going any fucking where. She's stuck with me, forever if she'll have me.

I'd like to know more about Leo, have some time to talk with him. But more than that, I think she needs time with him. He didn't look like someone who had deserted her tonight. He was protective and clearly loves her.

I ease away from Meg, careful not to wake her, grab my phone from my slacks and descend the stairs of Meg's townhouse as I dial Luke's number. It's late, but they're probably still at the reception.

"Williams," Luke answers. I can hear the band in the background, and people laughing and talking.

"Hey, I need a favor."

"Name it," he answers quickly, and I grin. Natalie picked a good guy.

"I need Leo's number."

"He's still on stage, Will," Luke answers dryly.

"Don't be a smart ass."

Chapter Twenty-Eight

~Meg~

I wake to a heavy arm wrapped tightly around my waist, a nose pressed to my cheek, and a large, muscled leg draped over mine.

I sigh and wiggle, trying to stretch without untangling myself from Will. He feels good, and after last night, I need his closeness.

He almost left me.

And I can't blame him.

"Good morning," he whispers.

I turn my head, rubbing my nose against his and grin. "'Morning."

"Sleep good?" He asks and hugs me tight.

"Yeah. You?"

"I did."

"I like waking up with you."

He leans back and offers me a confused smile. "You wake up with me all the time."

"No I don't," I shake my head. "You're always up before me."

"Hmm." He kisses my temple and links my fingers with his and we just lie here and wake up. "You okay?" he whispers.

"I'm good."

"So," he begins with a sigh. "Tell me about Leo."

I frown at him, confused as to where this is coming from. "I already told you about him last night."

"No, you told me about how you met him. I want you to tell me about *Leo.*"

"Why?"

He shrugs. "Call it curiosity."

"Will, he's just like a brother to me…"

"Stop," he presses his fingers against my lips and smiles reassuringly. "This isn't a pissing contest. I'm really curious to know more about him."

I search his face, and rub my hands down my face, turn on my side and face him. "Okay, I'll give you the cliffs notes version."

Will chuckles. "Okay."

"He went into foster care at the age of twelve, after both his parents were killed in a car accident. There weren't any relatives to take him." I sigh as Will scowls. "He could have gone down some bad roads. But he just lost himself in music, and then he had me to worry about, and thank God he is so fucking stubborn, or I shudder to think what kind of a mess he could have made out of his life."

I clear my throat and trace Will's shoulder with my fingertip. "He moved to Seattle when he turned eighteen, armed with his guitar and a trust fund that was set up with the insurance money from when his parents died. That's how he was able to help me pay for school and basically take care of me for so long. He's a smart guy. And he's so talented."

I smile at Will. "It was fun singing with him last night."

"You two are great together."

I nod. "It was like no time has passed," I whisper. "I've missed him."

"Why did you lose touch when he went to L.A.?"

"Because I'm a brat." I smirk at Will's frown.

"You are not."

"Oh, yeah, I am. I threw quite the fit when Leo told me he was leaving for L.A." I shake my head. "I acted like a kid who wasn't getting her way. I just didn't want him to go. And it hurt my feelings that he didn't give me the option to go with him."

"From what you told me, it sounds like he was looking out for you."

"He was," I nod in agreement. "But it still hurt. I loved him, and he left. And I was too stubborn to stay in touch with him after he was gone. And then when the mad wore off, and I wanted to hear his voice, I felt like too much time had passed, and I didn't think he'd want to hear from me." The last sentence is said with a whisper and brings tears to my eyes.

"I'm quite sure that's not the case," Will murmurs and brushes a tear off my cheek with his thumb. "No matter how stupid Jules acts, I'd always want to hear from her."

"Yeah," I mumble, not knowing what else to say.

"I think we should get up." Will pulls away from me and bounds out of bed, all naked and rumpled from sleep.

"I think you should get your sexy ass back in bed." He grins wolfishly at me and pulls the covers away from my naked body.

"Nope, up."

"Hey! It's cold."

"Get your hot ass out of bed and into the shower. I have a surprise for you." He rolls the blankets into a ball and throws them on the floor, stomping into the bathroom to start the shower.

"What about morning sex?" I yell after him.

"In the damn shower!" he yells back.

"You mean we can have morning sex in the shower?" I yell.

Will appears in the doorway and leans his shoulder against the jam, crosses his muscular arms over his chest, naked as a baby.

"I love it when you're naked," I tell him happily from my position on the bed.

"I'm happy to hear that," he smiles and crosses one leg in front of the other, looking all relaxed. "Are you going to get in the shower under your own power, or do I need to carry you in there?"

"Why are you so bossy this morning?" I ask with a laugh.

"I'm bossy every morning, babe. Now," he pushes away from the door and saunters to the bed, grabs my ankle, and pulls me to the edge of the bed. "Let's get in the shower."

"Okay," I hold my arms up, and he pulls me to my feet, but rather than letting me walk into the bathroom, he lifts me onto his shoulder and carries me.

"I can walk," I tell him wryly and slap his firm ass.

"Not fast enough."

"Tell me about this surprise," I slap his ass again just before he sets me on my feet.

"No. You said something about shower sex." He grabs my shower gel and lathers up a wash cloth.

"I'll have shower sex with you if you tell me about the surprise," I offer and have to grip his biceps to hold steady as he glides the soapy cloth over my breasts and down my stomach, landing between my legs.

"Are you sure?" he asks.

"What was the question?"

* * *

"Where are we going?" I ask from the passenger seat of Will's car.

"You'll see. We're almost there."

"I don't like surprises."

"I'm getting that. You're really bad at just shutting up and letting me do my thing, sweetheart."

"You should never tell me you have a surprise for me."

"Lesson learned," he mutters and parks the car in front of the café with the twelve-egg-omelet.

"Breakfast is the surprise?" I ask with raised eyebrows.

"Shut up, Megan."

He exits the car and opens my door for me, pulling me up by the hand, wraps his arm around my waist and plants a hard kiss on me, right there on the sidewalk.

"You can shut me up like that anytime, football star."

He winks and leads me into the restaurant, through the shabby booths and to the back where a guy is sitting with his back to the room, beanie on his head, hoodie on, tattooed hands holding a cup of coffee.

Leo.

My wide gaze finds Will's and he just shrugs.

Leo looks back at us and smiles, stands, and holds his hand out to Will. "Hey, man."

"Hey. I'm gonna let you guys catch up. Do you mind giving Meg a ride home when you're done?"

"You're leaving?" I ask him, butterflies swarming crazily in my stomach.

"I'm a third wheel, and won't understand your inside jokes anyway." He brushes his hand down my face, leans in and whispers in my ear, "You'll be fine. I love you. Call me if you need me."

"I love you too," I murmur and watch him walk out of the restaurant.

"Have a seat," Leo gestures to the other side of the booth, and I automatically plop down in it and just stare at him. His beanie is pulled low across his forehead, covering his eyebrow piercing. His grey eyes are happy, but guarded as if he doesn't quite know how I'll react to him.

He's gripping onto his coffee with both hands.

"You have new tats on your fingers," I murmur.

"You have a new tat on your arm," he returns.

I smile. "I've had it for a while."

"What song?"

"*Dare You To Move.*"

He nods, understanding why. "The floor line?" he asks.

"Yeah."

He nods again.

"How long are you in town?" I ask, trying desperately to start conversation. It's never been hard to talk to Leo. I hate that it is now.

"A while. The tour is done, and we're taking a hiatus."

"I thought you lived in L.A. now." I frown.

"I have a place there, but I miss home." He shrugs and offers me a half smile and I can't help but zero in on that silver hoop in his lip. It actually looks really hot on him. "I miss you, Meg-pie."

"I miss you too," I sigh and nod at the waitress as she offers me coffee and sets menus in front of us. "I'm sorry."

"It's not your fault."

"Yeah, it is."

"No, it's not. I have your number. I never called you either."

"Why?" I ask.

"I didn't think you'd want to hear from me."

"I guess we were both wrong," I murmur and smile at him. "So you're gonna be here a while, huh?"

"Yep. Gonna work on the next album, and just regroup."

"Good."

"So, Will Montgomery?" He sits back in the booth and narrows his eyes on me.

"Yeah." I smile shyly and look down at my coffee.

"You love him?" he asks, cutting to the chase.

"More than anything." I confirm.

Leo nods, watching me. "He makes you happy." It's not a question.

"Very."

"Is Sylvia still around?"

My eyes shoot to his in surprise. "How did you…?"

"I'm not stupid, Megan. I knew you were paying her. Is she still around?"

"No, Will paid her off."

"Looks like he makes me happy too." Leo takes a sip of his coffee, and I laugh, my stomach finally settling.

"What about you? Settling down with any groupies?" I ask sweetly and he throws a sugar packet at me.

"No settling down. Sex, fine. Relationships, no."

"Leo…"

"No." His face is hard, and I know the subject is closed.

"Stubborn ass."

"Just like the rest of the women in the country, you adore me," He gloats and takes a swig of coffee, smacks his lips and smiles smugly.

"I'm glad to see you're still modest." I shake my head at him, so happy to be with him again.

"So, tell me about Will, and why I shouldn't break his throwing arm for touching my sister…"

Epilogue

~Will~
Two months later…

"Why didn't we hire a moving company again?" I ask as I carry the four-thousandth box off the moving truck into the spare bedroom.

"Because, they aren't careful. I don't have much, but what I do have I don't need getting broken and ruined." Meg is sitting on the floor in the guest room, going through a box.

"Can you help us finish unloading the truck before you start unpacking boxes?" I ask her, hands on my hips.

"Hey! Where are you guys?" Caleb and Leo both come into the guest room with scowls on their faces.

"You guys do not get to go have sex while we unload your truck," Caleb says, pointing at us.

"Dude, that's my sister," Leo crosses his arms over his chest and Meg laughs.

"Come on," I hold my hand out to her and pull her to her feet. "Let's go, lazy bones."

All of the brothers are unloading the truck, the girls are directing us on where to put the boxes, as if we're all illiterate and can't read *bedroom* written in black sharpie on the side of the box.

Women always need to boss us around.

I love them.

Megan joins Nat in the kitchen, merging her things with mine, and my chest swells with happiness. It took me six long weeks, but I finally talked her into moving in with me.

"You know," Meg announces to the room at large. "You didn't all need to come help. I don't have that much stuff. Leo and Will could have handled the big stuff."

259

"Thanks so much for volunteering me," Leo mutters. "Why didn't we hire a company again?"

"That's what I said," I agree, and we both earn glares from Meg. She looks so hot when she's irritated with me.

"So, Sam," Leo saunters over to Samantha, who's trying to decide where to hang some artwork Meg brought with her. "What are you doing later?"

"I won't be doing you," she mutters and we all bust out laughing.

Sam is a hard-ass. She's no-nonsense, and tells it like it is. She's also gorgeous, and I can't blame Leo for trying.

"Uh, I wasn't offering, honey." Leo smiles smugly. "I was wondering if you'd like me to take you to have that stick pulled out of your ass."

The girls gasp, and Luke's eyes go hard as stone, but just before he makes the move to kick Leo's ass, Sam laughs and shakes her head.

"Nope, I like my stick right where it is."

"Let me know if you change your mind."

"You'll be the first to know." She hammers a nail into my wall and hangs the picture at her feet. "But just so you know, I don't date famous people."

"Neither do I," Leo winks and saunters into the kitchen, pulls a beer out of the fridge and takes a sip. The girls are all smiling broadly at him, and I have to say, I want to high-five him.

There's no way in hell he'll talk her into going out with him.

Finally, after what feels like days, everyone leaves. I thank everyone for their help as they climb in their cars and drive off, shut the front door and go in search of my girl.

I find her in the guest room again, going through that same box from earlier.

"What are you looking at?" I ask her and lean against the door jam. She looks so young, sitting there on the floor in my old jersey and her black yoga pants, hair pulled up in a ponytail and no makeup.

"I found these pictures that Nat took of me when we were in college." She thumbing through the photos, and I frown in confusion, and then it hits me. Natalie takes naked pictures.

Naked pictures of Megan.

"Show me." I push away from the door and lower myself to the floor behind her, my legs on either side of her and pull her against my chest, her sexy ass snuggled up against my groin.

And then my world stands still.

The photos are black and white. Meg is holding her guitar, and not wearing a stitch of clothing.

"Holy hell," I mutter as she shuffles through them slowly. There must be two dozen of them, Meg in different poses with that guitar. Her hair is down, framing her face. She was slimmer then, in the way women are when their bodies are changing from being a teen into a woman. I much prefer her rounder breasts and hips now, but damn, even then she was a knock out.

"How old were you?" I ask.

"Nineteen," she replies shyly, looking at the photos.

She comes to the last one. She's sitting cross-legged on a bed covered in white sheets that have been messed up. Her arms are wrapped around the guitar, and it's covering her completely, but it's the sexiest photo of the bunch. Her face is sober, her wide eyes staring into the camera, and she's biting her bottom lip.

"Can I keep that one?" I ask.

"Sure. You can keep them all."

"Really?" I run my hands up and down her arms and kiss her neck, just below her ear. I'm sure she can feel how much these photos have turned me on.

"I don't need them." She leans into me and turns her sweet face to me. I run my fingers down her cheek and kiss her nose, her dimple and then her lips.

"You are beautiful, Megan. Then and even more so now."

"I'm glad you think so."

"I'm glad you're here, in our home with me."

She smiles widely, her eyes happy, and I will do whatever it takes to keep that happiness there for the rest of her life.

"Me too. Can we get naked now?"

"I thought you'd never ask, sweetheart."

THE END